Thoroughbred Legacy

The Preston

Scandal
of the Preston
to return this hors... ...cle!

Available December 2008

#9 *Darci's Pride* by Jenna Mills
Six years ago, Tyler Preston's passion nearly cost him everything.
Now he's rebuilt his stables *and* his reputation, only to find the
woman he once loved walking back into his life.

#10 *Breaking Free* by Loreth Anne White
Aussie cop Dylan Hastings believes in things that are *real*.
Family. Integrity. Justice. In his experience, the wrong woman
can destroy it all. So when Megan Stafford comes to town,
he knows trouble's not far behind.

#11 *An Indecent Proposal* by Margot Early
Widowed, penniless and desperate,
Bronwyn Davies came to Fairchild Acres looking for work—and
to confront her son's real father. This time she'll show her lover
exactly what she's made of...and what he's been missing!

#12 *The Secret Heiress* by Bethany Campbell
After her mother's dying confession,
Marie walks away from her life and her career...only to
find herself next door to racing-world royalty. Wealthy
Andrew Preston may make Marie feel like Cinderella, but
she knows men like Andrew don't fall for women like her....

Available as ebooks at www.eHarlequin.com
#1 *Flirting with Trouble* by Elizabeth Bevarly
#2 *Biding Her Time* by Wendy Warren
#3 *Picture of Perfection* by Kristin Gabriel
#4 *Something to Talk About* by Joanne Rock
#5 *Millions to Spare* by Barbara Dunlop
#6 *Courting Disaster* by Kathleen O'Reilly
#7 *Who's Cheatin' Who?* by Maggie Price
#8 *A Lady's Luck* by Ken Casper

Dear Reader,

There's something special about being involved in a continuity like THOROUGHBRED LEGACY—a sense of something bigger, richer. And this one spans the globe.

From the bluegrass of Kentucky to the vineyards of California, from England to the Middle East and now to Australia's stud-farm capital, the Upper Hunter Valley. Here, a clash of values pits a single-dad cop who just wants to hold on to his family and his home against the wealthy Thoroughbred-racing set, and the heroine in particular.

But no matter where in the world we may be, or who we are, the concept of home is a universal one. And a powerful one.

My characters might start by squaring off hotly over an interrogation table, but when they finally start working as a team, they'll realize they all want the same thing.

A sense of true family. Love. A home.

I hope you enjoy their journey.

And I'd love you to stop by my Web site—a small window into my own home—and drop me a comment at www.lorethannewhite.com.

Loreth Anne White

Thoroughbred Legacy

BREAKING FREE

Loreth Anne White

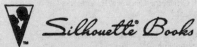

Published by Silhouette Books
America's Publisher of Contemporary Romance

SILHOUETTE BOOKS

ISBN-13: 978-0-373-19935-8
ISBN-10:   0-373-19935-X

BREAKING FREE

Special thanks and acknowledgment are given to Loreth Anne White for her contribution to the Thoroughbred Legacy series.

Visit Silhouette Special Edition and Thoroughbred Legacy at www.eHarlequin.com.

Printed in U.S.A.

LORETH ANNE WHITE

As a child in Africa, when asked what she wanted to be when she grew up, Loreth said a spy…or a psychologist, or maybe a marine biologist, an archaeologist or a lawyer. Instead she fell in love, traveled the world and had a baby. When she looked up again she was back in Africa, writing and editing news and features for a large chain of community newspapers. But those childhood dreams never died. It took another decade, another baby and a move across continents before the lightbulb finally went on. She didn't *have* to grow up. She could be them all—the spy, the psychologist and all the rest—through her characters. She sat down to pen her first novel…and fell in love.

She currently lives with her husband, two daughters and their cats in a ski-resort town in the rugged Coast Mountains of British Columbia, where there is no shortage of inspiration for larger-than-life characters and adventure.

Readers can find out more about Loreth at her Web site, www.lorethannewhite.com.

To Gillian Murphy,
who breathed life into the Hunter Valley,
and who did it with characteristic Aussie humor and flair.

Chapter One

Hands tense on the wheel, Detective Sergeant Dylan Hastings drove his squad car along the undulating ribbon of tar that bisected miles of brittle-dry stud farm acreage dotted with stands of tall eucalyptus.

He was going to arrest Louisa Fairchild, the grande dame of the Australian Thoroughbred racing scene, a woman who thought she was above it all, who figured Commonwealth justice was the best money could buy.

Dylan was about to show her different.

This time.

Because he'd seen Louisa buy "justice" before—when he was just eight years old. It had changed his life forever.

It had made him become a cop.

It had made Dylan determined to fight for justice for all—not just the stinking rich.

He turned off the Hunter Valley highway, heading for Fairchild's nine-hundred-acre estate along the Hunter River.

The route passed several miles of vineyards. It was March, and autumn colors quivered, brittle on the vines, metal windmills turning lazily in the hot wind. Here and there horses ran wild over the drought-brown hills, tails held high, frisky in the hot, smoke-tinged breeze.

It was all seemingly calm despite the political tensions simmering in Sydney, yet the ominous ochre haze over the blue hills of Koongorra Tops spoke of a different kind of threat.

The constant whispering reminder of bushfire smoldering in deep gullies just beyond the ridge across the Hunter River didn't bode well for a valley coming off a long, hard summer of unseasonable drought.

The homicide and arson case at Lochlain Racing, coming on top of these already tinderbox conditions, had left the town of Pepper Flats and the surrounding community wire-tense and baying for blood. The fire at the stud farm had been ugly. Real ugly. And the community wanted someone to pay.

Soon.

Dylan was about to make Louisa Fairchild do just that.

Still, like the smoldering hotspots across the Hunter, a small coal of doubt flickered quiet and deep inside Dylan. He knew he didn't have enough to officially charge her. Yet.

But his superintendent had issued the order to bring her in ASAP.

A gas bomb had detonated in the Sydney central business district less than two hours ago—part of the APEC protests. It had gone off just as the U.S. President was landing at Sydney International for the leaders' portion of the Summit. The U.S. Secretary of State was already in town, at her hotel, where a second device had been primed to detonate simultaneously.

Techs had managed to defuse that one, but the death toll from nerve gas in the first explosion had already hit thirty-two and was climbing fast. The New South Wales police force had received threats from one of the radical protest groups that there were more bombs out there. Riots were now erupting, and part of Sydney had been quarantined. According to Super-intendent Matt Caruthers—Hunter Valley Land Area Com-mander—the Australian Prime Minister was about to go on air to declare a state of emergency.

Caruthers had also informed Dylan that the Prime Minister was calling in the military, and that the NSW police commis-sioner had ordered the majority of the state police force to the capital ASAP—including just about every officer in the Hunter Valley Land Area Command. The homicide team working the Sam Whittleson–Lochlain arson case had also been recalled.

All that remained in the Upper Hunter was a skeleton staff for rotational patrol.

Dylan had been left to twist solo in the dry wind until the APEC dust settled.

This arrest was unorthodox. Everything about it.

And Louisa's lawyers were going to be all over it.

But Caruthers was worried Louisa Fairchild would use this very opportunity to slip through the cracks. She was already a flight risk, and so far, everything the homicide squad had found to date pointed right at her.

She had the motive, opportunity and means to shoot Sam Whittleson, her sixty-one-year-old neighbor and owner of Whittleson Stud, whose charred remains had been found at Lochlain the night of the fire.

Louisa and Sam had been fighting like dogs over rights to Lake Dingo for the last two years. The lake straddled their estates, but the farm boundaries themselves were in dispute, and Louisa had already shot and injured her neighbor over the water issue ten months ago. She'd shot Sam in her library, with her Smith & Wesson .38. He'd survived, but there were witnesses who'd heard Louisa say she "should have killed the bugger properly the first time."

That was a death threat in Dylan's book.

And now Sam Whittleson *was* properly dead.

The first shooting had never gone to trial, a fact that irked the hell out of local cops, including him. Louisa Fairchild with her overpriced lawyers and swanky PR team had claimed self-defense, wangling a deal with Whittleson's legal counsel that saw Whittleson dropping charges against Louisa for fear of being prosecuted for trespassing and assault himself.

But the homicide team now had witnesses who'd seen Louisa Fairchild's dark-gray Holden fleeing Lochlain the night of the blaze and murder. The soil in the tires of her truck confirmed she had been there.

And the fire-damaged murder weapon had finally been recovered from the crime-scene rubble—a Smith & Wesson .38. The gun was currently being processed by forensics techs, and a serial number should be legible before the day was out, which meant the weapon could be traced.

Quite possibly right back to Louisa Fairchild.

Dylan would have been happier to have known for a fact the murder weapon belonged to Louisa.

Instead he'd been sent in prematurely. To squeeze her, bring her in for questioning, rattle her cage, find anything that would allow the NSW police enough to hold her for trial while they built their case.

Right. And who was going to take the fall if the weapon wasn't hers, if the charges didn't stick?

Dylan pinched the bridge of his nose.

He could see himself going down as the scapegoat on this one. Once those APEC stories started dying back from national headlines, *this* was going to be the news.

A small fist of tension curled in his gut as he caught sight of the bronze-and-red Fairchild logo emblazoned on massive stone pillars flanking the entrance to the estate. Dylan's jaw tightened as he signaled to the guard his intent to enter and swung into a driveway lined for almost a mile with mature jacarandas that knitted branches in a canopy over the hard-packed dirt.

On either side of him white fencing trailed across acres of dry grassland that was being cut to the quick for fear of bushfire, the tractors boiling soft clouds of dust that blew like spindrift. But as he neared the manor house and saw sprinklers shooting long white staccato arcs over lush emerald-green lawns and vibrant flower beds, Dylan's acrimony bit deeper.

Louisa Fairchild defied even the drought.

There were severe irrigation restrictions on the river. She was likely pumping water from Lake Dingo which belonged, allegedly, to a dead man.

A man she might have killed. For this very water. For the stud farm she was still trying to snatch out from under his family.

Dylan reminded himself to bury his personal hatred of Louisa Fairchild. It could cost him down the road if his animosity got in the way of her arrest.

The mobile phone on his belt buzzed as he pulled into the circular gravel driveway.

He reached for it, checked caller ID. Heidi. Probably calling to pester him about that party she was desperate to go to tonight. Or the private art school in Sydney she suddenly so passionately wanted to attend.

Dylan let the call flip to voice mail, feeling the tension in his gut wind tighter as he pulled to a stop.

His kid might be as fickle as the wind, but she'd also had a rough ride lately, nearly losing her own horse in the Lochlain fire. Yet no matter how Dylan tried to help, Heidi was throwing up barriers, acting out, making additional demands. She'd just have to wait until he got home tonight, because right now he had a potential career-breaker on his hands.

And Heidi wasn't going to have a future if this case ended up taking him down.

He got out of the squad car, adjusted his gun belt, and put on his hat. It was unusually hot for an autumn evening. He squinted into the haze, waiting for backup from the neighboring Scone station to arrive.

He'd asked for a female cop to help him execute the warrant. What he'd gotten was Ron Peebles, a probationary constable on the job for all of three weeks.

Already things were going sideways, Dylan thought as he watched a plume of dust rise behind the squad car approaching in the distance.

Constable Peebles drew up alongside Dylan's vehicle, got out, his movements taut. It was the young rookie's first arrest and it showed.

"Ready?" Dylan said.

Dry gum leaves clattered suddenly in a gust of hot wind, and a flock of lorikeets burst from the branches in an explosion of color as they took flight and darted through the sprinklers.

Peebles tensed, cleared his throat. "Yeah, I'm ready," he said, looking everything but.

Boots crunching over the gravel driveway, they made their way to the entrance of the massive stone-and-stucco mansion, built ten years ago. Dylan still remembered the old house. He'd played on this farm as a kid with his brother Liam and their friend Henry. That was many years back, before Liam had been murdered.

He climbed the stairs to the door, chest tightening.

He glanced at Peebles standing slightly to the side of the door, feet planted square, hand near his weapon. Peebles nodded.

Dylan rang the bell.

A great booming clang resounded inside the house, and the door swung open, two blue heelers barreling out.

"Officer Hastings?" Louisa's housekeeper, Geraldine Lipton, regarded them with a frown.

"G'day, Mrs. Lipton," he said. "Is Miss Fairchild in?"

Her eyes darted to Peebles, then back to Dylan, hand tight-ening on the brass doorknob as she pulled the door slightly closed. "Miss Fairchild is busy riding," she said tersely. "And then she'll be busy packing. She leaves for London to-morrow."

Dylan flashed Peebles a look—a definite flight risk. "It's important we speak to her immediately, ma'am," he said.

The pinkness of irritability reached up Mrs. Lipton's neck and into her cheeks. "Why don't you wait in the library, officers?" she said curtly. "I'll see if Miss Fairchild can meet with you."

Dylan removed his hat as they followed the stout house-keeper in her starched navy-and-white uniform through a vaulted hallway decorated with broad-leafed plants, sleek sculptures and breezy rattan furniture. The decor had been redone since Dylan had been here last winter. It looked cold to him. But then they didn't pay him to pick out color swatches and match drapes. That was his ex's department.

The thought of Sally shot a familiar jolt of annoyance through him that compounded his feeling of ill will toward Louisa, the past suddenly crowding in on him.

Mrs. Lipton threw open a set of solid old jarrah-wood doors, ushering the two men into the library of polished wood, leather furniture, antique tomes, old art and a general aura of established wealth.

Dylan immediately eyed the elaborate, glassed-in gun col-lection beyond the fireplace. If Louisa's Smith & Wesson was in that cabinet he was going to have a problem. It would mean the pistol they had in the lab belonged to someone else.

Again, he cursed that he'd been forced to move prema-turely. He needed the serial number on that murder weapon.

"Can I send for some tea while you wait?" The house-keeper's voice remained tight.

"No. Thank you," Dylan said, striding into the vast room where Sam Whittleson had come damn near to getting himself shot to death the first time.

Late-afternoon sunlight streamed in through French doors open to the patio, the water in the pool outside shimmering as if someone had just dived in. But Dylan made straight for the cabinet, pulse quickening as he noted a vacant spot on the red velvet where Louisa's .38 had rested last June.

It was missing.

But as he leaned forward for a closer inspection of her collection, the library doors swung open with a crash and Louisa Fairchild's voice resounded through the room.

"What in hell do you people want now!"

Dylan straightened, turned slowly to face her, projecting a powerful confidence and calm he didn't quite feel.

Framed by the double doorway and flanked by her stubby housekeeper holding her black velvet riding helmet, Louisa Fairchild cut a tall, sophisticated and formidable figure for her eighty years—spine held stiff, crisp cotton stock-tied blouse high at the neck, tan breeches, dusty leather riding boots and silvery hair pulled back in a sleek chignon. She had handsome features and the very tanned and lined face of an Australian outdoorswoman. Her hands were brown, too. Veined, but elegant. Strong. Working hands, if rich ones.

Louisa was a blend of what defined this country in many ways. A woman of the land, one who'd made her wealth from it. Descended from a family that had risen from common stock brought over on boats to the penal colony to become rich in a warm climate of equal opportunity.

If Louisa had the same respect for equal justice as she had for opportunity, if Dylan didn't hate her so much for what she'd done to his family, he might even find a grudging respect for this matriarch. He thought of his own frail mother, of this formidable woman's indirect role in unraveling her.

"G'day, Miss Fairchild—"

"Cut to the chase, Detective Sergeant," she snapped. "What do you want?"

He noted the strain in her neck muscles, the way she held her riding crop tight against her thigh, and he let silence hang for a few beats, just to rattle her further.

"We'd like to ask you some questions, Miss Fairchild," he said, walking slowly toward her. "We'd like to know, for example, where your Smith & Wesson revolver is."

Her eyes flicked to the gun cabinet and back. Her hand clenched the crop tighter. "If you're here about that Sam Whittleson thing—"

"You mean his homicide?"

"I have nothing to say about that. And I must insist you get off my estate."

"Perhaps you'd like to come down to the Pepper Flats station then, just to answer a few questions?"

"Are you arresting me, Detective Sergeant?" Her chin tilted up in defiance. "Because if not, I have no intention of going anywhere with you, and I'm ordering you off my land. Now. Before I call my lawyers."

"Then I'm afraid we'll have to do this the hard way, ma'am," Dylan said, reaching for the cuffs at his belt.

"Miss Louisa Fairchild," he said, reaching for her arm, "I'm placing you under arrest for the murder of Sam Whittleson."

Megan Stafford stepped out of the pool, wet hair splashing droplets at her feet as she reached for her towel, the evening sun balmy and soft against her bare skin.

She began to towel herself as she studied the purplish-yellow haze on the horizon. It looked as though a thunderstorm was brewing, but she knew better. The haze was from the Koongorra fires.

It reminded her of Black Christmas when bushfire had raged across New South Wales for almost three weeks—the longest continuous bushfire emergency in the state's history. No one in this region took the threat of mega fires for granted after that, especially with drought conditions like this.

Especially after the scare at Lochlain Racing, a neighboring stud farm owned by Tyler Preston.

Megan and her brother Patrick had arrived at Fairchild Acres two days after the murder of Sam Whittleson and the tragic Lochlain blaze. Sam had been shot in the Thoroughbred barn at Lochlain, late at night. One shot in the chest, one in the back. His body had then been dragged into a vacant horse stall, doused in turpentine and set ablaze. The fire had spread quickly through the H-shaped barn buildings, devastating the farm with losses into the millions.

Several prize Thoroughbreds had died; nearly forty others were left injured and incapable of ever racing again.

The barn had been under closed-circuit-camera surveillance, but the CD containing the footage from that night was missing.

Now emotions in the region were as brittle as the rustling dry gum leaves—the whole valley fearing an arsonist and murderer was loose among them.

Megan bent sideways, trying to knock water out of her ear. It had been an awkward time to arrive. She felt strange to be here at all.

She and Patrick had come to Fairchild Acres at the behest of their estranged great-aunt Louisa, who wished to determine if her only living relatives were worthy of her inheritance.

Louisa's blunt letter had been a slap in the face to Megan.

She knew the woman by reputation only as a cold-hearted and phenomenally wealthy battleaxe with a prized talent for spotting winning horses. She also knew her great-aunt had—for some unspoken reason—banished her own sister Betty from Fairchild Acres many, many years ago, totally severing that branch of her family. Megan's gran had never spoken about the incident. Neither had Megan's mother.

And the family secret had died with them.

Megan had adored her Granny Betty, and she had no interest in the fortune of the noxious old dame who had shunned her gran.

If it hadn't been for some serious argument on the part of her pragmatic brother, who claimed Betty had been denied her rightful share of the Fairchild estate, Megan would not have taken time off work, packed her bags and been standing barefoot at the Fairchild pool right now.

But the Fairchild legacy Megan had really come seeking was not money. She'd come to find an answer to that old family secret. She wanted to know where her gran had really come from, and why she'd been banished. It was a sense of birthright, of belonging, that Megan hungered for.

But her thoughts were suddenly shattered as the unflappable Mrs. Lipton came barreling out of the library. "Megan! Megan! Come quick! It's Miss Fairchild! They're arresting her!"

Megan stilled, towel in midair. "Arresting Louisa? What for?"

"Murder!"

Megan dropped her towel, grabbed a pool robe from the deck chair, and yanked it over her arms as she raced up the flagstone steps to the library.

She froze in the doorway.

A large sandy-haired cop was ushering a handcuffed Louisa out of the library as a skinny young policeman moved towards the gun cabinet.

Megan's heart started to hammer. *"Louisa?"*

They all spun round.

The tall officer holding her aunt narrowed eyes like hot blue lasers onto Megan. Steady eyes. The most startling cornflower blue she'd ever seen. Eyes that sucked her right in. And held her.

Her stomach balled tight and her heart began to patter.

Part of her job as a legal consultant and art buyer was to evaluate instantly color, form, function. The artist in her appraised the cop just as fast.

He was tanned, well over six feet, features ruggedly

handsome. He had the lean, hard lines of an endurance athlete—a sign of mental resilience, the kind that could too easily translate into obstinacy. But it was the overall impression—his electric aura—that shocked her to her toes. The impact was total, complete.

And it made her mouth turn dry.

"Thank God you're here, Megan," Louisa said, trying to twist out of the cop's grasp. "Get my lawyer, Robert D'Angelo, get him on the phone. At once!"

Megan felt herself hesitate. The directness in the cop's clear gaze was unnerving, commanding her attention in such a way she was barely able to register anything else in the room.

She cleared her throat, her eyes beginning to water with the effort of meeting his penetrating gaze. "I'm Megan Stafford," she said to the cop. "Louisa is my great-aunt. What's going on here?"

His eyes dipped quickly over her damp body, her skimpy bikini, bare feet. Megan pulled her robe closed, belting it tightly across her waist.

"Detective Sergeant Hastings," he said. "And this is Constable Ron Peebles. The constable is here to execute a search warrant on the property. It's on the desk over there. Your aunt is coming with me. She's under arrest in connection with the murder of Sam Whittleson." He began to escort Louisa out.

"Wait!" Megan surged forward, grabbed his arm. "You've made a mistake," she said, locking eyes with his. "My aunt is eighty. She…she didn't do this."

His eyes narrowed. "Hindering an officer is an offense under the law—I don't want to have to take you in as well, Ms. Stafford. Now if you'd please step back."

She withdrew her hand slowly, adrenaline zinging through her, and with it came the first stirrings of hot anger.

The officer walked Louisa out of the library.

"Megan!" she called over her shoulder as the man led her

into the hall. "Just get D'Angelo, will you? His number is on the library desk. Tell him to meet me at the Pepper Flats station at once. And watch that numbskull search," she demanded. "Don't let him touch a damn thing! Mrs. Lipton—"

"This way please, Miss Fairchild."

"Mrs. Lipton, get Patrick," Louisa shouted, craning her neck round as the cop opened the front door, escorting her out. "Tell him to speak to the managers. Tell them…tell them I'll be back in a few hours." Louisa's voice was strained, her features pinched.

But it was the parting look she shot Megan that unnerved her grand niece the most.

Megan barely knew her estranged aunt, but the woman's iron reputation preceded her. Louisa Fairchild was unshakable.

Unsinkable.

Except now. Megan could see in her steel-blue eyes that this macho cop had rattled her aunt. Badly.

He'd shaken something deep and hot in Megan, too.

Adrenaline tightened her stomach. With it came an uncomfortably cold whisper of doubt. The cop had to have something on Louisa to actually arrest her.

Could her aunt be involved in murder?

She exhaled, trying to steady her hands. Right. Call Robert D'Angelo. Then get Patrick. Her brother could help gather the farm managers together.

She scrabbled through the papers on Louisa's library desk. She'd met D'Angelo at dinner last week. He'd reminded her of a hungry beak-nosed bird of prey. Damn, she couldn't find his cell number anywhere in this mess. Louisa's private office was being redecorated, her boxes stacked in one of the outbuildings while most of her immediate paperwork and files had been temporarily relocated to this oak rolltop.

"Do you have the keys for this gun cabinet, ma'am?" Constable Peebles asked.

Her eyes shot to the young, dark-haired cop. "No. I don't."

He broke the lock. Tension fluttered through her stomach and perspiration began to prickle over her brow. "Mrs. Lipton! Where's th—" She found an address book in the drawer. "Oh, I got it!" She flipped it open to D'Angelo, Fischer and Associates, quickly dialed the firm's number in Sydney. He wasn't there, but they gave her his mobile number. She dialed again.

Robert D'Angelo answered on the first ring. And the knot of tension tightened in Megan's stomach as he told her he was miles away, on the outskirts of Sydney, and that APEC security blockades were going up along all major arteries because of the bomb blast. It was unlikely he'd make it through anytime soon.

"You need to get down to the Pepper Flats station yourself, Megan," Robert instructed in his reassuring baritone. "And tell Louisa not to say one word. Anything she says while in police custody can be used against her in court. Drive that home to her, understand? I cannot stress this enough."

Megan knew this was going to be a tall order. Asking Louisa to keep her mouth shut and her abrasive opinions to herself was akin to asking the sun not to come up.

"The police have four hours within which to officially charge her and to get her in front of a magistrate," Robert said. "If they want to hold her longer, they'll need to apply for another warrant. Watch this. Let them know you know it. And you *must* be allowed to speak to her in private."

Megan nodded to herself, thinking ahead. She knew the basics. She'd started studying criminal law at university herself, before dropping it in favor of art and corporate law. The combative nature of the criminal justice system wasn't a fit for her personality. She'd learned that pretty quickly.

"Keep me updated via mobile," Robert told her. "I'll start assembling a criminal team at the town office."

"You…think it's *that* serious?"

"It is if they believe they have enough to take her in. My

team will commence background checks on the arresting officer right away. What did you say his name was?"

She glanced up at Peebles, now rifling through cabinet drawers, and she thought of the cop with the steady blue eyes. "Detective Sergeant Hastings."

"By the time I'm done, Hastings won't have a job. And you let him know it."

Megan hung up picturing the tall, swarthy and cerebral Robert D'Angelo squaring off with the physically robust and tanned cop. And a shimmer of electricity rippled through her belly at the thought of having to square off with him herself.

She was no substitute for the formidable lawyer.

And no match against that determined hunk of police officer.

Chapter Two

"Mrs. Lipton, get someone to bring a car round for me!" Megan yelled as she raced up the sweeping marble staircase.

She flung open the cupboard in her guest room, grabbing a sleeveless shift dress, the creation of a young up-and-coming Sydney designer, urban casual.

All Megan's clothes were the work of emerging artists— fledgling designers she predicted would become household names. She liked to support them at the start of their journeys. It had become her trademark philosophy, and her sartorial style on the Sydney art gallery circuit had begun earning her a familiar spot on the social pages of the city newspapers and glossies. That in turn had garnered attention for her clients.

Attention for her clients was good. It fed her business.

She shimmied into the dress, not wasting time to take her bikini off. Quickly sliding her feet into sandals, she grabbed her purse, and stalled in front of the mirror as she caught sight of her wet hair still plastered to her head. She cursed, grabbed a silk scarf off the dresser, flinging it over her hair as she snagged her large sunglasses, and clattered down the broad staircase, and out the front door.

"Biltong" Laroux, Louisa's rugged broodmare manager, had brought her aunt's champagne-colored Aston Martin DB9 convertible round to the front door.

Megan stalled, eyes whipping to his. "You want me to take *this?*"

"Patrick's got the sports ute. The other cars are either out or in the shop."

"It's…not an automatic," she said.

Biltong pushed his felt hat farther back on his head, a glint of amusement in his warm brown eyes. "Do you need someone to drive you, Ms. Stafford?"

"Of course not," she said reaching for the door handle. "Just…hold fort here, please."

Megan started the ignition and promptly stalled the high-end sports car. She cursed, hotly aware of Biltong watching her from under the brim of his bush hat. She knew how to drive a stick shift. She just hadn't done it in a while.

She depressed the clutch and turned the key, setting the engine purring again. She shifted into First gear, and jerked sharply forward, almost giving herself whiplash before taking off down the driveway in a blast of dust, Louisa's blue heelers yipping at the wheels.

Damn.

Louisa rarely went anywhere without her two cattle dogs, and they were going to get hurt if they kept this up all the way down to the estate gates.

Megan hit the brakes, kept the engine running as she reached over to open the passenger door. "C'mon. Get in Scout, Blue!"

The blue heelers scrambled excitedly onto the butter leather, settling next to her in the two-seater.

Megan engaged gears, releasing the clutch as she simultaneously depressed the gas pedal, having to consciously think in order simply to drive. Finding her rhythm, she gathered speed down the mile-long driveway under the jacaranda trees, billowing fine red Australian dust in her wake.

As she neared the gates, a group of horses kept pace at a canter in the adjacent field.

She wheeled the sports car onto the farm road, picking up more speed as she headed for the small town of Pepper Flats. Dusk was settling over the dry valley, and her heart hammered in her chest as she mentally prepared to face the physically disarming cop again. She wondered just how the hell she'd gotten to this point in the space of a week.

Dylan had been born in Pepper Flats. For the past ten years he'd worked the area as a local cop, and not once during that time had he ever heard mention of a Fairchild niece.

And a woman like Megan Stafford wouldn't go unnoticed in this valley, he thought as he led a stone-faced Louisa into the station charge room, ordering her to sit while he entered her into the system.

A long-lost niece conveniently popping out of the woodwork with her great-aunt tipping the wrong side of eighty seemed a little too contrived for his liking. She was probably after the old dame's fortune, and the thought turned Dylan's blood cold.

He knew Megan's type—all warm surface gloss and seductive appeal on the exterior, but calculating and devoid of compassion on the inside.

He'd learned the hard way just how deceptive a gorgeous-looking woman like her could be. He'd married one. And he had spent the past ten years of his life raising his kid alone as a single dad, when all he'd dreamed of was a real family.

It was a mistake he was not likely to make again.

He handed Louisa two forms outlining her rights and began setting up the recording equipment in the interview room while keeping an eye on his octogenarian charge sitting thunderously silent.

She'd gone ash-pale under her tan and refused his offer of water. A small wedge of worry edged into Dylan's chest.

It was a custody manager's priority to watch for signs of ill health that might arise from police detention, and with Peebles executing the search warrant, Dylan was doing double duty as both custody manager and investigating officer in a station that wasn't even a designated holding facility.

D'Angelo would have his balls over this "transgression" alone. But given the state of emergency and the police shortage, Dylan had no choice but to wing this as best he could, and hope that Crown prosecutors would argue extenuating circumstances on his behalf should D'Angelo try to nail him for it.

"This way please, Miss Fairchild?" he said, taking her arm. "I need to get your fingerprints."

"You have one hell of a hide doing this, Hastings," she snapped. "I know your sort. You—"

"You know nothing about me," he said, leading her smartly to the fingerprinting station along the brick wall.

You destroyed my family and you don't even remember who I am.

Not that she'd care if she did.

"Hold still, please," he said, taking her wrist and pressing her thumb into the ink pad, rolling it from one side to the other.

No, he thought as he held her inked thumb apart from her other fingers and moved her hand over to the blank sheet, Louisa knew nothing about him at all.

He rolled her thumb over the white surface until the print was complete. She muttered a colorful oath under her breath and pulled back as he began to thoroughly smear her index finger with ink.

"Would you hold still, please?" He tried to tamp down the irritation spiking sharply through him. But as Dylan began to roll Louisa's next finger through the ink, a movement outside the window caught his eye.

He glanced up to see an Aston Martin DB9 Volante coming to a bone-jerking halt in front of the station, the high-performance engine stalling. Dylan felt an odd reflexive rush as he recognized Megan Stafford, looking like some Hollywood star in a casually elegant short dress, silk scarf, bare sun-bronzed arms and giant shades, Louisa's two blue heelers on the seat beside her like Lord and Lady Muck.

He saw her mutter what could only be an expletive as she swung open the convertible's door, extending long athletic legs. And Dylan felt a smile tempt the corners of his mouth.

He tried not to watch those lean legs walking towards the entrance of his station, tried to focus on Louisa's prints, but at the same time he was compelled to sneak another peek, grudgingly acknowledging that Fairchild's grand-niece really was hot, even with clothes on.

Heat coursed softly through Dylan as the image of Stafford in that barely there bikini reformed in his consciousness—and his body hardened in instant response. He banked down the unbidden and annoying rush of physical anticipation, reminding himself Stafford had probably come to the station to wheedle herself into Louisa Fairchild's good graces—if there were such a thing—and right into the octogenarian's will.

This helped steel his focus.

But as she entered the reception area he felt the chemistry of the smoke-tinged air in the small brick station shift, and his pulse quickened anyway.

"Louisa?" Megan called, leaning her body over the counter. "Are you all right?" Her mouth opened in shock as she saw her aunt being fingerprinted down the hall, and her green eyes flared at Dylan. "I need to talk to her," she demanded. "In private."

The cop speared her with those intense blue eyes of his. "It's her right, Detective Sergeant Hastings. I…I'm a lawyer."

His brow crooked sharply up, and Megan felt her cheeks grow hot. She swore to herself. She had no idea what had possessed her to say that. The man flat-out unnerved her.

"Would you take the dogs outside, please, Ms. Stafford? And I'll let you in the back as soon as we're done with the prints here."

Megan muttered another curse as she returned Scout and Blue to the car. He was playing power games with her by ordering her out with the dogs like that. It was probably also a ploy to rattle Louisa.

Megan reentered the station, removing her scarf and using it to tie her damp hair back into a ponytail as she did. She wished she'd managed to get out of her wet bikini before coming. It was now uncomfortable.

Detective Sergeant Hastings unlocked a door to the side of the reception counter, admitting her into the working part of the police station.

It was deserted at this hour, and his presence seemed to suck up all the air in the place. Megan suddenly felt nervous. But when she peered beyond his broad shoulders and saw the normally statuesque Louisa looking so frail and vulnerable as she tried to scrub the ink from her hands at a grimy, gray, industrial-sized enamel sink, a fist of anger curled deep in Megan's belly, squeezing away the nerves.

"I need a moment with her," she said quietly. "Alone."

He held out his hand. "Room down on the left."

"Come, Louisa," she said, taking her aunt's arm, feeling the cop's eyes burning into her back as they went down the corridor to the interview room. He had a way of stripping her naked just by looking. It made her legs feel like jelly and she had trouble concentrating on the simple act of walking.

"Leave the door open so I can see you both," he called out as they were about to enter the windowless neon-lit room.

She glowered at him.

Dylan checked his watch. The longer he left them, the

more chance D'Angelo had of showing up before he could squeeze Louisa. Yet he was legally obligated to give them time alone. He unhooked his phone from his belt, was about to punch in his home number and let Heidi know he wasn't going to make it for dinner, when his mobile beeped.

He flipped it open. "Hastings."

"Sergeant, it's the lab. We've managed to lift the serial number of the murder weapon. The Smith & Wesson .38 that killed Sam Whittleson is registered to Louisa Fairchild."

Bingo!

This was going to make things a hell of a lot easier. He'd now be remiss *not* to have brought her in.

He flipped open his phone, relief rushing through him as he called his daughter.

Megan placed her hand gently over Louisa's slender veined one. It felt as fragile as a bird under her own, and beneath the harsh fluorescent lighting her aunt looked much older, drained. It wasn't surprising. No innocent person deserved to be fingerprinted like that, to be forced into an airless and sterile room with one-way mirrored glass, seated at a table that had been bolted to the floor. *Especially* not an eighty-year-old woman of Louisa's stature in the community. "How are you holding up, Louisa?" she asked softly, studying her aunt's blue eyes.

"Where the blazes is Robert?" she snapped. "I'll be fine as soon as he gets me out of this hell hole."

Megan hesitated, not wanting to upset her aunt further by telling her Robert might not make it through the APEC barricades tonight. "He's…on his way. He instructed you not to say a word, Louisa. Silence cannot be held against you, but anything you do say can be used in court—"

"Oh, for Pete's sake, Megan, this is not going to get to court!" But a flicker of fear in her eyes belied her bluster.

Megan glanced at Detective Sergeant Hastings talking on

his phone down the hall. "He must have *some* reason to hold you here, Louisa," she said in a whisper.

"Impossible!"

"Then why do you think he brought you in?" she said calmly. "I mean, they already questioned you after the Lochlain fire, and cleared you, didn't they?"

Louisa went silent, her eyes suddenly uncertain, and without the habitual steel they were startlingly reminiscent of grandmother Betty's eyes. And of Megan's mother's eyes. An acute sense of love and loss rustled so sharply through Megan that it put a catch of emotion in her throat.

This irascible grande dame really was her family.

And a sense of family was something Megan yearned for.

"I didn't kill him, Megan."

"I know that, Louisa."

"Do you?"

Conflict twisted through Megan. She wanted to say yes. But in all honesty she knew very little about Louisa.

For a moment she couldn't answer.

"I did *not* shoot Sam, Megan," Louisa insisted, eyes narrowing. "I did not set fire to that place. I had nothing to do with the old bugger's death." She smoothed back a stray wisp of hair that had escaped her chignon as she spoke, and Megan noticed that her hands were shaking. Louisa's face also had a strange sheen to it, her skin unusually pale save for two little hot spots forming high along her cheekbones. In spite of her stiff spine and the defiant tilt of her chin, her aunt was unraveling.

Megan needed to get her out of here soon.

"Would you like me to get you some water?"

"Just get me Robert, for mercy's sake. What are we waiting for?" Her breaths were coming too fast, too shallow. She was perspiring.

"I'm getting you some water," Megan insisted, standing up.

She marched along the passage to where Detective Sergeant Hastings stood talking on his phone, and her whole body instinctively braced, adrenaline beginning to hum in her chest as she approached him.

But he angled away from her slightly as she neared, lowering his voice as he spoke into his mobile so she wouldn't hear. "Listen, chook," he said softly. "I'll explain when I get home. I'm really busy right now—"

"My aunt needs water," Megan demanded, standing square in front of him.

He glanced up, a flash of irritation in his eyes that shifted quickly into something quite different as he took in the faint damp patches her wet bikini had formed on her dress. He pointed to the water cooler next to a desk on his right, his eyes dark.

Megan swallowed, cursing the effect his look had on her as she went to get water.

"We'll talk when we get home, okay, kiddo?" he said almost inaudibly, the gentleness in his voice catching Megan by surprise. She stilled as she bent over to fill a cup at the cooler, unable to stop herself from listening in on his phone conversation.

"There'll be other parties—no, listen—" He hesitated. "Sweetheart, wait—"

He swore suddenly, and flipped his phone shut, eyes narrowing as he saw Megan watching him.

"Your daughter?" she asked, standing up, cup of water in hand.

He shoved his mobile back into his gun belt, his eyes flat, inscrutable. "Shall we proceed with the interview now?"

But Megan held her ground. "You're a dad, aren't you? A family man. Can you not find it within yourself to show my aunt some compassion? She's eighty, for goodness' sakes."

"She's also rich. Is that why you're here out of the blue, Ms. Stafford? Because she's pushing the wrong side of eighty and has amassed a small fortune?"

Her eyes narrowed sharply. "Damn you," she whispered.

"I'm worried about my aunt's welfare, not her money, and if you don't charge her immediately, I insist you let her go."

He held out his hand, showing her the way. "Let's get this over then."

But as they entered the room, Louisa stood up shakily, pressing her hand against her sternum as she tried to brace herself against the table. Her face was ashen, her skin damp.

"This…this is ridiculous," she said, her voice coming out in a rasp. "This cannot be happening. I need…to leave—" She tried to walk, wobbled, and gripped the back of her chair to steady herself.

Megan rushed forward, taking her by the arm. "Louisa, please sit—"

"Where's Robert?" she said hoarsely, panic straining her features. "I…I won't go through this. I will not be subjected to this. I…refuse to do this without Robert. He wouldn't let this happen. He would not let it get this far."

Hot tension whipped through Megan. She shot a look at Hastings as she helped Louisa back down into the chair. "I'm not sure counsel of her choice is going to make it here in time. Could…could you do this tomorrow? Louisa needs air. This room is too hot."

"You said you were her lawyer."

"*A* lawyer. Not *her* lawyer. Besides, I'm not a criminal one."

That sandy brow of his crooked up again.

It fuelled her anger. "I'm a corporate lawyer for an art gallery cooperative in Sydney," Megan snapped. She was furious she was even explaining herself to this stubborn hunk of a policeman. "And I find your attitude disrespectful. My aunt is an esteemed member of this community. She deserves better treatment than this—"

"She deserves *equal* treatment, Ms. Stafford."

Megan wavered slightly at the veiled menace in his tone. "She does have a right to counsel of her choice before you question her. And she's not well—"

"She has no such *right,* Ms. Stafford."

"But you do allow it—"

"We're running out of time." He depressed a button to start recording the interview. "Now if you'll please calm down and take a seat, I'd like to advise Miss Fairchild that she is entitled to refrain from answering my questions, and that anything she does say can be used in a court of law. Miss Fairchild." His eyes focused on Louisa, a muscle pulsing along his jaw. "Can you explain how your Smith & Wesson .38 came to be found in a melted fertilizer drum near the body of Sam Whittleson?"

"What?" Megan slowly took a seat, staring at the cop. "That's not possible," she whispered.

His laser-blue eyes turned on her. "It's a fact."

Megan shot an inquiring look at her great-aunt. "Louisa?"

"Someone…must have stolen it," Louisa said, pressing her hand harder against her upper abdomen, her breathing shallow.

Desperation surged through Megan. Her eyes whipped back to Detective Sergeant Hastings, tension crackling through her body as she jerked to her feet. "This is enough, Sergeant! This is pure harassment. You're on a fishing expedition, otherwise you'd have charged her already. I insist that you either do so now, or let us go, because my aunt has nothing more to say. And she's clearly not well."

Before he could respond, Louisa swayed, clutched hard at her chest, rasped for air, and slumped off her chair.

"Louisa!" Megan dropped to her knees, fumbling to loosen her aunt's high collar. Louisa's skin was cold and clammy. She'd stopped breathing. "Oh, God, she's having a heart attack!" Megan yelled as she tried to ease Louisa onto her back. "Dial triple zero—get an ambulance!"

She felt Detective Sergeant Hastings taking her shoulders, forcing her back from her aunt as he keyed his radio.

"We need an ambulance, Pepper Flats police station," he barked. "Cardiac arrest. Maybe MI. Eighty-year-old female—"

He gave a rapid-fire series of details as he knelt beside Louisa and began ripping back her restrictive blouse, feeling for a pulse at her neck.

"No pulse," he told dispatch. "She's non-responsive. Commencing CPR."

He tilted Louisa's head back, checking her air passages.

Tears filled Megan's eyes as she looked on in horror.

"Get out front!" he yelled at her between CPR breaths and compressions. "Flag the ambos outside—tell them we're in here. Move it, *now!*"

Chapter Three

Heidi stood at her bedroom window, staring into the dark night, thinking about stuff.

Her father still wasn't home and she could hear her gran stirring down the hall as she went to the bathroom. A strange mix of concern and irritation flushed through her.

She hated feeling this way about her family.

It had gotten worse after the night she'd stood at this same window, watching the strobe lights pulse over the night sky, hearing the distant bullhorn—knowing Lochlain Racing was burning.

She'd smelled the bitter smoke on the wind, and she knew Anthem was in there, in the blaze. Her dad, too, fighting the fire with the other villagers, and her heart had been so sick with worry.

She'd wanted to be there. To help. But she'd been ordered to stay with Granny June. Just as she'd been ordered by her father to stay home tonight.

And now Zach had gone to the B&S ball without her.

She swiped a stupid tear from her face. Damn, why was she so emotional?

Granny June's health wasn't helping. It was draining Heidi. Her gran was forgetting things, getting more confused. Wandering off. Leaving water to boil, running the bath and not shutting off the taps. And Heidi's freedom was increasingly restricted because of it.

Apart from her riding, she could never do anything after school because her dad was worried something would happen if they left June alone too much now. And Heidi didn't want to feel like this—resentful about it. But her dad was putting more and more pressure on her to help care for his mother as work commitments pulled him away, and it was starting to wear her down.

She wanted out.

She wanted to go to private school in Sydney to study art. Like her mum, Heidi was gifted artistically. And like her mother, she hoped one day to work in an artistic field, in a big vibrant city.

She heard her gran going back to bed down the hall, and Heidi looked up at the splatter of stars, the thin sliver of moon, wondering how often her mother gazed up at the sky in London—the same sky.

So far away.

She wondered if her mum ever missed her family. Or if her dad ever wished he could see Sally again. Heidi could never tell what he was feeling. Whenever she mentioned her mother to him, he'd just get all bossy and change the subject.

He thought not talking about Sally was somehow shielding her from the fact her mother had walked out on them, from this very house, one night ten years ago.

After that her dad had invited his recently widowed mother to come and live with them, mostly to help care for Heidi, who was only four.

Now she was fourteen, and she was caring for her gran.

Another warm tear rolled down her cheek. Her dad didn't understand.

He never did.

He was always too busy being a cop, catching crims, protecting others. He had no idea how much of a burden Gran was becoming, how fast her illness was progressing. Heidi suspected a part of him didn't even *want* to see it.

She wrapped her arms over her stomach, feeling so alone.

She missed Zach.

She missed riding her horse, and prayed Anthem was going to make it. She wanted to be with her mare, and they'd told her she couldn't be anymore. That she should only come at the vet's visiting hours, because everyone had their hands full at Lochlain and she was getting in their way.

She sniffed, rubbed the back of her hand across her nose, and went down the hall. Edging open the door to her grandmother's room, Heidi listened carefully, hearing only the sounds of soft breathing in the dark. "Gran?" she whispered.

No answer.

She hesitated. Her dad would kill her.

But she didn't care.

She left the house, closing the front door very quietly. Going round to the garage, she got her bike out, and began cycling the twelve miles along the dark farm roads to Lochlain Racing, her bike-light a small halo in the Australian night.

It was almost midnight when Dylan pushed open the door of Elias Memorial's dimly lit waiting area.

Megan had dozed off in a chair at the far end of the room, the television mounted near the ceiling silently flickering with highlights from the latest country cup race at Muswellbrook.

Someone had given her a blanket and she'd pulled it up to her chin. The scarf that had tied back her hair was gone, and the wet strands had dried into thick soft blond waves that fell both seductively and innocently across her cheek. Louisa's blue heelers lay sleeping at her feet. One of the dogs cocked open an eye, regarded him warily.

He knew their names now—Scout and Blue. He'd persuaded the clinic staff to allow the animals into the waiting area while Louisa had been wheeled in for emergency angioplasty. It hadn't been a tough sell. Jenny, one of the emerg nurses, was engaged to Mitch Ogden, an old mate of Dylan's. Mitch, Henry, Dylan and his older brother Liam used to hang together as young boys.

It was a time when Dylan was still a Smith, not a Hastings.

A time when he still had a brother.

Dylan's step-dad had officially adopted him much later, long after Liam's murder. Long after the family moved to Sydney, where his real father had turned into a morose drunk unable to come to terms with his son's brutal death, and Dylan's mum had finally remarried.

Dylan hesitated at the waiting-room doors, oddly conflicted by the old memories that really had no relevance to this moment, other than being somehow tied back to Louisa Fairchild. Arresting her had stirred it all back up to the surface. And it wasn't something he wanted to deal with.

But at the same time, the soft and unexpected compassion blooming in his chest as he studied Megan sleeping in her chair was almost pleasurable.

She didn't look so slick right now. She looked vulnerable. Dylan was born to care, to protect. To defend. And he felt these instincts rustle in him now.

It had been almost two hours since he'd left her here and gone back to the station to prepare the formal homicide charge.

He'd brought a copy with him.

Megan was going to be furious.

He removed his hat, dragging his hand over his hair before

stepping into the room. He felt tired. Responsible for Louisa's heart attack.

He'd judged Louisa's stress at the station to be a display of guilt. Had he been too intent on hammering her for personal reasons—for a sense of retribution—to notice the warning signs?

Self-reproach bit at him.

As much as Dylan despised the old dame, he did not want to be the cause of her death. And with guilt came an even deeper sense of unease. This incident was going to provide D'Angelo with a devastating round of ammunition when he finally made it through those APEC barricades and saw first-hand what was going down with his client.

This case really could end up costing Dylan his job.

He'd seen it happen to better cops than himself. The firm of D'Angelo, Fischer and Associates had gone after a couple of Newcastle officers for alleged police brutality last year and won on procedural technicalities. Bloody pack of dingoes.

Dylan couldn't afford to lose this job. It was his life. He'd returned to Pepper Flats specifically for this posting. It had been his way of trying to hold on to his family ten years ago, after Sally's affair. And even when Sally had split before the first year was out, it had still proved a good place to raise his child.

And right now Dylan's discomfort was compounded by the fact he hadn't been able to make it home to talk to Heidi before she went to bed—because of this case. Because of Louisa.

He needed to get home in time to catch his kid before she left for school in the morning.

Pressure weighing heavy on him, Dylan took a seat near Megan, watching her, wondering if his involvement with Louisa Fairchild's clan would, again, cost him life as he knew it.

Megan stirred, and something weird tightened in his chest.

Her eyes flickered open sleepily, then flared wide as she sat up sharply, startled to find him looking at her.

"Any word yet?" he asked. Waiting for Louisa to come out of surgery had bred an uneasy, if temporary, truce between them.

"No," she said, pulling the blanket higher. She looked cold. And about as exhausted as he felt.

With all Louisa's minions, Dylan wondered why Megan was the only one here tonight. Was the old woman really so alone?

"You the only family Louisa has in town at the moment?" he said.

She pushed a thick wave of hair back from her face and moistened her lips as she weighed up his reasons for asking. Beautiful lips, thought Dylan.

"My brother Patrick was here while you were gone," she said. "He went back to the estate to look for some of Louisa's medical papers. The doctors think she might be on a medication that isn't documented in her clinic files. They want to be sure."

"So you and Patrick must be the grandchildren of Betty Fairchild?"

Interest flared in her green eyes. She sat straighter. "You know about Betty?"

"I was born here. I grew up in the valley. Old-timers talk."

She studied him, curiosity beginning to hum about her with a kinetic energy that stirred something dark and quick in Dylan. She clearly wanted to ask more about Betty, and he wondered why. Surely she knew about her own grandmother.

"How come we haven't seen you out in these parts before?" he said.

"You going to accuse me of gold-digging again?"

"Just wondering what brings you here, and where home is for you, Megan."

She studied him in silence. "Sydney," she said finally. "Our side of the family was estranged from Louisa for some time.

She wanted to get to know us better, so we came to visit a
her invitation."

He nodded. He wanted to believe in her.

Then he thought of Sally, and glanced away. Be damne
if they weren't similar in looks. The kind of looks that reall
did it for him.

A doctor passed, and they both tensed. More minute:
ticked by. Dylan got up and went to the nurses' station to asl
how things were progressing, and they said he should take s
seat, that the doc would be out as soon as he had word.

He paced the waiting area like a caged lion, Mega
watching him.

Another half hour passed.

He checked his watch, stopped pacing. "You want a coffe?
Or tea or something? There's a machine round the corner."

Relief visibly rippled through her, and she smiled. "Coffee
would be heaven."

He brought it back to her, and their fingers brushed as she
took the cup. Energy crackled so sharp and sudden between
them that her eyes flashed up to meet his. Dylan swallowed.

He took one seat down from her, bending to scratch Scout
behind the ear with one hand, holding his coffee in the other,
discomfited by what was clearly a powerful and very mutual
physical attraction between them.

"How old is your daughter?" she said, cradling her cup in
both hands, blowing steam.

Dylan slanted his eyes to her. "Fourteen," he said.

"You're a single dad, aren't you?"

"What makes you say that?"

She lifted her shoulder. "The way you were talking to her
on the phone."

A wry smile tempted his lips. "You'd make a good detective, Stafford."

"I'd know better than to arrest my aunt for murder if I was
one."

His smile faded. He continued to hold her eyes. "I'd be remiss not to have brought her in, Megan," he said quietly. "I do have a job to do."

"Right." She looked at her coffee. "So what kind of party did your daughter want to go to?"

"You heard that much from the phone call?"

"I was standing right there."

He sipped his coffee, realizing he'd underestimated this woman. "It was a B&S ball," he said. "Being held out on one of the farms north of here. They're—"

"Bachelors and Spinsters. I know what they are. People dress up in fancy gowns and gumboots or whatever, drive for miles to some really isolated rural area, sit in some shed or paddock in mud or dirt and drink a ton of beer from kegs around a big bonfire while decked out in all their finery."

This time he did smile. "And then they do burnouts in their parents' sports utes on some poor farmer's field."

"Great big drunken orgies," she said.

His jaw tensed.

"I'm not surprised a father wouldn't want his teenage daughter to go. I wouldn't either." She assessed him quietly for a moment. "Does her mother have a say?"

He raised his brows. Megan was fishing. And very directly so. "Her mother hasn't been around for the last ten years," he said carefully.

"I'm sorry."

"Don't be. She walked out one night, never looked back." He swallowed the last of his coffee. "She's a big-shot interior designer in London now. Exactly where she wants to be."

"And you?"

He got up, feeling intensely uncomfortable. "I'm also exactly where I want to be," he said, scrunching his cup and tossing it forcibly into the rubbish bin.

She watched him, her curiosity clearly piqued, and the fact she was personally interested in him sent a hot frisson through

Dylan's gut. Discomfort, or pleasure, perhaps an odd mix of both—he couldn't be sure.

"You've been with the Pepper Flats station awhile, then?"

"Ten years."

"That is a long time."

He knew what she had to be thinking, that someone of his age and tenure should be working higher up in the Land Area Command, or handling one of the big-city beats. Not manning a rural three-man station.

Truth was he'd had it with metropolitan policing. His stint with the Sydney narc and homicide squads had eaten up his life like a cancer, sent his marriage down the tubes, and he'd had his fill of the grit, the death, the drugs, the graveyard shifts and overtime. Marriage problems on those beats were an occupational hazard. His had been no exception. Sally's affair on top of the usual stress had been the real killer.

Dylan had taken a demotion in order to move his young family back to the Hunter Valley, where he'd hoped to make a last-ditch go of his relationship with Sally. He'd wanted to give his kid a *life*—a yard, a dog, a swimming pool, access to the bush. Country values.

As unconventional as it sometimes seemed these days, he'd always dreamed of an honest-to-God traditional family.

Perhaps it was because his own family had been decimated in childhood.

Hell alone knew why, but it was what he wanted, and he'd taken the career-killing move to do it.

He'd stayed for all those same reasons, for Heidi, even when Sally couldn't hack it. He inhaled deeply. He sure as hell wasn't going to tell Megan Stafford all that.

"I believe in community policing, Megan," he said simply. "I believe in this town." He checked his watch, and got up, suddenly needing space. He'd said too much. It was fine for him to ask questions—that was his job. But her asking questions felt personal. Too personal. And this woman made him *want* to share. That freaked him. He never shared this stuff.

"It's got to be tough," she said. "Being a single parent."

"Why? You have kids?" he answered much too aggressively.

She snorted softly. "No, I don't. But I was a fourteen-year-old girl once. So I do know something about that." She looked up at him and smiled a smile that made Dylan's heart tumble in spite of himself.

"And I had a father. A real alpha dad who pretty much wouldn't let me do anything." She regarded him with a shrewdness that wormed way too close to home. "He'd have liked to have kept his 'baby' girl in cotton wool for the rest of his life…" Her voice caught, a poignancy crossing her lovely features, and then she gave a half shrug. "He never got that chance. I lost him when I was about your daughter's age."

Dylan immediately wanted to ask what had happened, but just then the ward doors swung open with a crash, and the surgeon came striding out, removing his mask.

Megan surged to her feet, reached her hand out, and for an insane second Dylan thought she was going to grasp his own for support. But she caught herself, wrapping her arms tightly over her stomach instead. He was even more stunned to realize he'd have welcomed her touch, taken hold of her hand in that moment, and comforted.

That knowledge made his heart hammer, soft and steady, as he searched the approaching surgeon's features for a sign of positive news.

"She's going to be just fine," Dr. Jack Burgess said with a warm smile as he neared.

"Oh, thank God!" Megan cupped her hands over her mouth, her eyes shimmering with emotion as they flashed to Dylan's. But she froze at the look on Dylan's face.

He knew why.

His cop mask was back, the moment between them lost to the night.

She turned back to the surgeon. "What exactly happened?" she asked.

"She had a myocardial infarction—your basic heart attack," he said. "We performed an emergency angioplasty, inserting two drug-eluting stents, which are basically little medicated wire baskets that will help keep the arteries open. As long as Louisa rests and takes regular medication, she could be up and about within three or four days. It's a fairly common procedure, and recovery is generally swift."

"When can I see her, talk to her?"

The doc smiled at Megan. "You can see her now. The process was done under local anesthetic using a catheter inserted into her left femoral artery. But we did sedate her, so she'll be a bit woozy."

"So you expect her to be discharged in about four days, then, Jack?" Dylan asked. He was on first-name terms with the doc, as he was with most people in town.

"We may want to keep her under observation a little longer because there were a few minor complications. Otherwise, yes, about four days. She's a fighter. But—" He directed a warm grin at Megan again, which for some reason irked Dylan. "That's going to be part of the problem. Louisa needs to relax, and you're going to have to be there to make sure she does, Megan."

"What…kind of complications?" she asked.

"Her white-cell count was a little low, so we'd like to watch that—keep an eye out for infection at the site of insertion. We also want to make sure there are no drug interactions, but we should know more when Patrick gets back. And we want to watch for internal hemorrhaging. The potential for another heart attack still remains with this procedure, which is why she must stay calm."

Dylan cleared his throat. "And when will she be fit to see

me, doc?" he asked, feeling Megan's eyes boring hotly into him.

The surgeon pursed his lips, his brow furrowing slightly. "You mean...in a professional capacity?"

"She remains in police custody." Dylan raised the papers in his hand. "I do need to officially charge her as soon as—"

Megan whirled to face him. "You cannot possibly still be thinking of charging her?"

"—as soon as she's well enough," he finished his sentence, eyes remaining firmly on Jack.

"I'd wait until tomorrow, Dylan," said the surgeon. "Check in with me then and I'll be in a better position to make a judgment. Now—" he smiled again "—if you'll both excuse me, I do have another patient. Megan, Jenny will show you to Louisa's room. If you have any questions, ask her. She'll page me if it's urgent."

"Of...of course. Thank you, doctor." She spun to face Dylan as the surgeon left. "You're insane." She glowered at him. "I want to know how on *earth* you can think Louisa burned that barn full of horses? What makes you so certain she killed a man?"

"The murder weapon is registered to her—"

"Doesn't mean she pulled the trigger! It's just not logical to think an eighty-year-old is going to sneak out of her house late at night to go kill her neighbor in someone else's barn miles away. And there's no way in hell Louisa—a woman everyone *knows* loves horses more than people, and who owes her livelihood to the industry—would burn someone else's Thoroughbreds." Frustration burned into her eyes, making them crackle deep emerald against her tired complexion, and all Dylan could think about was sex.

"What else do you have on her?" she demanded.

"Megan, we have a witness placing her at Lochlain Racing shortly before the blaze broke out. The description of the slate-gray Holden seen fleeing the arson scene matches her truck. The soil in her Holden's tires was also a match to Lochlain soil. The courts had been about to rule in Whittleson's favor on the Lake Dingo ownership issue. Phone records show Louisa called Whittleson's mobile at Sydney airport just before he was due to board a plane for a safari in Kenya. Then he mysteriously abandoned that flight to head to Lochlain, where he was killed in the barn. With her gun. A weapon she used to shoot him before."

Her brows drew low. "Oh, and tell me why she might have lured Sam to Lochlain Racing?"

Dylan had no idea. It didn't make sense. Yet.

However, Whittleson's phone records showed he'd placed a call to his son Daniel, the head trainer at Lochlain, just prior to receiving Louisa's call at the airport. The incoming call before that had come from Whittleson's lawyer, who later confirmed he'd called his client to let him know the lake-ownership issue was likely going to come down in Whittleson's favor. Whittleson could conceivably have tried to call his son with this good news, and upon getting Daniel's voice mail, decided to abandon the safari and drive to Lochlain to tell him personally. It was, after all, news that would save Whittleson Stud, which had meant absolutely everything to the debt-ridden sixty-one-year-old. Life had finally been on the upturn for the Whittlesons the night Sam was murdered.

"You're not her lawyer, Megan," Dylan said quietly. "And I really am not at liberty to discuss the investigation further with you."

"Damn you," she muttered in exasperation. "For a moment there I…I thought…" She dragged her hand through her hair, and Dylan noticed she was shaking. "I don't know what I thought. That maybe you were a nice guy, or…something."

Her words cut deeper than he should allow them. "I'm a cop, Megan. Just doing my job."

Her jaw tensed with sudden resolve. "Robert D'Angelo will be here within a few hours," she said, eyes searing into his. "And I'll tell him how you pressured Louisa in that interrogation room, without the benefit of her legal counsel. It was obvious she wasn't well. That fact was caught on your own interview tape. You totally disregarded the fact she is eighty years old—elderly—and thus vulnerable. You precipitated her heart attack, Sergeant. You nearly killed her." Megan's voice was clear and firm. "And if you continue to pursue this case against my aunt, I can guarantee D'Angelo will take you down for it."

Something very personal, and very hot flickered through Dylan. "Is that what *you* want, Megan, to take me down?"

She swallowed, something reciprocal flickering darkly in her eyes. "What I want," she whispered, "is for you to stay away from my aunt. You heard what Dr. Burgess said. She needs to relax. I don't want you going in there and giving her another heart attack and actually killing her this time."

He stepped closer, a combative anger beginning to hum deep in his gut as he bent close to her ear, lowering his voice to make sure he was out of anyone's earshot except hers. "Seeing as you've taken the gloves off, Ms. Stafford, I have to admit I'm asking myself who'd benefit if she *did* kick the bucket? Or is it a bit too soon for you and your brother? Is that why you want me to drop this case, so you and Patrick have a bit more time to kowtow to the grande dame before she cashes in?"

"Oh, that is low."

She was so close, he could smell her, kiss her if he dared, and she was making him hot enough to do it. "If you didn't come for the inheritance, Megan," he said, his voice thick, low, "then why are you really both here out of the blue?"

She blushed, eyes flickering.

And Dylan knew a liar when he saw one.

He'd stomached his fair share in police interrogation rooms, and her reaction made his heart turn cold, his unbidden lust for her simply hardening his resolve to win this one.

"How much do you *really* know about your aunt, anyway?" he said, watching her eyes closely, waiting for them to give her away again, trying to ignore the faint scent of sun lotion that lingered on her skin, reminding him of family summers at Bateman's Bay, of happier times. "Because I suspect I know Louisa a helluva lot better than you do, Megan Stafford. I know just what she *is* capable of. I've seen the Thoroughbred set close ranks around their own. I've seen her and D'Angelo's father buy 'justice' before."

He'd seen it thirty years ago, when he was eight years old, and his brother Liam eleven. It had been the incident that tore his family to shreds, forcing them from their modest home in the Hunter.

It was what had ultimately made Dylan become a cop.

And now that he was back, now that it was within his power, he was not about to let her kind get away with murder—again.

"If you want to be a part of the Fairchild team, if you want to take me down personally, then, Megan, you and I are going to be at war."

He turned and headed for the doors, heart thudding. He needed to focus. He needed to cut Megan from his mind. She'd already proven an emotional distraction he couldn't afford right now. His priority was to find officers he could rotate on twenty-four-hour guard outside Louisa's door, and he knew it was going to be an issue. He couldn't use Peebles. He was a probationary cop. It was against protocol.

His phone rang as he reached the hospital doors. He unhooked it from his belt, snapped it open. "Hastings," he barked.

It was an officer at the Scone station. He said a Scone patrol officer had picked up Heidi on her bike. She'd had an accident, but she was fine.

Dylan froze on the spot. "Where is she?"

"We took her home."

Confusion spiraled through his brain. Heidi was supposed to have been at home, asleep. *"What happened?"*

"She was cycling along a dark section of Burumby Road a couple of hours ago when an oncoming sedan swerved to avoid a wallaby, running her bike into a ditch. The vehicle didn't hit her, but she's quite shaken up. The driver called it in, tried to help her. He was worried about a young girl that age being out alone at night on that stretch of road."

White-cold fear and anger lanced through Dylan.

He shot a look at Megan, who was watching him intently from the nurses' station. And he felt suddenly, inexplicably, naked. Vulnerable.

Furious.

With himself. With her. With everything.

He hadn't realized just how much he'd needed to talk, to lean on someone with his family issues. *She* had made him feel that need.

And suddenly her compassion, her interest, the way she'd drawn him out, felt deceptive. Deceitful. He felt cheated. Lured.

He spun on his boot heels and stormed through the hospital doors into the pale dawn, the threads of his life unraveling at his feet.

Be damned if he was going to let the Fairchild clan take him down again.

He wasn't going to lose what little control he still had left over his family.

Over himself.

This time his family would not run. He would stand up and fight. And this time there would be only one winner.

Him.

His family.

Chapter Four

Dylan arrived home as Heidi was getting ready for school. She was pale, eyes avoiding his as she ate her cereal at the round oak table in front of sliding glass doors that overlooked their garden and the fields beyond.

He had to forcibly tamp down a surge of anger. She was safe. That was the main thing. He closed the front door quietly behind him, and entered the kitchen area, struck suddenly by how much his daughter's thick blond hair resembled Megan's—and Sally's—drawing another parallel between the two women he didn't care to see.

He'd made a terrible mistake falling for Sally.

They'd both been too young to start a family, and completely incompatible on any long-term basis.

Sally had been sexy, flirtatious, artsy, full of vibrant laughter and energy, and it had translated into a dynamic experience in bed. But outside the bedroom her craving for the continual excitement of a metropolis, alternative lifestyles, and the flattery of men, had begun to cost them.

Sally had *needed* to be the centre of attention, and loved going out to parties all the time.

Dylan was more traditional. He liked the outback, bushwalking, the ocean. Winter nights by the fire. He liked things simple. Wholesome. Sally called it boring.

But by then they were married, and things had started going sideways.

And when she'd become pregnant at twenty-four, she'd felt overweight, unhappy and lonely with Dylan doing long, gritty hours of overtime to support them.

When Heidi was born Sally had detested being cooped at home with only other young mothers for company. She'd rebelled and had a raging affair, seeking validation in another man, an artist.

Her infidelity had completely broken Dylan.

He was a one-woman guy. A lifer. When he fell, he fell hard and forever. And falling for Sally had cost him a mighty big chunk of his life.

He'd avoided getting involved with other women while raising Heidi solo. He'd dated, but only superficially. His focus was his family.

"Hey there, kiddo," Dylan said gently.

Heidi said nothing, just stared at her cereal.

He heaved out a lungful of air, removed his Glock, locked it in the gun safe, and undid his heavy gun belt, setting it on the counter with a soft clunk. He sat down, rubbing his neck, his back stiff.

"Talk to me, Heidi."

She pulled her mouth into a tight pout, glaring at her cereal bowl, stirring milk with her spoon as she hunkered down behind the super-size cereal box.

Dylan moved the box aside. "Heidi, I'm not going to be

mad," he said, struggling to hold on to his temper. "I just want to know where you were going last night."

Silence.

Irritation itched at him. Their dog Muttley scratched at the glass door, and Dylan got up to let him out. His mother usually let Muttley out first thing in the morning, but she hadn't come down for breakfast yet, which was unusual for her. Tension knotted in his shoulders.

He took a seat opposite Heidi. "Were you going to the party?"

Her eyes flashed up at him. "No. I needed to see Anthem."

He waited a beat just to make sure his voice came out neutral. "Why so late? Why didn't you wait until this afternoon, after school?"

Her bottom lip started to wobble a little. Dylan's chest tightened. "Heidi? Talk to me. Please."

She looked up slowly, and was about to say something when they heard Dylan's mum coming down the stairs.

Heidi cast her eyes down, then suddenly pushed her chair back from the table, grabbed her schoolbag and started for the door, unfinished cereal left on the table.

"Heidi!"

"I'm going to miss my bus," she snapped, and the door slammed shut behind her.

Dylan cursed and looked up at the ceiling.

"Morning, Timmy," said his mother, moving towards the kettle and filling it. "Did you sleep well?"

"It's Dylan, Mum."

She looked momentarily confused. "Of course," she said softly, plugging in the kettle. "I know that."

Dylan got up to let Muttley back in, his heart sinking. He felt flat. Tired. His mother was worse than he thought. This was the second time in a week she'd called him by his brother's nickname.

A brother who'd been dead for thirty years.

He needed to take June for another checkup. That would require a trip to the city, impossible right now. He also had to find a way to break through to Heidi. And he had to get back to work. He'd had no sleep, but no one else would be in the station today.

Dylan had also been left with no choice but to place Peebles outside Louisa's hospital room for the first shift, short of doing it himself. And that wasn't going to happen—he still had an investigation to conduct, because no matter how he looked at it, things were just not adding up with Louisa the way he'd like them to.

He stood for a moment at the glass door, absently studying the smoky haze in the distance as he rolled the facts over in his mind again.

As much as he hated to admit it, Megan had hit on the key thing troubling him. It *was* possible Louisa's gun had been stolen from the cabinet, and that she hadn't been the one to pull the trigger.

But she could also have hired someone to do the job. That might explain the arson. Because again, he was forced to agree with Megan—he didn't see Louisa as capable of torching horses.

He needed better evidence against her, or evidence of an accomplice, or they were going to end up having no case.

And there was that other nagging question in his mind. Why Lochlain? Why had the murder and arson happened there? He needed to find *that* link. The only connection he could see with Lochlain Racing so far was that the homicide victim was the father of Daniel Whittleson, who worked as Lochlain's head trainer.

Secretly, Dylan was relieved Louisa was in hospital.

It bought him time to dig deeper before having to officially charge her and get her in front of a magistrate.

He rubbed the back of his neck again, trying to ease the stiffness. What he really needed was a full-on homicide team

working this, as would ordinarily be the case. But until the
APEC stuff eased off, he was it.

And that was the other thing Megan was right about—
D'Angelo was going to go for him personally, potentially
crucifying him on points of police procedure, like putting the
probationary cop outside Louisa's door.

Damn, but he was in a no-win situation.

Megan sped along the country road, autumn wind in her
hair, the vineyards, vibrant with reds, oranges and gold,
flashing by in a blur.

She'd spent the morning with D'Angelo and Louisa at
Elias Memorial, rehashing the arrest, going over every little
detail that had led up to the heart attack. When they'd finished,
D'Angelo had pushed his glasses up his Roman nose and
told them with his classic trademark equanimity that he would
personally make Detective Sergeant Dylan Hastings his target
in getting this arrest overturned.

D'Angelo had been particularly pleased to discover the
probationary rank of the constable guarding Louisa's door.
He'd noted this was against NSW policing regulations, adding
that police staffing problems in the Hunter LAC were going
to be their ace in the hole.

So was the fact Louisa had not yet been officially charged.

D'Angelo's criminal team was now in the process of
putting together a case to nullify the arrest, focusing on police
ineptitude, Dylan's in particular.

Megan felt conflicted by this.

That wasn't justice. Not in her book. That was legal chess.

It went to the heart of why she'd dropped criminal law.

In her mind, the one and only way to exonerate her aunt
and put a simple end to this was to find the real killer, and the
cop sure as hell wasn't going to be looking any further—he
thought he had his suspect.

Which was why Megan was on the road to Lochlain Racing

now. She wanted to see the arson site herself, speak to owner Tyler Preston, find something—*anything*—that might help solve this case.

But a cold and faint finger of doubt touched her again as she turned onto a dirt road, slowing for some riders, the sun warm on her arms.

What had Dylan meant by saying Louisa had bought justice before? And why *had* Louisa's pistol been used as the murder weapon?

Megan drove up the Lochlain driveway, and pulled up under a tall stand of gum trees alongside one of the farm outbuildings. As she got out of the car, the first thing she saw was a young teen in a navy-and-white school uniform on some risers near an empty dressage ring in the distance. She was bent forward, face buried in her hands, crying. Not just crying, but sobbing, her frame physically racked by emotion.

Megan glanced around. There was no one in the immediate vicinity. She hesitated, then walked up to the girl. And as she neared, something in her heart squeezed.

The child reminded her of herself at that age.

Perhaps it was the thick honey-blond hair in two pigtails, the proximity of a dressage ring, the scent of horses in the air—all combining to prod loose a certain memory thread. It was at about the same age as this girl, Megan had lived to ride.

Dressage had been her performance class, a passion passed down from Granny Betty to her mother to her.

She'd lost touch with the sport after her mum and dad's accident. Life had changed after that. She'd been sent off to boarding school, the horses sold. But right at this moment she felt the old passion stirring oddly, deeply, inside her once again.

"Hey there," she said, edging onto the wooden bench alongside the girl. "You okay?"

The teen stilled, then sniffing and wiping her face, looked up cautiously. Her cheeks were streaked and blotchy, but she had incredibly beautiful big green eyes. Again an odd sensation gripped Megan. She had a weird feeling of looking back in time, at herself.

"My name is Megan Stafford," she said softly. "Can I help?"

The girl swiped her eyes, looking embarrassed, then shook her head.

"Did something just happen?"

She glanced away, stared at the empty ring, her gaze shifting slowly towards the fire-damaged barns that had been cordoned off with construction fencing and checkered blue-and-white crime tape. Her eyes brimmed with fresh tears and she moistened her lips. "My horse, Anthem—" she said, eyes fixed on the charred ruins "—was injured in the fire."

Megan's heart clutched. "Oh, honey, I'm so sorry. Did… did you lose her?"

The girl bit her quivering lip as tears spilled silently down her cheeks again. "I…might. She's got smoke inhalation damage. I don't know if she's ever going to be okay, and…" She was racked by another deep sob. "I can't be with her because the vet is in there with the other horses now. Anthem was doing all right, and…and then suddenly there was a whole lot of fluid in her lungs yesterday…" Her voice choked as a wrenching surge of raw emotion took hold of her.

Megan instinctively put her arm around the teen, drawing her close, just holding her, stroking her hair. She recalled how many times in her own youth she'd wished her mother had been around to do just this, hold her—how alone in the world she'd felt after her parents had died.

Megan hadn't thought about this in a long while.

After a few minutes the girl looked up sheepishly with red-rimmed eyes. "Thank you," she said, wiping her face. "I'm sorry. I…I just couldn't hold it in anymore."

"It's okay, hon. You need to let these things out." Megan had a sense the child had also desperately needed the tactile comfort of another human. "Are you here all alone?"

She nodded. "I got off the school bus here because I was hoping they'd let me see Anthem. I usually ride her on Tuesdays, but…" She sighed deeply. "They're so busy with all the other horses and Anthem is not a Thoroughbred. I'm worried they're not watching her closely enough." She glanced up. "Anthem's depressed. I think she needs special attention or…she might just give up."

"I'm sure they're treating all the horses the same, sweetie."

She shook her head. "I don't think so. If we had money, I'd take her someplace she could get individual care. I bet if she was an expensive racer they'd have gotten her out of the fire earlier. She wouldn't have been left until last."

"I'm sure it didn't happen like that."

She looked up with an expression that made Megan's heart ache. "I'm sure it *did*."

"Why is Anthem stabled here?"

The girl sucked in a shaky breath as galahs, pink and white, flitted and chattered in the tree above. "Tyler Preston, the owner, was giving me lessons."

"Dressage?"

"No, Anthem and I have been working on that ourselves. Tyler teaches a couple of us local kids the basic stuff. He's really good—he used to have his own TV show. He gave my friend Zach a part-time job as a groom, and his payment is the lessons. Zach uses one of Tyler's horses when he rides here, but he has his own at Huntington Stud, where his dad works as a trainer. And because *my* dad has a *stupid* job and doesn't make enough money, *he* can't afford stabling costs or lessons anywhere, so Tyler offered for free." Her big green eyes flashed up to Megan. "You see? Anthem is not a priority, and I'm worried the vet is going to neglect her since he's so busy with the prize horses."

"I tell you what, I'll talk to Tyler and get the low-down, how about that? I'm here to talk to him about the fire anyway."

The teenager stared at Megan in bemused silence as she

digested this. "Why would you do that for me?" she asked very quietly.

The question caught Megan off guard. "Why wouldn't I?" She hesitated a moment, then smiled gently. "Besides, you remind me of someone I used to know, someone who used to love riding with all her heart."

"What happened to her?"

"She forgot to follow her heart. Come—" She held out her hand. "We'll go talk to Tyler, and then I'll give you a ride home. Where do you live?"

"Pepper Flats, near the village," she said, getting up, dusting off her school uniform. "My name is Heidi. How do you know Tyler, Megan?"

"I don't. Louisa Fairchild is my great-aunt and I'm visiting, and...well, I'm helping her out with a bit of a problem."

They walked together over the gravel driveway toward the main house. "So you're not riding at all at the moment, Heidi?" said Megan.

She shook her head.

"You know, Louisa has some really good dressage horses and she might be able to spare one. Would you be interested in riding at Fairchild for a while? Just until Anthem is better, of course." She grinned. "Besides, I'd enjoy the company. I think I'd like to ride again myself."

"Why'd you stop?"

Megan sucked in a deep breath redolent with the scents of the fall air—eucalyptus, the tinge of distant smoke, hay, horses. It was a grounding scent, earthy. "I stopped when my parents died," she said. "They were killed in a car accident, and my brother and I were sent to boarding school. Life sort of changed after that. We didn't really have a family anymore."

"I'm sorry."

She put her arm around the teen. "Hey, it's okay. Brookfield ended up being a great school and—"

Heidi jerked to a stop. "You have *got* to be kidding me! *You* went to Brookfield art school?"

"Yes."

Her hand went to her chest. "Oh, my gosh. That's where I want to go."

"It's a good school. I'm sure you'd like it."

She pulled a face. "We can't afford it."

"There are bursaries. I could always talk to someone."

She stared, open mouthed. "You *really* could do that?"

"Well, I might if you show me some of your art and tell me a bit more about yourself," she said with a warm smile. "You haven't even told me your surname—"

"Megan!" a powerful male voice called out to them.

They both turned to see a tall dark-haired man in a cattle-man's hat, his left arm in a sling, striding towards them, three border collies at his heels.

"That's Tyler. I thought you said you didn't know him?"

"I called ahead. He's expecting me." Megan grinned. "And I guess he recognized Louisa's Aston Martin." She laughed. "Louisa claims it's the Thoroughbred of motor cars."

"That's our place," Heidi said, pointing to a rambling brick house behind which a field of tall dry grasses bent softly in the breeze. In the distance kangaroos grazed under eucalyptus trees fringing a ridge.

Megan slowed the convertible, pleased to finally be getting the hang of changing gears. In spite of its flash she liked the way the car's manual shift connected her with driving—it made her feel more grounded. Everything about this valley seemed to be changing her in subtle ways, reminding her who she really was. What she liked.

Turning into the driveway, Megan caught a glimpse of a swimming pool at the rear of the house. She pulled to a stop in front of the brick garage. A tire swing hung from the branches of a gnarled deciduous tree, dog toys dotted the front lawn, and someone had carefully tended a lavender-fringed bed of iceberg roses that were peaking with a soft blush of pink. Feminine flowers, thought Megan. "Your mother must have a real green thumb," she said, opening the driver's-side door.

Heidi shot her an odd look. "My gran planted those."

"They're beautiful." In fact, there was something genuine about the whole scene. It held a warm sense of family so welcoming and simple that it snagged Megan's chest forcibly, and she had to stop for a second to analyze why.

Perhaps it was because she'd come to the Hunter Valley looking for her own roots and a sense of her own family, hoping to find it by discovering what had happened between Betty and Louisa. Maybe she even harbored a subliminal desire to bond with her great-aunt herself.

But as Megan climbed out of the convertible, the front door of the house flung open, and she froze.

Storming out of the house, bare-chested, damp tousled hair, bleached jeans slung low at his waist, a hairy mutt at his heels, and daggers in his clear blue eyes was...Detective Sergeant Dylan Hastings.

Her jaw dropped.

"Is that your dad!" she whispered to Heidi. Then it hit her—he'd said he had a fourteen-year-old child.

She'd just given the cop's daughter a ride home.

This warm family house belonged to the detective trying to nail her aunt for murder, the man who'd declared personal war on the entire Fairchild clan.

Her heart began to hammer and her body turned warm at the sight of the half-naked, sun-bronzed cop stalking over the lawn towards the Aston Martin. She swallowed, bracing for a confrontation because it sure as hell looked like that was what he had in mind.

But he went straight for Heidi, lifting her feet off the ground as he bear-hugged his kid with all his might. "Jesus,

Heidi!" he said, setting her down and stepping back, taking her face firmly in his large hands. "You have *got* to stop scaring me like this. Enough is enough, okay? I've been calling the school, your friends." He hugged her close again, his blue eyes glimmering with powerful emotion.

A lump squeezed into Megan's throat and she felt a strange pang of yearning. He glanced at her then, over his daughter's blond head, and his eyes turned cold, hard. Angry. He stepped back from his child slowly. "Go inside, Heidi. I need a word with Megan."

Heidi's eyes lit up as she glanced between the two of them. "You know Megan?"

Neither Megan nor Dylan said anything.

Heidi wavered, confused. "Dad…Megan has offered me a horse on Fairchild Acres. She said I can ride every day after school until Anthem is better. And you'll never guess what."

"What?" he said quietly, eyes focused on Megan.

"Megan went to *Brookfield!* She said I could maybe get a bursary, that she could talk to someone with the alumni association."

"Go inside, Heidi. I want to talk to Megan. In private."

Exasperation filled Heidi's eyes. "Why?"

"Just do it. Now."

"You never let me do *anything*, you know that! I know what you're going to say to her, that you don't want me going to boarding school in Sydney, that you want to trap me in this damn house and valley forever, babysitting my grandmother!"

He looked at his daughter in shock. "What did you say?"

"It's always no, no, no!" Tears began streaming down Heidi's face again. "My *mother* wouldn't do this to me!" she yelled, stomping towards the house.

Dylan's neck and shoulder muscles bunched visibly as he clenched his jaw, fists closing at his side.

Megan stepped forward. "Heidi, wait—"

But Dylan shot her a fierce warning glare that hummed with such angry tension it physically slammed Megan back.

As Heidi reached the front door, a woman in her late sixties stepped into view. "Timmy? Is everything all right?"

"I'll be right in, Mum," said Dylan. "Just…give me a minute."

The woman faltered, glanced at Megan, then shut the door.

Megan felt her jaw drop.

This handsome, stubborn hunk of a cop lived with his mother. And he hadn't batted an eyelid at being called Timmy.

"What is this?" he demanded, wagging his hand between the two of them as soon as they were alone. "You trying to get at me through my kid now? Trying to insinuate yourself into my investigation, my life, by involving my *family?* I don't want her to be a part of this investigation, understand? And I do not want Heidi on Fairchild property. Not now. Not ever."

He turned to go, but spun right back, clearly not finished. "It's that D'Angelo, isn't it? He put you up to this. Because that would be his style. Underhanded schmuck." He marched towards his front door.

"Dylan, wait, please."

He stiffened at her use of his first name, turned slowly to face her, his sun-browned muscles now gleaming under the hot autumn sun.

"Give her a break, Dylan. She's suffering over the near-loss of Anthem. I had no idea she was your daughter when I offered her a horse."

He blew out air, dragging both hands through his damp hair, clearly exasperated. And so damn hot. Megan couldn't take her eyes from the gold chest hair covering his dark tan, the way his biceps rolled under his skin, the way his abs rippled down into his jeans when he moved his arms up. The way his jeans were slung so low she could see the fine trail of darker blond hair running down to his groin.

A complex heat burned through her belly, and Megan swallowed, trying not to gawk at how his jeans were faded around his fly, trying not to think of how every molecule in her body wanted to be naked and pressed up against this man.

She didn't think she'd had the pleasure of personally encountering a male specimen this ripped in quite a long time. Or being turned on sexually so fast by a man's chemistry.

She forced herself to meet his eyes, heart beating faster, wondering if he'd seen her reaction, the flush in her cheeks. "I…I honestly had no idea until I saw you coming out that door who Heidi was," Megan said, clearing the huskiness from her throat. "I'm sorry. But I can't take the offer back now, and you can't take it from her either. She needs this."

"And just who in hell do you think you are to tell me what my daughter needs?" he said, his voice dangerously low.

She reached nervously behind her for the car door. "Why won't you let me help her, Dylan?"

"Because we're on opposite sides of a homicide investigation, *Stafford*. That's why. And you're the one who wants to take me—" he flung his hand back towards his house "—and my family down, remember? I'm the sole supporter here, and any involvement with you in whatever capacity could seriously cost me down the line. So, please, get the hell off my property."

She hesitated, realizing how her battle to save Louisa had in fact just become a battle to undermine this home, this gorgeous single father who clearly had more than he could handle on his plate.

But something else surfaced through her conflicted feelings—her own stubborn need to get through to people. To make them understand where she was coming from. To make them *like* her.

"Just let her ride at Fairchild, Dylan," she said softly, in spite of the blood pounding loudly through her veins. "Heidi needs this. And—" She raised her hand to stop him from speaking. "And don't tell me I don't know what a fourteen-year-old girl needs, because I have the edge on you there, Sergeant."

He swore softly, and Megan knew she'd hit a sore spot. Despite the fact they were on opposite sides of a murder case, Megan was undeniably drawn to him by something quite apart from the lust burning in her belly—compassion.

She'd never dreamed the tough macho Aussie cop would live with his mother and daughter, a scruffy hairy mutt, and pink-white roses and lavender in his front garden.

This was a traditional and fiercely protective family man, and she found that utterly compelling. Seductive in so many ways.

The fact that he looked like a half-naked Greek god without his shirt didn't hurt either. He was melting her from the inside out in all sorts of ways.

"I think you should leave," he said quietly, ominously.

"Only if you'll agree to let Heidi ride with me," Megan said. "For her sake."

He was silent for a beat. "Why do you care so much?"

"Because I was there. I was her once."

A muscle pulsed at his jaw as he studied her. "Fine," he said finally, quietly, pushing the word out around clenched teeth. "She can ride."

Well, that was about all the thanks she was going to get. Megan nodded curtly. "Fine," she said as she opened her car door. But she stopped suddenly. "You know what I don't understand, Sergeant," she said, turning back to face him, her voice oddly thick, "is why a man like you, clearly committed to family and community values, is so bent on hurting my aunt. What is it that you have against her? Why do you need to humiliate her like this? Why is it so personal?"

He stepped really close, placing his large hand on the open convertible door, closing her in, and she felt her muscles tense.

"Don't kid yourself, Stafford. Your aunt doesn't give a damn about family and community values, so don't try and pull that one on me again. She's a callous woman who thinks Australian justice is the best money can buy. And—" he paused, watching her, his lips so close, his warm scent enveloping her "—besides her *charming* personality, all the evidence points straight to her. It's not personal. It's my job. Pure and simple."

"Perhaps you see nailing the great Louisa Fairchild as a feather in your career cap," she countered, unable to stop herself.

That muscle in his jaw throbbed steadily as his voice dropped another octave, dangerous in its quietness, yet darkly seductive at the same time. "If I wanted to climb career ladders, Megan, I'd have stayed with Sydney homicide." She could smell his shampoo, the faint scent of aftershave, the heat on his skin. "I'm here to catch criminals, not climb career ladders. I sacrificed my career to move here to build a family. Not that that would mean anything to someone like you."

That cut. So very deep he had no idea. She nodded slowly, watching his mouth, not trusting herself to speak. She believed him on one count. This was a man who'd protect family at great cost. Even if it meant sacrificing a career.

D'Angelo had said Detective Sergeant Hastings' demotion to Pepper Flats might well have been precipitated by some misstep, some disgrace that had been buried years ago. Something the lawyers would find and use against him in court.

But Megan was beginning to see it differently.

"And your talk of art school is threatening my family, understand? I don't want my daughter going to school in Sydney."

"It's just school," she said, her voice thick. "She'd come home weekends, still be able to ride."

"This has nothing to do with you, and I'd appreciate it if you left. Now." He paused, a sexual current thrumming between them. "Before we both regret it."

She nodded again, her cheeks flushing deeper. "Fine," she said. "But maybe the next time she's sobbing alone by an empty paddock, *you* should be there for her instead of a stranger."

"Maybe," he said slowly, "if your aunt hadn't shot someone, Megan, I would have been."

His eyes skimmed her bare legs as she got into the car, then met hers again. "What were you doing at Lochlain anyway?" he asked as she banged the door closed.

"Your job," she said, putting the car in gear. "Finding the real killer so you will see that my aunt is innocent."

And she backed out of his driveway.

Chapter Five

Dylan cursed as he watched the pale-gold Aston Martin disappear down the undulating ribbon of road, heading toward the prime stud farms in the region.

Seeing his kid pulling up in a Fairchild luxury convertible had unhinged him. And the hero-worship he'd glimpsed in Heidi's eyes when she looked at Megan had frustrated the hell out of him.

That's all he needed. Another coltish blonde messing up his life and libido—a glamorous Sydneyite with big-city ideals, and a privileged member of the Australian Thoroughbred set to boot.

Sydney and a blonde had damn near destroyed him once already. He had no stomach for it.

So why in hell was his body defying him like this?

Why was he feeling this physical magnetism toward Megan Stafford when she represented everything about a lifestyle he'd rejected?

And she'd stood there next to her sports car so darn cool and aloof while he'd been burning up with lust and anger inside. He swore again. Heidi hadn't seen her mother in ten goddamn years. Now she was throwing Sally back at him, and Dylan was convinced it was because of Megan.

How ironic would that be? To have struggled for the last decade to build Heidi a life out here, only to have her follow her mother's path, regardless.

He didn't want Megan around.

For too many damn reasons to count.

Especially given the scope of this case, and what it could cost him if it went down the tubes. Dylan turned to go back into the house, whistling for Muttley as the mobile on the belt of his jeans rang. He flipped it open. "Hastings."

It was Superintendent Matt Caruthers. "Hastings, we've had an anonymous tip come through our crime line. Some guy calling from a prepaid disposable maintains that Louisa Fairchild killed Sam Whittleson."

Dylan stilled.

"He claims Fairchild has a lackey on regular retainer to do unpalatable jobs for her, and this bloke was allegedly called into service the night of the Lochlain fire. Our tipster says Fairchild shot Whittleson in a fit of rage because she'd just gotten word the courts were going to rule in his favor over Lake Dingo."

"Go on," Dylan said, frowning.

"This guy claims Whittleson went to Lochlain that night to personally deliver the good news to his son, Daniel. Fairchild knew this because she'd just called him at the airport to try and offer him a settlement. Whittleson allegedly refused. She was furious, drove to Lochlain, confronted him in the barn, and things went south. She shot him, realized she'd actually killed him this time, panicked, and had this lackey of hers on scene within two hours to cover up her mess and remove the security footage. He used her truck, apparently, which is why it was seen fleeing the blaze."

Dylan's frown deepened. He rubbed the stubble on his chin, autumn sun hot on his bare torso. "So what's stopping this guy from coming forward to make a statement?"

"Hell knows. But the pieces sure fit."

They did. And the arson would certainly make more sense. "How do we know this tipster is for real?"

"We don't. But—and this is the clincher—he said Fairchild, in her panic, tossed her Smith & Wesson into a fertilizer drum in the maintenance area of the barn. She told her guy to retrieve it, but he couldn't locate it in time. Thing blew in a chemical fire."

Dylan's pulse quickened. The location of the murder weapon had not been released to the public.

Either this anonymous tipster had got his information direct from the homicide cops, or he really *did* know who'd killed Sam.

"What's in it for this guy?" said Dylan.

"We don't know yet. But whatever his motivation for spilling the beans, it gives us something to work with. And the pieces do fit."

"An anonymous tip is not going to get us a warrant to get at Fairchild's payroll and bank records to see who she might be paying under the table, Matt."

"Try squeezing the family, rattling her staff, see if you can shake anything loose about the identity of this lackey. Really put the pressure on, and something may give. Let Fairchild know you're going to get a bedside hearing into Elias Memorial and charge her as soon as she's well enough. Make her believe that when she does leave that hospital it'll be straight for a correctional centre in Sydney where she'll await trial without bail. Make her think that if she coughs up her accomplice there could be a plea bargain on the horizon. Then we work the accomplice into giving her up, play one off against the other."

Dylan hooked the phone back onto his belt and called for

Muttley again as he climbed the stairs to his front door, flagstone warm under his bare feet.

Caruthers was right. It did fit. Almost too perfectly. He could rattle Louisa's cage on that one, especially if she felt guilt over the horses.

He needed to question Fairchild and the Lochlain staff again, see if he could find out who might be working under the table for Louisa. *If* this tip was genuine, her accomplice would likely be someone who knew his—or her—way around Lochlain Racing well enough to know where to find the security CD. He or she was probably also a recognizable face around both farms.

Whoever the tipster was, he clearly wanted to see Louisa go down for this, and it added another uncomfortable dimension to the case for Dylan. Because if the guy wanted her nailed so badly, could it be remotely possible she was being framed for some reason?

This homicide was beginning to feel a lot bigger than a simple feud over water.

Dylan changed into his uniform, and went to find Heidi. She was watching TV, her sketch pad on her lap, and on the page was an evocative black-and-white impression of Anthem being led by a woman with long hair. A woman who looked an awful lot like Megan.

"Nice," he said, looking over her shoulder.

She said nothing.

"Who is the lady?"

"Mum."

Dylan's heart bottomed out. Heidi hadn't seen a photo of her mother in years. She was superimposing Megan's image onto something in her imagination. He swallowed against the tightening in his throat. "It's a nice drawing."

She remained silent.

He ruffled her hair, and she pulled away, staring at the TV.

Dylan inhaled deeply, went into his office and pulled out

the papers from the old divorce kit. He set them on his desk and stared at them—papers Sally had long ago signed and returned for him to initial before forwarding copies back to her.

He never had.

He wasn't sure why not.

Perhaps it was his innate resistance to divorce in general. He'd seen firsthand what it could do to a family. Or perhaps it was because he was a lifer—for him marriage simply meant forever.

Or maybe it was because he had wanted somehow to leave the doors open for Heidi to connect with her mother.

That hadn't happened.

And the way Heidi was bringing her mother up now was unhealthy. She was going to get burned if she tried to reconnect with Sally at this point. If Dylan was truly honest with himself, he'd known in his heart from the night Sally walked out that she would never have anything more to do with either of them again.

Ever.

He looked up, out the window, stared at the gums on the ridge, the family of kangaroos grazing there. And he couldn't say why, but he picked up that pen, and scribbled his signature across the requisite pages.

Then he unlocked his top drawer, pulled out his address book, flipped it open and copied Sally's London address onto a large white envelope. He slid the papers inside.

And he blew out a heavy breath.

He'd get it into the mail tomorrow.

He walked out the door, feeling an odd lightness inside. In spite of everything else going on in his life, part of him had just broken free.

Megan lobbed the ball back at Patrick, muscles burning, sweat plastering her tennis dress to her stomach, breath rasping in her lungs. He returned it with a sharp crack of a backhand, and she burst into a sprint to the left of the court, missing the ball as it singed the asphalt in a puff of fine dust just inside the line.

"Christ, Patrick—" she rested her hands on her knees, panting, laughing "—you've really been keeping in shape all these years."

He chuckled from the other side of the court, bouncing another ball, getting ready to serve again. "You're getting soft, little sister."

"I am not!" She stood, shoving damp tendrils back from her forehead, relishing the warm burn in her body. She'd needed to hit something and work up a sweat after encountering Dylan half-naked yesterday. She hadn't got that wound up about a man in a long time. Her body was still humming with pent-up adrenaline.

"Ready?" he called from the other end of the court.

"Oh, yeah, I'm ready," she called back, widening her stance, bending her body forward, rocking slightly from side to side, both hands on the racket, eye on the ball.

He tossed it up into the air, sliced at it with his racket. She lunged, swinging at empty air as the ball zinged past in a yellow-green blur.

He laughed. "Give up yet?"

She swiped the back of her wrist across her forehead, smiling. "Not on your life, baby."

And he lobbed another ball, this time easy and well within her reach. "Tell me about this cop," he yelled as he swung through.

And she missed instantly.

"Damn it, Patrick," she yelled, angry more at her complex feelings for the cop than the fact he'd made her lose focus and miss the ball. "What do you mean, anyway?"

He came up to the net, gorgeous, tanned, healthy, his brown hair gleaming under the sun. "A tad defensive, are we?"

"Comes from missing the ball," she retorted.

He grinned. "Good game, sis. Thanks."

She walked alongside him on the other side of the net. "It's been a long time, hasn't it?"

"Much too long." He shot her a look. "Told you it would be good to come."

She set her racket on the court bench, and picked up a towel, dabbing it to her neck. "Well, I didn't come for her inheritance, Patrick."

"I know." His hazel eyes held hers. "But we're her blood, Megs, the only living family she has left. Granny Betty and Mum were unfairly cheated out of the Fairchild wealth, and if Louisa wants to set things right now by leaving her legacy to her sister's grandkids instead of the government, you should be more practical about it. The woman has amassed a fortune."

Exactly what Dylan had said.

Megan glanced toward the horse barns in the distance, the white-fenced paddocks and corn-colored fields that rolled endlessly down towards the twisting brown Hunter River, the dusky blue haze of the gum-forested hills of the Koongorra preserve on the opposite bank.

Patrick followed her gaze. "Imagine owning all this some day, Megs?"

"Sergeant Hastings really seems to think Louisa is capable of this," she said distractedly.

"*Murder?* You don't believe that."

"I don't know what to think right now, Patrick," she said, tossing her towel onto the bench. "I honestly don't believe she would have set fire to Lochlain, but…Dylan seems to know something about Louisa's past that we don't."

"Dylan? We're on first-name terms now?"

She pulled a face. "I met his daughter. She's a nice child. I gave her a ride home before I knew she belonged to the cop."

His hazel eyes turned serious. "Megan, be careful. This could get messy. D'Angelo plans on nailing this guy big-time."

"He's just doing his job."

Patrick arched a brow as he reached for the jug of ice-cold lemonade that Marie Lafayette from the kitchen had set on the table for them. "*Is* he?"

"He's got no staff," she added.

"Doesn't mean we should be shortchanged justice," he said, pouring the lemonade, ice chinking against glass.

"This state of emergency situation is putting us *all* into a surreal position, Patrick. It doesn't mean we have to gun for the cop and his family personally, either."

He studied her intently for a moment. "He's got to you, hasn't he, this detective and his kid?" he said, handing her a glass.

She took it, glancing away.

"Megs?"

She faced him. "You know what this should be about, Patrick? It should be about proving Louisa's innocence, about finding the *real* killer. Not about crucifying the sole detective on the case for botched procedure."

"Well, finding the real killer *is* the detective's job, Megan. And he's clearly not doing it if he's looking no further than Louisa. That doesn't leave us with much choice, does it? He's making himself a target."

Megan took a deep swallow of lemonade, cool and welcome against her parched throat. "Well, whatever you think, it's in *everyone's* interests to try and get the police to drop this before D'Angelo starts dragging it too far into legal mud."

"You're right." He gave her a wicked smile. "We won't be able to prove to the old dame that we're worthy of her legacy if she's sitting in the slammer without bail awaiting trial by jury, will we?"

"Patrick!"

He grinned. "It's a joke, sis. Lighten up."

She glared at him. "You're not helping."

He nodded, eyes turning serious and shrewd again, the stockbroker mind at work. "Did the police search of the house when she was arrested turn up anything?"

"Not that I know of."

"And the murder weapon is definitely registered to Louisa." It was more statement than question.

Megan nodded, taking another sip. "But D'Angelo is not worried about that. When we met with him at the clinic yesterday to go over the arrest details that precipitated the heart attack, he said just because the pistol is registered to Louisa, it doesn't prove she shot anyone."

"They must have something on her, though, to arrest her."

"D'Angelo is not acknowledging the arrest as legal. He said the police will have to disclose whatever they do have on Louisa when they charge her and get her in front of a magistrate, but he's going to make sure it doesn't get that far. He left for Sydney last night. He's going to negotiate a Thoroughbred sale for Fairchild, and while he's there his criminal team will be putting together a case to have the arrest overturned."

"So in the meantime all we need to do is keep Louisa's doctor on side, Louisa in hospital and the police at bay so they can't charge her."

"Right. D'Angelo also said we might want to make an official burglary complaint, and get on record that Louisa's gun was stolen."

Patrick snorted softly. "Which will give D'Angelo ammunition in court if it ever gets that far, making a jury see theft as a viable scenario, one the police investigated themselves." He set his glass down. "That lawyer is worth his weight in gold."

He saw the look on her face. "What is it?"

"I'm remembering all the reasons I dropped criminal law. D'Angelo's strategy has less to do with justice than a strategic game—one he actually appears to be relishing. He doesn't give a damn about burying someone as long as it means getting his client off and winning."

"And that client is your rich great-aunt, sis." Patrick looped his arm over her shoulder as they left the tennis court. "D'Angelo's strategy will get Louisa out of the woods, and us back on track, proving we are worthy of her legacy."

She pulled away. "Dammit, Patrick." Her eyes tunneled into his. "This is not just about Louisa and us. A man was killed. A trainer lost his father. Tyler Preston's livelihood is in ruins. And do you know that the cop's daughter's horse was also injured in that blaze?"

He frowned. "All the more reason for the detective to be less objective about this case, Megan, if he's got an ax to grind."

"He's a single dad! Nailing him is nailing his family."

Patrick's expression turned serious. "He really did get to you, didn't he?"

She said nothing, turned and marched across the springy green lawn and up the stairs to the house. "I'm going to see Louisa," she called over her shoulder.

Patrick watched his younger sister storm up the stairs, a combination of athletic elegance and sheer energy, blond ponytail swinging, brown legs lean and tanned. And he had a sudden flashback to when they were kids.

He smiled, his heart filling with warmth.

She'd always been the idealist. The kind one. The crusader. And he'd loved her for it.

He was the pragmatist. A businessman—a stockbroker who focused on the bottom line, the outcome. He hadn't always been practical. Life had made him that way by necessity. And coming to Fairchild Acres to sound Louisa out on a potential inheritance made solid financial sense to him. But it had also given him something unexpected. Something special. A chance to reconnect with his sister. And an opportunity to get to know his great-aunt. Despite what everyone said about Louisa, there was something in Patrick that connected with her, and he was actually beginning to like the charismatic old dame. Thorns and all.

Coming to Fairchild had given him a sense of family he hadn't even realized they'd lost.

Megan set a large vase of belladonna lilies on a stand under the hospital window. While Louisa lay sleeping, she rearranged the fragrant trumpets she'd cut herself on the farm this morning after her game of tennis with Patrick. The March blooms thrived in the dry Upper Hunter climate, and they'd just come into their full glory, a time when many other flowers had passed their prime for the season.

She picked up the newspaper she'd brought with her, and took a seat near Louisa's bed, thinking that a garden was one of the things she missed most about living in an apartment. As beautiful as her Sydney flat was, overlooking the ocean, she didn't have a piece of earth to call her own.

Megan flipped open the paper, scanning the headlines. The unrest in the city was calming down a little. That could mean a return of police presence in the Hunter Valley. She glanced at Louisa, wondering if that was a good or a bad thing. D'Angelo was using the lack of police as his trump card.

Then again, having a proper homicide task force reinstated could help find the killer faster. Tension whispered through Megan, tightening the complex knot of conflict growing in her belly.

Louisa stirred, opened her eyes, saw Megan and scowled. "How long have you been sitting there watching me?"

"A few minutes. How are you feeling?" Megan asked.

Louisa struggled to sit. "I'd kill for an espresso," she muttered.

"The doc said no more caffeine. You were having too much."

"Bollocks. And I want that idiot cop removed from my door. I won't have it—I'm not some common criminal." She threw back her covers. "Pass me my clothes. I need to get out of here."

Megan moved to her side. "Louisa," she said, restraining her gently. "You need to stay calm, and you need to stay in hospital. The doctors are worried about infection." The doctors were also concerned about what other drugs Louisa might be taking. The health records Patrick found showed nothing, yet they knew from her blood work that Louisa was using some kind of stimulant, apart from caffeine.

"I'm fine. They can come check me at the estate."

Megan lowered her voice. "It's not just your health, Louisa. If the police think you're fine, they're going to charge you. D'Angelo wants to get this arrest overturned before that happens. The longer they take to charge you, the more ammunition in his favor, and the more he can say they've breached protocol. And with all this APEC stuff going on we can also try and keep your arrest out of the media, avoiding a circus. Which will be better for stud business." Megan smiled encouragingly. "So you stay right where you are, and remain low-key. For your own good."

Louisa's steely eyes held hers for a long beat. "You keep bossing me around, girl, I could cut you from my will."

Megan snorted. "There's one thing you better know about me, Louisa. I'm not here for your money."

"Pshaw! Everyone says that."

"I'm not everyone."

The older woman looked at her strangely. "What are you here for, then?"

Megan wavered for a moment. "Family."

"What rubbish!"

"They told me you were blunt."

"What else did they say?"

"That you have a charming personality, for an eighty-year-old," Megan said with a wry smile.

"No one wants *me* for family, girl. It's my money and old age that keeps everyone around. I'm no fool."

Megan pulled up her covers. "No one said you were. Marie

Lafayette sent you some fruit. I put it on the counter over there. Let me know if I can bring you anything else."

Louisa studied her in silence for a long while. "You remind me of her," she said finally, quietly.

"Who? Marie?"

"No, Betty."

Megan's pulse quickened. "How so?"

"You're gentle like her."

"And this is a good thing?" Megan cocked a brow. "Coming from you, Louisa, I imagine you see that as a weakness."

Louisa actually smiled, and it reached with a nostalgic glimmer into her blue eyes. "Didn't mean Betty couldn't be stubborn as a mule."

"What happened between you and Betty, Louisa?" Megan asked cautiously. She didn't want to push too fast, nor did she want this opening to slip by completely.

Louisa's eyes shuttered and she was quiet for a few moments. "That's in the past."

Megan took a seat next to the bed. "It's my past, too, you know."

"So that's really why you came here, is it? To dig around in the past?"

"Like I said, I want to know more about my family, my heritage."

Louisa looked away. "It's easier to deal with people who want money," she said. "Or objects."

"Well." Megan leaned forward. "If it'll make things simpler, I do want to ask you a favor. I'd like to borrow a couple of horses."

Louisa's eyes flashed back to hers. *"Racehorses?"*

Megan laughed. "No, dressage horses."

"What for?"

She inhaled deeply. "I used to ride competitively when I was kid," she said. "I tried just about every equestrian discipline out there but settled on dressage as my performance class." She paused, watching Louisa. "It was Granny Betty who passed a love of the sport down to my mum, and then to me. Those were special moments we had, all three of us riding together sometimes." She glanced away, staring at the belladonna lilies, the memories strangely raw after all this time. "I thought I might get back into it," she said, turning to face Louisa.

Those steely eyes were unreadable, but Megan could see she'd shaken Louisa deep down somewhere. "Betty and I also used to ride together," she said, very quietly.

Megan remained silent, hoping Louisa would offer more. She didn't.

"You said two horses. Why?"

"I met this young girl," Megan said, carefully steering around the truth. She couldn't possibly tell Louisa one horse was for the daughter of the police officer trying to put her away for life.

"She reminded me of myself at that age. She has a tangible passion for dressage, but she doesn't have access to a horse at the moment. Her family is not wealthy, so I...sort of offered."

Louisa chuckled. "Bleeding heart you are, just like Betty. I used to tell her that she'd never amount to much if she gave everything away..." Her expression grew distant, then suddenly turned shrewd and sharp again. "How well do you ride?"

"I was going places on the circuit." Megan grinned. "At least in my own mind. Granny Betty said it was in the Fairchild women's blood."

"She did, eh?"

Megan nodded.

"And the girl? How good is she?"

"She's learning."

"Take Lady Manners for the girl, a nice solid bay mare and

a bit on the small side. I ride her myself—steady as a rock, she is. Get the grooms to bring her to the stables near the house." Her eyes narrowed. "You take Breaking Free."

"The black stallion?"

"He needs the work. Good horse. Excellent dressage skills. Still has a tendency to carry his weight forward, though."

A surprising excitement shimmered through Megan at the thought of working with a horse in the ring again, especially a stallion like Breaking Free. "Thank you."

Louisa shrugged, as if to say *We'll see,* then winced from the pain the movement caused her.

"You okay?"

"Fine. I want to be alone now."

Megan hesitated.

"Good grief, don't look so worried, girl. I'm not about to kick the bucket. Yet," she added, closing her eyes and lying back. "Still haven't decided if you and your brother are worthy of my legacy."

Megan smiled. The woman was something else. She actually liked her frankness. And Megan sensed a softness buried deep down under Louisa's brittle veneer. It was that hidden part of Louisa that Megan could feel herself connecting with. Yet this was also a woman who'd been trying to bankrupt her debt-ridden neighbor with a battle over water rights so she could snap up his farm for a song.

And now he was dead.

She went to the door, thinking one could never really know another person's heart, what broke them down, or what gave them strength. Or how they defined courage, rebellion, success.

She paused, looked back.

"Louisa?"

"What now?"

"Do you know Dylan Hastings?"

Her eyes shot open. "Is this a mental test? You think there's something wrong with my mind now? Of course I know him. He's the fool who arrested me for bloody murder."

"No, I mean…from before. He said he grew up in this area."

She huffed. "So did a lot of people. Doesn't mean I know them all. Now leave me be. I need some rest. And do me a favor. Get that guard away from my door."

Megan nodded, and left, the door swinging silently shut behind her.

Louisa sighed, closed her eyes, and lay back on her pillow, feeling for the first time in years how nice it was to have someone who cared. Just because they were family. But with that thought came a strange and uncomfortable sense of vulnerability.

Or perhaps that was just her damaged heart.

Chapter Six

The next morning Dylan ran lightly up the stairs of Elias Memorial, frustrated that already three full days had passed since Louisa's arrest and he still had nothing. But he stopped in midstride when he noticed a media van pulling into a parking space under trees across the street.

He turned and watched as two more media vehicles drew up. They were following a shiny black sports ute. He frowned, put on his shades. What was this? Slow day with the riots?

The door of the ute swung open and Dylan instantly recognized the tall black-haired man who alit from the vehicle—Daniel Whittleson, head trainer for Lochlain.

Sam's son.

Daniel slammed the door, his posture aggressive as he stalked toward a small group of reporters beginning to gather outside a TV van.

Damn, he must have called this himself.

Dylan watched as Daniel waved for the journalists to

follow him, and began to run up the Elias Memorial stairs, two at a time.

Dylan quickly started down the stairs and halted him midway. "Daniel, what's going on here?"

Daniel pointed up at the hospital. "Have you charged her yet?" he demanded.

Dylan lowered his voice so the reporters wouldn't hear. "Relax, mate. Why'd you call these people? They're not going to help."

"The woman who killed my father is in there, Sergeant," he said loudly, wagging his finger at the hospital windows. "Lying in all her privilege with one of the most aggressive law firms in the country closing ranks around her. They call D'Angelo, Fischer and Associates the cop killers, do you know that, Hastings? Because of the way they nailed those two Newcastle cops last year. They don't give a rat's ass about justice. And what about my father? Where's the bloody justice for him?" The normally quiet man was shaking with anger as he pushed his words through clenched teeth. "I have had it with that woman, Hastings. She's messed with one too many lives this time."

Daniel swung round to face the media crews who were scrambling to catch the confrontation between the cop and the victim's son on camera.

"What about justice for the folk of the Upper Hunter!" Daniel demanded loudly. "What about the farmers who could have lost billions to flames if the Lochlain blaze had spread to neighboring studs and vineyards? What of the horses we lost at Lochlain—"

Dylan grasped his arm firmly. "Look, mate," he growled quietly. "I want resolution as much as you. We'll get it, but not this way."

"You haven't charged her yet, have you? I heard you didn't get a chance to before she conveniently went into cardiac arrest."

"It was a heart attack."

"Well, *did* you charge her?"

"She's not well enough. Doctor's orders."

Daniel glowered at him, then yanked his arm free, and began storming up the steps toward the hospital doors.

Dylan spun round and immediately caught sight of Megan barring the hospital doors, eyes wide, skin pale.

As Daniel reached the doors, she stepped in front of him. "You can't go in there," she said.

"And who the hell are *you?*"

"I'm Megan Stafford," she said, green eyes fierce, body stiff with tension. "Louisa's niece."

Daniel looked momentarily rattled.

"If you go in there and confront Louisa now," Megan said, "she could die."

"You may be her niece," Daniel said, voice thick with an acrimony and pain of his own, "but the man she killed was my *father.*"

"She didn't do it, Daniel."

Protective instinct surged through Dylan and he moved quickly up the stairs, knowing his every move was being recorded for television from behind.

Daniel shot Dylan a look as he reached them. "You *are* charging Louisa Fairchild with murder, right?"

Dylan cursed to himself, sensing the cameras rolling behind him. He was being backed into a corner, and had to head this off now before things got out of hand. Daniel's incendiary remarks could spark a media lynching of Louisa Fairchild. That wasn't justice.

Acting fast, he took Daniel by the arm, drawing him to his side as he slipped his hand around Megan's waist, pulling her firmly to his other side.

Flanked by the son of the victim, and the niece of the accused, Dylan turned to face the media crew from atop the Elias Memorial stairs, the NSW flag snapping in the warm wind behind them. He was fully aware of the image he was cutting on behalf of the men in blue statewide, aware he alone could end up the scapegoat for this, that this photo could come back to haunt him.

"I'm going to make a brief statement," he said firmly. "So listen up, because I'm not taking questions."

He spoke smoothly, projecting a powerful presence that caught both Daniel and Megan off guard. Cameras clicked. Wind gusted, cracking the flag against the blue sky. Megan's hair teased across his cheek, and immediately Dylan became conscious of her curves against him.

He focused intently on the journalists below, not on how good she felt in his arms. Not on her scent, nor the texture of her blouse under his fingers, the sensation of her waist pressed against his gun belt.

"New South Wales police are doing everything in their power to bring a killer and an arsonist to justice," he informed the small media cadre. "This is a complex investigation, and it comes at a complex moment in our state's history. We have deaths and riots in our capital, and passions are running high all round." Another camera clicked.

"The important thing is to stay focused on commonwealth justice being fair, and being there for all—"

"What about Louisa Fairchild!" called one reporter, nosing forward with his mike. "She shot Sam Whittleson before. Has she been charged with homicide?"

Megan's body tensed against him.

"Louisa Fairchild is a person of interest in this case, but this remains an ongoing investigation. I can make no further comment at this point. Thank you all."

He turned to go, hand firmly on Megan's hip, guiding her up the last step and steering her through the clinic doors, away from the media spotlight. Daniel was hot on their heels.

The automatic doors slid quietly shut behind them, cutting

out the sound of the crowd. Megan exhaled in relief and looked up into his eyes.

Silence grew thick between them.

Dylan slowly removed his hand from her hip, holding her gaze for a long beat. Megan blushed, clearly feeling the same physical pull he was, and that mutual awareness burst through his chest in a sudden hot rush, an awesome feeling of sky-high exhilaration, one he hadn't felt in a long, long time. And now was such a wrong time.

He stepped back, momentarily shaken.

She was too. He could see it in the way her eyes flickered, as if searching for a way out. She brushed a strand of wind-blown hair off her face, glancing at Daniel, then back at him. Her hand was trembling.

"Thank you," she said softly, eyes lucent. "You could have lambasted her out there. I'm grateful."

"Don't be," he said, acutely conscious of Daniel glaring at him. "When Louisa does leave Elias Memorial it will be for a Sydney correctional centre."

"What...do you mean?"

"I plan to bring her before a magistrate at a bedside committal hearing right here in hospital and charge her as soon as Doc Burgess says she's medically able. That's why I'm here, to see the doc."

She stared at him, the soft gleam in her eyes turning cool, her mouth flattening. She turned, walked off.

Dylan's insides twisted. As much as he wanted to nail Louisa, he hated having to say what he had to Megan.

Daniel immediately strode after her, but Dylan grabbed his arm. "Dan, I know this is tough. I can only imagine what you're going through, but let the wheels of justice turn on this one." And he hoped to hell they would.

Daniel swallowed, his body still visibly humming with adrenaline, dark eyes hot and angry. "You're not totally convinced she did it, are you?"

"I'm convinced that if you go in there now, you're going to hinder my investigation."

"You going to arrest me if I do?"

Dylan glanced at the door that led to the wards, saw Megan had stopped to watch him. "Yeah, I will," he said, his eyes locked with Megan's across the room. "But you're not going to force my hand, are you?"

Daniel moistened his lips, gathering himself. "If I can be of any help…"

Dylan nodded, eyes still fixed on Megan. "I'll let you know."

With another angry glance at Megan, Daniel stalked off.

Megan held Dylan's eyes for a moment longer, then she turned, and pushed through the doors. They swung shut behind her.

Dylan blew out a hard breath, and rubbed his brow.

He was between a real rock and a hard place now.

Megan marched straight back into Louisa's room. If the small press scrum outside the Pepper Flats hospital was anything to go by, they were in for the full national media circus when the chaos in Sydney quieted down. And now the prospect of a bedside hearing.

She brushed past the young constable sitting outside Louisa's room, and walked through the door, her conviction faltering only slightly when she saw how tired and gray her aunt still looked.

"Louisa, you have got to talk to me. We don't have time to play games anymore."

"What?"

Megan pointed to the window. "There's a media crew waiting outside. Detective Sergeant Hastings could have trashed you out there. We're damn lucky he didn't—"

Her aunt huffed dismissively. "He's protecting his own bloody hide, that's what, because he knows I'm going to turn up innocent." But Megan could see the shimmer of unease beneath Louisa's bluster.

"He kept Daniel from barging in here, too, you know."

"Sam's son?"

"Yes, Sam's son."

Louisa's eyes shimmered, her features tightening. "I didn't kill Sam, Megan."

"I know that. We all know—"

"No," she said. "We don't all know. That cop, Hastings, doesn't know. The press doesn't know—"

"Then we need to prove it, instead of just gunning after the police and looking for legal loopholes in the arrest. What happened to your Smith & Wesson, Louisa? Why was it used to kill Sam? How did it end up being the murder weapon?"

Louisa's eyes turned a stormy blue. She didn't like being confronted like this. "It's obvious," she said. "It was stolen."

"No, it's *not* obvious. We need to prove it. We need to get the police into your library to dust for prints."

"And what will that show? That my staff and the constable with the search warrant touched everything?"

Exasperated, Megan dragged her hand through her hair. "The constable was wearing gloves, Louisa. And it's a start. It could force the investigation in another direction. If nothing else, it'll provide the ammunition D'Angelo wants if this goes in front of a jury."

Louisa's jaw tensed and she glowered at Megan, but she wasn't able to hide the hint of worry in her eyes.

"Yes, Louisa, it's *that* serious. The rate this is going, you could be charged, brought before a magistrate right here in this hospital room, and end up leaving Elias Memorial and going straight to prison, where you could sit without bail to await a Supreme Court murder trial. I think we should file an official claim of theft, let the cops in to dust the gun cabinet."

Her aunt's face turned thunderous, her hands began trembling. "I will not have them in my house."

Megan exhaled and spun sharply to face the window, crossing her arms over her stomach. The woman was impossible. She was so damn stubborn she was going to end up obstructing police efforts to find the real killer. And she was probably going to land in prison because of it.

"That detective is just pushing your buttons, Megan, because he knows he's not going to get a warrant to go anywhere near my estate again. Filing a report of theft would give him the access he wants."

"What are you so damn scared of, Louisa, if you have nothing to hide?"

"It's the principle. I'm innocent and don't deserve to be harassed. My home is my sanctuary, and D'Angelo has ordered my staff not to talk to the cop. He said silence is best. I trust him."

Megan just shook her head. Little did Louisa know she'd already invited the cop's daughter to ride at Fairchild. Boy, she was in a real double bind now, tangled up and feeling the pressure from all sides.

She thought of the look on Daniel Whittleson's face. As aggressive as he'd been, he'd lost a father.

He had a right to his pain, his anger.

She thought of the mixed messages in Dylan Hastings' touch, how his large and capable hand had felt against her hip. The way he'd handled the crowd.

He had one hell of a balancing act to pull off in a small community like this. And out on those stairs he'd come across as a cop doing his level best to serve his entire constituency, equally. Fairly.

She thought of how Louisa had been trying to drive Sam under by cutting off his access to Lake Dingo water, forcing him to sell Whittleson Stud to her for a song. What kind of woman did that? Her aunt was one hard lady.

She spun back to face her. "It's always about *you*, isn't it, Louisa?"

He aunt stared stonily back. "If a woman doesn't protect herself, who's going to do it for her?"

"You've been standing on your own too damn long, you know that?"

"And you're too sensitive, girl. Like your grandmother. No one is forcing you to take this on. It's not like it's going to get you into my will, either."

"Damn you," she whispered. "Leave your money to the bloody government, a charity, I really don't give a hoot."

"Then why *do* you care? Why are you standing there fighting with me now?"

Megan closed her eyes, inhaling deeply. "And why do you keep pressing *me* on this, Louisa? I told you, I'm here for family. But I guess even I have my limits." She turned to go, hesitated. "Maybe you are right. Maybe I am too sensitive. Maybe I just don't want to see an eighty-year-old woman hauled to Silverwater Correctional Centre in prison garb. Family or not!"

She shoved open the door, turned back one more time. "And you know what else? If you didn't shoot Sam, somewhere out there is a real killer. And just maybe you could stop thinking about yourself long enough to help the police catch him."

She pushed through the door without looking back.

Louisa watched the door swing shut, adrenaline buzzing through her tired body. She needed caffeine. She needed her herbs. And the incision in her groin was throbbing sore. More than anything she was furious. She'd been falsely arrested, accused of something she didn't do, stuck in this hospital bed, and now Megan Stafford had the chops to claim *she* was making things difficult for the police.

She closed her eyes, fatigue and the shakes swamping her. Megan's words bit into her harder than they should. Maybe the child was right. Maybe she had been alone too long, in too many ways.

Maybe she'd forgotten *how* to care.

* * *

The first thing Heidi saw as she entered her dad's office looking for a pencil sharpener was the big white envelope sitting squarely on his desk.

With her mother's name on it.

Written in her dad's bold hand with thick black pen.

Her heart stilled.

She glanced quickly over her shoulder, saw her gran was busy in the kitchen.

What could her dad possibly be sending to her mum?

She reached for the unsealed envelope and slipped the contents out onto the desk. Her throat turned dry as she realized what she was looking at—divorce papers. Signed by both her mother and her father. Official.

Over.

Her eyes moistened inexplicably.

She couldn't say why the papers affected her like this, but they did. She quickly returned them to the envelope, hands shaking.

For several minutes she just stared at the bold black address on the white paper. She hadn't known until this very moment exactly where in London her mother lived.

Her eyes shifted over to her dad's address book. It was lying open next to the envelope. She shot another look over her shoulder, making sure Granny June was still busy in the kitchen. Her dad would be livid if he found out she'd been rummaging in his things.

She set down her broken Snoopy pencil, grabbed a pen from a container on her dad's desk, and quickly copied her mum's address onto a notebook, e-mail addy and all. She tore the page from the notebook, folded it over several times, and slipped it into her pocket, heart racing.

As she left the office, the seed of an idea was forming in her mind.

* * *

Dylan rang the doorbell.

A tall, fit and tanned man in white tennis gear opened the door, momentarily taking Dylan aback.

"G'day, mate—Detective Sergeant Dylan Hastings," he said, noting the quick flicker of recognition in the man's face at the mention of his name. "I'd like to speak to the Fairchild Acres manager. Is he in?"

"You can speak to me," the man said, eyes narrowing. "I'm Patrick Stafford, Louisa Fairchild's nephew. I'm handling the administrative side of things in her absence."

Megan's brother.

Dylan could see the resemblance. Even though their coloring was different, both Patrick and Megan exuded a calm athletic energy. And the easy air of wealth.

"I need to interview some of the Fairchild staff," he told Patrick. "I'd like to start with the manager."

"You have a warrant?"

"Do I need one?"

"I'm afraid Miss Fairchild's lawyer insists on it. None of our employees can talk to police without a court order." He began to close the door, but Dylan halted the action with his boot. Patrick's eyes darkened.

"D'Angelo gives the orders around here now, does he?"

"No. I do."

Dylan crooked a brow. "I must have missed something. Did you inherit the place while your aunt was in surgery?"

Anger corded the muscles in Patrick's neck. "I must ask you to leave."

"Is D'Angelo here, perhaps?"

"He's in Sydney, negotiating a deal. The estate still has business to run, Sergeant. Now if you'll excuse me—" He began to push the door closed.

But Dylan raised his hand casually against the side of the jamb. "Then I'd like to see Megan."

A ripple of surprise crossed Patrick's features, then a spark of irritation flickered in his hazel eyes. "I don't think you understand me, Sergeant. *No one* affiliated with Fairchild can speak to you. Not without a warrant."

"I don't need a warrant to speak to Megan. The business I have with her is personal."

A phone rang in the hall. Patrick's eyes darted agitatedly to the left. It rang again. "How about I tell my sister you stopped by?" he said tightly, closing the door and forcing Dylan to step back.

Dylan left the front porch and ambled round the side of the massive stone-and-stucco mansion, counting on the phone call to keep Patrick busy. Megan appeared to have taken temporary ownership of Louisa's Aston Martin, and he'd seen it parked round the back.

His boots crunched softly over gravel, then packed dirt swallowed the sound of his footfall as he followed a track that led toward the stables nearest the house where Louisa kept her personal riding horses.

The late-afternoon sun angled through the haze on the horizon, and he could see Blue and Scout lying under a stand of tall wattle trees near a dressage ring tucked behind the outbuildings. Dylan's gut told him Megan would be with them. She seemed to have taken on Louisa's dogs as well as the convertible.

Her brother, however, appeared to have taken the farm.

Megan didn't have a clue what a service she'd done him by inviting Heidi to ride here. While he detested the idea of his daughter's involvement, it did give him a personal reason to be on the estate.

Dylan strode quietly, purposefully toward the outbuildings, wind starting to rustle through the wattles. A truck drove across the estate in the distance, dust boiling behind it as it headed towards a group of bungalows near an exercise area for the Fairchild Thoroughbreds.

Blue saw him approach first and the dog came running, body held low, ears half cocked in warning, half anticipating a pat. Dylan crouched down and ruffled the cattle dog's soft, mottled fur. Scout, however, remained under the trees, flat on his belly, transfixed by something in the paddock beyond Dylan's line of sight.

Suddenly Megan came into view around the side of the barn mounted on a massive black stallion that was all rippling muscles, shining coat, stomping hooves and snorting breath.

Dylan's heart stalled.

He stood up, very slowly, mesmerized by the sight of her astride the powerful gleaming animal.

Dressed in a tight white T-shirt that left little to his imagination, frayed jeans, dusty riding boots, black helmet, and with her hair hanging in a gleaming untidy gold braid down her ramrod back, she didn't much resemble the slick urbanite he'd seen getting out of the convertible, or the fashionista in designer-casual who'd squared off with him on opposite ends of an interrogation table.

She was breathing hard, chest rising and falling fast, yet the rest of her body was taut, and her concentration fierce. Sweat dampened her back, and the horse had worked up a lather.

Bewitched, Dylan watched as Megan steadied the black stallion in the center of the ring, gathering the reins, her thighs pressing firmly against powerful flanks as the animal danced with barely bottled energy beneath her.

Forgetting the Fairchild employee list in his hand, Dylan moved on instinct into the lengthening evening shadows along the barn wall, not wanting to startle the horse, not wanting to distract Megan's focus. Wanting to watch, undetected, just a few moments longer.

She nudged the horse forward, gradually urging him into a springy canter as she held her spine perpendicular to the ground, her pelvis rocking easily in the saddle as the animal moved under her, the soft thudding of hooves in the ring raising puffs of fine dry dust that blew in the warm wind.

Perspiration began to gleam on her face and arms from the controlled effort as she slowed the stallion to almost a standstill, executing a turn on the forehand, then urging him forward and sideways at the same time. Sunlight caught a pool of sweat at the hollow of her neck as she turned, and Dylan saw that the horse's wild black eyes sparked with energy and his flanks shimmered in the glow of the setting sun.

Megan's mind, body, energy—everything was wholly attuned to the animal beneath her as their movements became one, and their efforts an equine ballet.

It clean stole his breath.

Dylan knew what sheer physical exertion and mental fitness it took to make dressage exercises appear so smooth, so effortless.

He knew because it was Heidi's passion.

Heidi had pointed out excellent technique when they'd watched the Olympic sport on television, and he was now entranced by the way Megan was working not against this stallion, but *with* him.

The animal was clearly flighty, his energy barely leashed. Yet Megan wasn't fighting to subjugate him in any way. Instead she was coaxing the horse to work with her, asking him to accept her intent as his own, giving him the idea that he had the freedom to run, but that it was his choice to behave under her. To become one.

It was a relationship of complete trust as much as it was one of power. A delicate balance of wills.

And it was flat-out seductive.

The subtle, sensual communication, body to body, mind to mind, the way she sat into him, spine erect, breasts thrust forward, shoulders back, hips rocking, responding to the horse as he responded to her—it turned him on in ways it shouldn't.

It made him hot. Hard.

Her hands tightened on the reins.

Dylan swallowed, pulse quickening, heat swirling low and dark in his gut.

Sweat became a gleaming lather on the horse's back as their movements grew more fluid, faster, her energy flowing like a river right though the animal as she galloped around the ring on the twenty-meter circle. And Dylan felt a reciprocal tug in his body, a pulsing in his groin, his heart pounding in beat with the hooves, his mouth growing dry, his pulse thrumming, tension mounting.

Then she brought the horse to a standstill.

Dylan released a shaky breath he hadn't realized he'd been holding.

Muscles almost quivering in forced relaxation, Megan gently coaxed the stallion to raise his head and tuck his chin in, rounding his spine, gradually gathering him into the compacted form of a highly collected dressage horse until she had him steady on the spot, his hooves pounding a three-time beat into the dust directly below him.

Dylan realized he was holding his breath again.

He'd just learned more about this woman watching her on that horse than he'd learned about others in a lifetime.

She had self-discipline, determination, control. Staying power. To her a relationship was about mutual respect, about allowing individual strengths to cooperate in a harmonious whole.

It was about freedom to make choices. Not a battle for control.

And in those moments observing her on the willful and spirited stallion, Dylan began to think he could just fall in love with Megan Stafford—or some idea of her.

Then a rough blur of movement caught his eye as Scout bolted from the wattle shade after something in the grass. The massive black stallion spooked, rearing up, eyes white and wild, hooves clawing at air, and he tossed Megan clean off his back. She landed on the ground with a gut-sickening thud, and a small bounce.

The horse whinnied, snorted, kicked backwards and bolted in a wild gallop around the paddock.

But Megan lay dead-still in the dirt.

Chapter Seven

She couldn't breathe.

And she didn't dare move. Pain was like fire in her chest, in her back. Her skull was ringing from the impact of her fall, the twilight sky spinning above, her vision blurred. She could taste dust, blood, in her mouth. From the corner of her eye she watched Breaking Free gallop round the edge of the ring. She prayed to God he wouldn't stomp on her.

He didn't.

He came to a standstill, snorting through his nose, sweat glistening over his body, bright eyes watching her intently.

Megan slowly managed to draw in one razor-sharp breath, then another, tears of pain tracking through the dust on her face. Gradually air returned to her lungs, and with a mad exhilaration, she realized she was going to be okay. She was alive, breathing, just badly winded, that's all.

She stared up at the violet sky and began to laugh through her tears. A release of pure adrenaline at first, then a real deep throaty chuckle as the irony hit her—*Louisa had given her Breaking Free as a test.*

That aunt of hers was something else.

Those shrewd calculating eyes had seen. She'd known. That Megan needed this, to be challenged, to find something vital at her core again—the part of her that had been lost along with her mother, Granny Betty, the horses she'd once ridden in her past.

And Megan *had* found it—her center, a moment of pure balance and peace when she and the animal had become one at the heart of the dressage ring, at that place marked X. A place where the rider was totally focused, yet fully aware.

It took a dressage rider to understand this, Megan thought as she rolled carefully onto her stomach and tentatively pushed herself up onto hands and knees, testing one limb at a time as she stood shakily.

Louisa spoke her language, a language she'd forgotten. Until this very moment.

And Louisa had given her the most challenging horse of all, her spirited black stallion, knowing that if Megan overcame her fear, or any doubt in her own abilities, and still chose to mount him, if she could find a way to communicate with Breaking Free, she'd manage to relate to her aunt, to her legacy.

To this place.

Megan snorted as she tried to wipe off the dust caked to her face with the back of her wrist.

Louisa Fairchild had probably wanted to see whether Megan's compassion and sensitivity translated into strength on that willful horse. Or if Megan was someone who'd fold under the challenges and pressures of a massive stud farm.

She slapped her hands on her jeans, trying to dust them off. It was futile really—dirt was sticking to sweat all over her body. She was now caked in the stuff.

She limped slowly over to Breaking Free, talking softly as

she neared him, her heart still hammering, blood rushing in her ears, her legs like wobbly jelly. The stallion studied her warily, twitchy as she approached, with a nasty glint in his black eyes that gave her a moment's pause. But she *had* to get back into that saddle. Just for a few moments. Or the horse would win.

Louisa would win.

She reached for the reins, clicked her tongue gently as she took hold of them, telling Breaking Free what she was doing. She mounted him and walked him slowly round the ring, rubbing his neck, whispering sweet nothings to him, settling them both.

That's when a familiar shade of pale blue near the barn snared her eye, immediately causing her to falter again. Detective Sergeant Hastings, in uniform, leaned casually against the barn wall, watching her, and only her, his features devoid of expression.

Megan's heart began to race all over again. And with the fresh dose of adrenaline came a hot spurt of anger. How long had he been standing there spying on her? She felt suddenly violated. Exposed.

She dismounted. "What do you want?" she snapped as she led Breaking Free to the stables.

He pushed off the barn wall and swung his legs over the fence, following her into the barn. "To talk to you."

"I've been ordered not to speak to you," she said as she led Breaking Free into his grooming stall.

He propped his shoulder against the wall inside the barn, hooking the ankle of one boot over the other. "You ride well," he said.

Megan concentrated on removing the stallion's bridle. She put on his halter and hooked him into cross ties, all the while feeling the burn of Dylan's eyes on her. His stance was casually arrogant and designed to provoke her, she was sure. But she refused to let him throw her.

"You want something, you go through D'Angelo," she said, crouching down to pull off Breaking Free's boots.

The air was warm and close in the barn. The horse's breath was hot, and the stallion was getting edgy with Dylan there, blocking the exit.

Megan was always acutely aware of an escape route when cloistered with a big horse in a tight environment. And that meant Dylan was making her feel trapped, edgy, too. As was the intensity in his eyes, the way he was tracking her every movement. The fact he was even here.

"I thought you wanted the truth, Megan," he said, watching her hands work the boot. "You won't get it playing D'Angelo's game."

She moved around the horse carefully, removing his other boots before going over to the cabinet of grooming supplies.

A young groom came rushing over, apologizing for not arriving sooner. "You want me to take him, Miss Stafford?"

She hesitated. She'd wanted to rub Breaking Free down herself, finish off their session properly, bond with him some more.

She glanced at Dylan, eyes laser-blue, waiting. Tension swelled in her. Whatever he wanted, Megan thought it better to get it over with.

"Thank you," she said to the groom as she rubbed Breaking Free's muzzle one last time. The stallion snuffled at her hand, looking for the peppermints she'd tempted him with earlier.

She dug deep into her back pocket, pulled out the last two and offered them to him. Breaking Free lifted the peppermints gently from her palm with his lips, letting a puff of warm hay-scented breath escape against her skin, then he just stood for a moment, resting his muzzle in her hand.

And Megan was a goner. She'd found a friend in this horse, a worthy challenge. And she'd just found a little part of herself.

It bolstered her confidence with Dylan.

"We can talk outside," she said, brushing past him, removing her helmet as she exited the stables. She pushed sweat-dampened tendrils back from her face, and kept on walking.

He followed her, as she knew he would, into a pool of balmy gold-red evening light. And he chuckled as he kept pace with her along the length of the paddock, dogs following at their feet.

"Something funny?" she said, slanting a look at him.

"You look good in dirt."

She suppressed the sudden tug of a smile. "I feel good in dirt," she conceded.

He regarded her oddly, as if seeing her for the first time. "You spooked me back there when he threw you, Megan."

"I was pretty startled myself, believe me."

Dylan stopped suddenly, forcing her to halt, too. "Why'd you laugh when you were lying on the ground?" He looked directly into her eyes, but at the same time he appeared to be cognizant of her hands, her lips, her legs—everything about her—in that all-consuming cop way.

Her pulse quickened. "I might ask why you didn't come to my rescue, officer," she said softly.

"I almost did. But as I reached the fence, and you started laughing, it dawned on me you were not the one that needed rescuing."

"Who did?"

Dylan was silent for a moment, then a dry smile crossed his lips. "Me, perhaps."

She angled her head, curious. "How so?"

"I was pretty mesmerized by you on that horse, Megan." *Why was he telling her this?*

She flushed unexpectedly, and a shaft of heat shot clear through to Dylan's groin. She turned, walked away. Too fast.

Dylan blew out a long, steady breath, gathering himself before going after her. The woman had a way of unhinging him.

"I laughed," she said as he caught up with her, "because I realized Louisa had given me Breaking Free as a test. She damn well knew he'd throw me. Eventually."

"A test to see if you are worthy of her cash?"

This time she halted, faced him square. Her green eyes sparked. "For the record," she said tightly, "my grandmother Betty left a sizeable legacy of her own. Sorry to disappoint you, Serge, but Patrick and I are not the desperate money-grubbers you seem to want us to be."

A volatile tension swelled thick between them as they locked eyes in silence.

"I'm sorry," he said finally.

She watched him for a beat. "Why *did* you come here today, Sergeant? What do you really want?"

You. Pressed naked against me, dirt and all. Right here, right now.

"The missing pieces of the puzzle, Megan," he said, his voice rough. He held up his list of Fairchild employee names. "I want to talk to the estate staff again. I need to know who might have had access to Louisa's .38."

A sharp flash lit her eyes. "So you *do* think her gun may have been stolen? That Louisa may have had nothing to do with Sam's death?"

He wasn't going to tell her they'd received a tip that her aunt had paid someone to cover up the murder, and that he was looking for an accomplice now.

"It's a possibility," he said, guilt edging into him as he saw hope widen her clear green eyes, their color even lighter, more bewitching, against the contrasting dark streaks of dirt on her face. Dylan could see she was going to develop one hell of a bruise on her chin. Her helmet strap had also cut a raw mark under her neck in the hard fall. The image of her astride the black stallion sifted into his brain again. "It would be easier to determine the truth, Megan," he said softly, "if your aunt quit throwing up legal blocks." He moved closer to her, every molecule in his body inexorably drawn to touching that bruise, every instinct warning him not to.

"If I could interview the Fairchild staff," he said, voice lowering an octave, "I might also learn who has a link to Lochlain Racing, because whoever took that security tape knew his or her way around Lochlain's systems." He shrugged abruptly. "But it looks like D'Angelo has put paid to that, because getting a warrant until I have more to go on could be tough."

He turned to go.

"Wait," she said suddenly.

He stilled, turned slowly back to face her, guilt deepening at playing her like this.

"Do you think I'm a fool, Sergeant?" She drew her shoulders back as she spoke. Under her snug white T-shirt her nipples were still tight from exertion, adrenaline. "Do you think I can't see you're manipulating me for information?"

She reached forward, snatched the list from his hand. "I'll look through it, let you know if anything jumps out at me."

"Why?"

"Because I don't want this to get to court, that's why. Because I want you to find who killed Sam, and to lay off trying to charge Louisa before D'Angelo makes a bloody legal mess of everyone's lives. Just don't play me for an idiot." Her eyes crackled with sexy anger. "I'm your last resort, and don't think I don't know it."

Silence thrummed between them.

He stepped closer, reached up suddenly, and touched her chin. "You should put some ice on that," he whispered.

Megan's mouth opened, soundlessly, desire rushing so hot and fast and heavy through her body, it rooted her boots to the ground.

And then he was gone.

She blew out a shaky breath, and Patrick's words whispered through her mind. *Be careful, Megan. This could get messy. D'Angelo plans on nailing this guy big-time...*

She stared at his broad back as he strode up the lawn with aggressive purpose. The sexiest darn guy she'd run into in years. What in heaven did she think she was doing getting into bed with him like this? Going against Louisa's law firm? Against her brother? She was playing with fire.

But her gut told her it was the right thing. They were all being as stubborn as Breaking Free when he'd first been led into that ring this afternoon.

But she'd brought the stallion round.

Could she do the same with the cop?

Or was she "overmounting," the term for choosing a horse beyond your expertise or skill.

If that was the case, she was in serious trouble.

"That police officer came by today," Patrick said over dinner.

Megan raised her eyes, stopped chewing for a moment.

It was just the two of them enjoying a quiet meal together in the solarium, specially prepared by Louisa's head chef François. Megan waited for François's assistant to pour the wine, tension shimmering softly as the liquid splashed into the glass, bouncing candlelight.

"He said he wanted to talk to the staff." Patrick's eyes held hers once the assistant had left.

She nodded.

"Then he asked if you were in. He said it was personal."

She poked at her salad with a fork. "I told you, I offered his kid a horse to ride here."

"Does Louisa know?"

"Not that she's his daughter."

"Megan—"

"Don't worry, Patrick. I can handle him."

"He's using you, Megan. He's using you to get at all of us."

She felt her cheeks warm. "Maybe, Patrick, *I* am using *him.*"

He regarded her steadily.

"Are you only concerned about the inheritance, Patrick? When did you get so damn cold?" She got up, threw her linen napkin to the table, and started to walk out.

"Megs—" He caught hold of her hand. "I'm concerned about *you*," he said in a big-brother-gentle tone she hadn't heard for years. It brought moisture to her eyes, and an unarticulated longing. She swallowed.

"He's a good-looking single guy, Megan," he said quietly. "But right now, he's also dangerous."

She studied Patrick. "He's dangerous to your money, that's what you're saying, isn't it?"

"You've fallen for him."

She moistened her lips. "If I'm falling for anything, Patrick, it's this valley. This farm. The horses. I'm beginning to think how nice it might be to raise a family out here, okay?"

He opened his mouth to speak, but she raised her hand to stop him. "And don't tell me you haven't thought the same thing. This place, this land, it's infectious."

"That's exactly why Dylan Hastings *is* a threat, Megs. If we let him put Louisa away, we could lose it all."

Dylan sat at the round oak table with his mother and Heidi, Muttley resting on his foot, and Megan on his mind.

"Dad?"

"What?" he said, irritated to have been distracted, once again, by the sensual memory of Megan on that horse. He'd become obsessed this evening with trying to articulate why the voyeuristic vignette had wrought such a mess inside him, why he'd dared cross the line by touching her face like that.

But deep down he knew why.

He'd fallen for Megan Stafford. A woman who represented everything he had no taste for.

And that meant he was in trouble. Again.

"Dad, are you *listening?* There's a big school dance

coming up. It's, like, the event of the year, and I'm giving you plenty of warning because Zach has asked me to go."

"Zach?"

"Zach Harrison."

Dylan made a mental note to vet the Harrison family as he cleared the dishes from the table. He should have done it ages ago.

"The dinner was wonderful," he said, giving his mum a kiss on the cheek.

"It was Timmy's favorite," she said.

Dylan stilled. "You're thinking a lot about Timmy, aren't you, Mum?"

He could feel Heidi watching as she packed the plates into the dishwasher. His mother's eyes clouded for a moment as she cast her memory back, her brow furrowing slightly in confusion. She looked embarrassed. "Not really. It's…just that it's autumn, and it was March when…when he…"

He cupped her cheek. "I know," he said softly. "But that was a long time ago."

"Sometimes it feels like just yesterday. It…muddles me up." Her eyes filled with moisture.

And that told Dylan she was feeling the pain all over again.

He went into his office to look up the number of the psychiatric specialist in Sydney. It was time his mother saw him again. They'd warned him her dementia might progress, that she might increasingly lose touch with reality, blurring the past with the present as her short-term memory went.

Her mental illness was a direct result of his brother's brutal sexual assault and murder. A part of his mother had retreated into herself that day. And her condition had gotten slowly worse over the years, exacerbated now by age.

It might never have happened if Louisa had allowed his family to see justice done. But because her high-priced lawyers had brilliantly—and successfully—defended a murderer and a child molester, his parents had been denied the chance to heal. To put Liam and the tragedy properly to rest.

And for that he blamed Louisa. He hated her.

As Dylan approached his desk he noticed Heidi's Snoopy pencil lying on it. He tensed. She'd been in here.

That meant she'd have seen the envelope addressed to her mother.

Had she opened it? Seen the signed divorce papers?

He flicked his gaze over the rest of his desk, noting his leather-bound address book was open at Sally's name.

He may have left it like that himself—he couldn't be sure.

He traced his fingertips softly over the surface of the notepad lying next to it, feeling the indentations. He ripped off the top page, held it to the desk lamp.

And he saw the impression left by Sally's residential and e-mail addresses. Written in Heidi's hand.

He went into the living room. Heidi was busy on the computer, and she quickly shut down a file as she heard him approach.

"What?" she said, confrontationally.

"You expecting e-mail?"

"My e-mail is private."

"Like my office?"

Her eyes gave her away.

"Do you want to talk, Heidi?"

"There's nothing to talk about," she said, getting up and marching towards the stairs on the verge of tears.

Dylan nodded, feeling once again that no matter how hard he tried to rein everything in, it was becoming impossible to stop his kid from slipping out of his grasp.

He thought of Megan astride that black stallion. She hadn't controlled the massively powerful horse through subjugation or force, but by letting him free in increments, with soft flicks of her wrist, trusting him enough not to bolt.

She could probably teach him a thing or two.

* * *

On her way up to bed, Megan scooped up the mail that Mrs. Lipton had left for Louisa in the hall.

She'd take it to the hospital tomorrow, as Louisa had requested. She flipped through the envelopes as she climbed the wide staircase to her guest quarters, pausing on the steps as a British stamp snared her attention.

Curious, Megan lifted the envelope to study the image. The red-ink postmark showed it had been mailed in Edinburgh. There was nothing unusual about that. Louisa's pile of mail consistently bore postmarks from as far afield as Dubai, London, New York—she did business around the world. But the design of the stamp had caught Megan's eye. It was the artwork of an emerging young Scottish impressionist whose work she'd bid on just last month in London for one of her private clients.

Megan smiled, immensely pleased to see "her" artist being nationally recognized this way. She still knew how to pick a winner.

She set the mail on her dresser and changed for sleep. She'd take the letters to Louisa before paying Dylan a visit at the Pepper Flats station tomorrow.

She'd seen several names on the employee list that would interest him, and she'd thought of a few more that were not on the list, casual hires who were paid under the table, according to Mrs. Lipton.

Nothing escaped that woman's attention.

Lying back on the freshly laundered Egyptian-cotton sheets, listening to the wind whispering in the gum leaves outside, Megan tentatively fingered the bruise on her chin, wincing slightly.

It was where Dylan had touched her.

In more ways than one.

Patrick was right.

She'd fallen for the cop. In the most basic way. And she couldn't get him out of her mind.

Chapter Eight

Dylan was on the phone speaking to a volunteer firefighter mate about Zach Harrison's parents when Megan entered the Pepper Flats station.

Outwardly calm, he felt his heart kick at the sight of her.

He raised his hand, motioned for her to let herself in and come round to the reception area. His civilian admin assistant had already left for the day and he was alone in the station.

From the corner of his eye Dylan watched her saunter up to his desk in the way that only some women could—with a mix of catlike elegance and casual grace, the whole mix simmering with latent sex appeal.

She was wearing faded designer jeans, strappy sandals and a sun-yellow shirt cut low at the neck. Freshly washed hair hung softly about her shoulders. She smiled at him, a toothpaste-ad smile that reached with a twinkle into her applegreen eyes, and Dylan's mouth turned instantly dry.

He cleared his throat and thanked his mate, blood pounding softly against his temples as he signed off and returned her smile. "Sorry about that," he said, standing up and holding out his hand. "Family stuff. Please, take a seat."

"Heidi?" she asked, taking the chair across from his desk, making him instantly aware of his body, the temperature of the room and the fact they were alone. Dylan wasn't sure if he was safe from himself around this woman.

He ran his hand over his hair, thinking she looked like a bloody health commercial—something that was supposed to be good for you. Except that what she was doing to his body and mind was purely bad.

For his case.

For his career.

For his family.

"Heidi has a big school dance coming up," he said, seating himself. "I was vetting a prospective date."

"Zach Harrison?"

Surprise rippled through him. "You know Zach?"

The corner of her mouth curved up, and be damned if he didn't go hot. "Girl stuff," she said. "Heidi told me about Zach and the dance when she came to ride at Fairchild this afternoon. She's really good on a horse, you know?"

So are you.

He shifted slightly in his seat, squaring his shoulders. "You left a message to say you found something on that employee list?"

"Yes." Megan opened her purse, and extracted the list. "Lady Manners is a great horse for Heidi, but she's still fretting over Anthem," Megan said, unfolding the piece of paper. "I've organized to have him transported to Fairchild—"

"What?" Dylan looked up in shock.

"With your permission, of course." She leaned forward, and he tried not to see what that did to her cleavage. "Heidi and I phoned the Lochlain vet this afternoon, and he agreed Anthem would benefit from an environment where she isn't subjected to the stress of the other injured horses and the scent of old fire. The vet said she's an unusually sensitive and intuitive animal, and a move to a calm environment like Fairchild Acres, with hand-walking several times a day and lots of love, could make a world of difference." Megan held his eyes steadily. "I have the perfect place for her, Dylan, and I have time to do that for Heidi and Anthem," she said. "If you'll let me."

Conflict twisted inside him. He felt railroaded. He rubbed the back of his neck. "Megan, this isn't a good idea—"

"For who? You and your case? Or for your child and her horse?"

"All of it, dammit. For you, too." He paused. "Look, I thought you came to talk about the employees on that list."

Her eyes held his for a long, heavy beat, a dark sensuality deepening their green color. Then she glanced down, and flattened the sheet of paper onto his desk. "This list you gave me doesn't include some of the casual hires who are paid in cash, or in kind, or in a labor trade-off between farms. Missing from the list is Wally Kettridge, Jim Banters and Bruce Budge. They all do casual labor during the busy seasons. I've added their names at the bottom there." She pointed. "And then there's Rick 'Sandy' Sanford, who has done carpentry inside the main house for Louisa, and he's fixed fencing on the estate. He's a full-time employee at Whittleson Stud, but he's freelanced at several other estates as well, including Lochlain. And there's—"

"Whoa." Dylan raised two fingers, swiveling his seat to face his computer. "Back up a bit, so I can enter those names into my system. Spell *Kettridge* for me."

She came round to his side of the desk, scraping her chair over the wooden floor to position it beside him, and he caught the scent of her perfume as she sat.

Swallowing against the dryness in his mouth, he entered the names as she read them, discovering it was close to impossible to type coherently with her watching over his shoulder, the sensation of her breath at his neck.

"No—" She reached over his arm, her hair falling forward and brushing his skin. His throat tightened.

"There's no *e* there," she said softly, way too close to his ear.

He deleted the letter, cleared his throat. "Go ahead."

"There are also two pupils from the Pepper Flats high school, both in year twelve. They work weekends and holidays as trainee grooms along with several university students who work during their long holidays." She hesitated, causing him to glance up. A mistake—her lips were so close. So kissable. His body began to hum with kinetic energy, and he saw her lids lower.

For an unbearably long moment silence hung thick, tense, the faint tinge of distant smoke in the air as the breeze drifted in through the open windows.

Dylan moistened his mouth, and she glanced away quickly, inhaling a little too deeply.

"I…I don't like thinking about the staff in this way," she said suddenly, swinging back to face him. "I can't imagine what it must be like to do your job, to always be suspicious, watching for something."

"You get used to it."

"To not trusting?"

He thought of her on that black stallion, and how vital trust was in a relationship. He wondered if he could ever trust again in that way. "What are those names you've underlined there?" he said, nodding to the list in her lap, forcing his focus back to his job.

She glanced down, visibly gathering herself, too. "Those are the full-time hires at Fairchild who have access to Lochlain Racing. The first is Marie Lafayette. She's from Darwin and a new hire in the Fairchild kitchen."

"She was around at the time of the blaze?"

"No, but she started just afterward. She was basically hired over the phone by Mrs. Lipton."

Dylan entered her name as Megan spoke, initiating a criminal check while he was at it. "What link does Marie have to Lochlain?"

"Her uncle Reynard Lafayette works there. I think he actually helped get her the position at Fairchild. He comes to the estate to visit Marie. He comes to see Mrs. Lipton, too."

Dylan shot her a look. "Mrs. Lipton?"

"I think she's sweet on him. He brings her fresh eggs every couple of days. He's a really odd guy, but he has a kind of roguish charm, I suppose. Yet there's…something strange about both him and Marie."

"Like what?"

She shrugged. "I don't know, it's…just a feeling." She laughed, slightly embarrassed, and it made her cheeks pink and her eyes glimmer. "They look at me funny."

"Funny?" A smile tugged at his own mouth, his eyes catching hers. And again, a silent communication swelled between them.

Her blush deepened. "It's nothing specific. They just seem overly curious about me. I catch them staring when they think I'm not looking. It…just doesn't feel normal."

He pursed his lips. "Does Reynard ever enter the main house?"

"The kitchen mostly. He has tea with Mrs. Lipton. She saves him brandy snaps that she bakes, apparently his favorite."

"And does Marie go and visit her uncle at Lochlain?"

"Pretty regularly."

"So all three—Geraldine Lipton and Marie and Reynard Lafayette—have access to the Fairchild gun cabinet, as well as a working knowledge of Lochlain Racing."

Megan blew out a breath. "I tell you, I really don't like

thinking like this. And I'm sure Mrs. Lipton would *die* before hurting Louisa. She'd do anything for my aunt."

Like cover up a murder?

Dylan finished entering the names. "And along with those casual hires you mentioned, they all conceivably have access to Louisa's gray Holden."

"Yes. Look, Dylan, I'm not thinking any of these people are guilty or anything. It's just possible that someone else took her gun and used her truck that night."

Or that Louisa paid them to.

But he wasn't about to tell Megan about the anonymous tip.

"How do you know about all these casuals if they're not on the official employee roster?" he asked. "You haven't been there that long."

"I asked Mrs. Lipton. She's up on all the comings and goings. Nothing escapes that woman."

"And she told you all this voluntarily?"

She pulled a face. "I wasn't exactly truthful in why I was asking."

Dylan studied her features, guilt and conflict and lust tightening inside him. He'd never have gotten this simple information without a warrant. And perhaps not even with one if there was no record of these people on the Fairchild payroll. He was indebted to her. And he was going to use what she'd given him to take her aunt down.

He was worried not only about that, but about what the Fairchild legal machine could do to her if they found out she was helping him.

"Megan," he said slowly. "You do know that D'Angelo will crucify you if he finds out you're telling me this."

"So? What can he do, sue me?"

"That shyster would sue his own mother. You're going against the powerful Fairchild clan here." He paused. "Against your brother, too."

"No. I'm not," she said, leaning forward earnestly. As she did, her hair fell in a curtain over her shoulder, releasing the scent of her shampoo. Her warmth.

"It's in *their* interests to have you back off from charging my aunt," she said, eyes piercing his, her breasts rising and falling softly in tune with his own rapid breathing. "No one is going to benefit if this goes to court."

Perspiration broke out over his chest at her increased proximity. He met her gaze steadily. "But if it does go to court, Megan, D'Angelo will drag you by the hair through the legal muck."

"And you, too. D'Angelo takes no prisoners, Dylan. That's why I need you to drop the charges."

Silence thrummed between them.

"You see?" she said softly, her eyes falling to his mouth. "I think we both want the same thing."

Heat shot clean through to his groin.

"We're just not agreeing how to get there." She leaned forward as she said it.

And at that moment his world began both to spin and to stand still. He was at the cusp, that dizzying instant before you leap and change everything—or don't. A line from which there could be no going back once crossed. And Dylan leaned forward, over that line, inexorably pulled towards her, his body acting quite apart from his mind, which couldn't even seem to register his surrounds as everything narrowed onto her.

She covered the distance, slowly, allowing his lips barely to skim hers.

Her breath mingled softly with his. He could taste her. She pressed her mouth more firmly against his, opening her lips under his, her tongue tentatively, seductively, entering his mouth.

Electricity cracked through him. Dylan grabbed the nape of her neck, cupping the back of her head, thrusting his fingers into her thick, soft hair, pulling her firmly against him as he moved his lips hungrily over hers.

He could feel her hand moving up his forearm, fingers exploring his skin, her body growing warm. Heat began to swirl and throb between his legs.

A car engine sounded outside, and Dylan pulled back, suddenly grounded, shocked at what he'd just done.

Megan looked at him, the expression in her eyes heavily seductive, her lips full and pinked from their kiss.

He jerked to his feet, dragging his hand over his hair.

He was in uniform, *dammit!* Functioning as the station sergeant, representing his state force, his town, his community, justice. He was up to the bloody hilt in potentially the most damaging case of his career—investigating this woman's great-aunt for murder, this woman he'd just gone and kissed. A woman who lived in Sydney, who stood to inherit a fortune. Who wanted things from life that were at odds with everything he stood for.

He just could not afford to do this. For so many goddamn reasons.

Yet he'd been incapable of stopping himself.

"This…this is wrong," he said, his voice thick, his head pounding.

She swallowed. "I…I should go." She stood, straightening her shirt, her nipples still hard nubs against the soft yellow fabric. Heat arrowed to his groin again, intensifying the swollen ache. He swore softly to himself and stepped back.

"Thanks." He cleared his throat. "For your help with the list."

She inhaled deeply, pressed her hand to her stomach as she gathered her trademark poise. "It's nothing," she said. "If I don't help you, I'm not going to get what I want. I won't clear my aunt."

"I'm a fair cop, Megan. Please don't forget that."

When I finally do convict your aunt and her accomplice.

She hesitated, then she turned quickly and walked to the reception door. He watched her rear move in those hip-hugging jeans, thinking just how much he'd like to get her out of them. But she spun to face him again, and he stiffened his spine.

"What about Anthem?"

"Pardon?"

"I have a Fairchild groom, driver and horse trailer organized for one-thirty tomorrow afternoon. Plus the vet has agreed to be on hand at Lochlain to help move her. That's if it's okay with you?" She smiled a nervous smile that made his heart tumble.

"Louisa is okay with this?"

"She doesn't know that Heidi is your daughter, Dylan, only that I have a friend who needs stabling for an injured horse."

"Why *are* you doing this, Megan?"

"I…I don't know," she said softly, honestly, an unexpected sadness filling her eyes. "Maybe it's just my way of putting things right between a father and a daughter. A chance I never had."

She turned to go, but not before he could see the sudden glimmer of emotion in her eyes.

"Megan—"

She stilled.

He studied her, liking her more and more by the minute, knowing at the same time he'd crossed a line they were both going to regret. How badly, he wasn't sure yet. He had to pull back, stop this, but he couldn't.

And here he was going another step further.

"Heidi will still be in school at one-thirty," he said.

"Meaning?"

"She'd want to be there when Anthem's moved."

"Oh." Warmth filled her eyes. "I'm so pleased you want to do this. But one-thirty is the only time I could get the trailer and staff this week. Plus the Lochlain vet will be available then. I…. I thought we could surprise her, Dylan, and have Anthem at Fairchild by the time Heidi comes to ride tomorrow afternoon."

Snared by Megan's enthusiasm, smitten by the way she wanted to make his child happy, slipping further into her world, knowing just how damn difficult it was going to be to extricate himself when the time came, he agreed. "I'll meet you at Lochlain tomorrow, then," he said, a whispering sense of foreboding shimmering along with anticipation in his gut.

He'd arrive at Lochlain early, use the time to question Reynard Lafayette, perhaps talk to Tyler Preston about some of the other casual hires on Megan's list, like Sandy Sanford.

"Deal." She smiled.

And Dylan felt he'd just sealed his fate.

Megan drove fast, too fast, the Aston Martin purring gloriously along the straight road, fields and fall colors blurring by.

She felt expansive, full. Exhilarated. A little wild. She smiled, tossing back her hair in the warm wind. She was experiencing the heady rush of first love, and there was nothing quite like it. Pure, intoxicating.

But deep down a whispering anxiety underlay the sensation. That was part of the thrill, she supposed as she turned onto the road that led back to Fairchild Acres. Because Patrick was right—there was always the risk she could lose it all. The danger almost made it more enticing.

Approaching the Fairchild gates, she slowed the convertible and wheeled into the driveway, thinking no matter what happened between her and Dylan, there *was* one thing she was certain about. Dylan stood at an intersection with his daughter.

Megan felt it intuitively.

Both Heidi and her dad were good, good people, but there

was a chasm growing between them, just like the one that had yawned between Megan and her own father.

And Megan's father had died angry. With her. And there was no way to explain what that had done to her, the void it had left in her.

If she could help bridge that divide between a father and daughter now, if she could help Heidi and Dylan through this rocky place in some small way, Megan might just make peace with her own dad.

With her past.

With herself.

And that would be worth it.

Chapter Nine

Dylan watched paint track down weatherboard as Reynard Lafayette, general handyman at Lochlain Racing, dragged his brush with a steady hand in spite of the edginess in his eyes.

Horses were being exercised in the distance, and the sound of construction punctuated the air—a farm slowly being pulled back together after the devastating blaze, the blackened, cordoned-off ruins of the crime scene a stark reminder of the road yet ahead.

A reminder they still had to get to the bottom of what happened.

"Yeah, so I'm from Darwin. What of it?" Reynard said, carefully dipping the tip of his wide brush into the paint tray, avoiding Dylan's eyes. "I already spoke to other investigators. Why are you questioning me now?"

He was hiding something. A sixth sense in Dylan was sure of it.

"You spoke to the arson squad," Dylan said. "This is a homicide investigation now, and we're just covering all bases. Marie Lafayette is your niece?"

A pulse increased at his neck, yet his hand remained steady as he tracked another broad streak of paint over the board. "What's that got to do with the price of eggs?"

"That's what you take Geraldine Lipton, isn't it? Free-range eggs from Lochlain. You visit Fairchild Acres what—a couple of times a week?"

"So, I know Mrs. Lipton."

"That's how you also knew there was a vacancy in the kitchen, wasn't it? Through Mrs. Lipton? You got Marie the job at Fairchild."

Reynard set his brush carefully on the tray, too carefully. He stood up, pushing back the peak of his cap, years of sun and hard living evident in his features. "My niece has nothing to do with this."

Dylan watched his eyes. He'd done a background check on all the staff Megan had drawn to his attention. None had criminal records apart from Reynard, although his was a spent conviction which, under Northern Territory law, basically meant he'd paid his dues to society and his slate had been wiped clean.

Dylan technically should not even know about it, but he'd learned of Reynard's past conviction from a confidential police contact in Darwin. The news had piqued his interest in the man. According to Dylan's Darwin contact, Reynard had lived a transient existence, and was a bit of a con artist who'd had several minor run-ins with the law. Then all of a sudden, after his slate had been wiped clean, he'd dropped off the radar.

Dylan's source had found it impossible to get anything more on Reynard from that point.

But Dylan had managed to ascertain from Tyler Preston that the Lafayettes came from a low-income background, and that Marie had worked at a hotel in Darwin until her mother had died recently—just before she'd moved to New South Wales to join her uncle.

"The Hunter is a long way from the Northern Territory," Dylan offered. "Why leave Darwin to come here?"

Reynard's eyes flicked ever so slightly to the right. "Look, mate, I resent this line of interrogation. I've told you coppers everything I know. I didn't see anything that night, and I know my rights. I don't have to answer any more of your questions."

"It would make your employer happy if you did," Dylan said. "The Prestons want this resolved as much as I do. Your head trainer Daniel Whittleson's father died here. If you have any information that—"

His eyes narrowed sharply. "I've said my piece, Sergeant. And you go harassing my niece, I'll hear about it, and I'll have her speak to that Fairchild lawyer. You'll be hearing from *him* then."

He turned his back on Dylan, dropped down onto his haunches, and poured more paint into the tray.

A Fairchild groom led a blinkered Anthem up a small ramp into a horse trailer emblazoned with the big red-and-bronze Fairchild logo. The smoky-white mare's tail and legs had been carefully wrapped, and the vet had given Megan the horse's medical file, which she'd pass on to the Fairchild veterinary consultant as soon as they arrived at Louisa's.

A driver waited inside the cab of the truck, ready to leave as soon as Anthem was loaded. Megan was busy thanking the vet when she saw Dylan in his uniform approaching under the gum trees. Her heart did a silly little tumble as she smiled and gave a quick wave.

She and Dylan had consulted Tyler together about moving the horse, and Tyler had expressed surprise that Louisa had actually offered stabling and veterinary care for Anthem. He'd told Megan that Fairchild was the only farm that had *not* offered to take in horses after the fire. He'd explained that even though Louisa did business with Lochlain, a latent animosity still ran deep between Fairchild Acres and Lochlain Racing because of Louisa's bitter feud with Sam.

Daniel Whittleson, Lochlain's head trainer, had naturally supported his dad in his rights battle over Lake Dingo, knowing full well that losing the water would send his debt-ridden father and the stud farm under, leaving Louisa to buy the land cheap. No one else would want it without water.

Louisa had also thrown her very vocal support behind Jackson "Jacko" Bullock in the race for presidency of the International Thoroughbred Racing Federation.

Tyler's cousin from Kentucky, Andrew Preston, was running neck and neck with Bullock, and Louisa seemed to feel Andrew's association with the Lochlain–Whittleson camp was reason enough to badmouth him. She'd made a big deal in the media about Andrew being a Yank, and not of true-blue Australian stock. She'd said the time had come for the international association to have a dinkum Aussie at the helm, someone who could finally bring their country-specific issues to the fore.

This information about Louisa had unsettled Megan.

There was so much about her great-aunt not to like, yet she still sensed that a buried compassion ran deep inside her—a mysterious side to Louisa that Megan was driven to connect with. Or was she just so desperate for a sense of family and belonging that she was looking for something where there was nothing?

Dylan came up to Megan and placed his hand proprietarily at her waist. Heat shimmered instantly through her. "Ready?" he asked.

More than he knew. "Good to go," she said with a light smile.

He thanked the vet and guided Megan to the cab of the truck, pausing at the passenger door. "I'm not good at this, Megan."

She looked up into his clear eyes, blue as the sky behind him. "Good at what?"

"Being indebted to a woman."

She grinned. "You got something against a woman being in control, Sarge?"

His features darkened, and his eyes turned serious. "I saw you control that horse, Megan. You tricked him into thinking he was in charge, that your will was his."

"It wasn't a trick," she said quietly. "Riding a horse like Breaking Free is about trust, not trickery. You each have to give up something, and allow yourself to become vulnerable because of it, but in return you become stronger as a unit."

"Trust can get a cop killed, Megan."

"I was talking about a horse, Sergeant."

He smiled wryly and opened the passenger door for her. "I'll follow you and the trailer in my squad car."

She hesitated, glanced over her shoulder. "Do you mind if I ride with you?" she said, lowering her voice. "I just learned something from one of the grooms that I think you should know."

Megan shifted in the car seat to face him. "Reynard Lafayette has been getting a regular and seriously hefty paycheck under the table, and it's not from Lochlain Racing."

Dylan's eyes whipped to hers, his hands tensing slightly on the wheel of his squad car as they followed the horse rig. "Who did you get this from?"

"The groom who helped me load Anthem."

"Go on."

"He said the guy who bunks with Reynard is a bit of a snoop, and when he saw Reynard was hiding something under his mattress, he figured Reynard was into porn, or something. So he took a peek while Reynard was out. He found pay stubs from a numbered company. Reynard is getting a regular monthly income from somewhere, and the groom said the gossip is that he's on someone's payroll."

"How come this groom told you this, Megan?"

"Maybe *he* trusted me."

Dylan threw her a look, and saw she was smiling, toying with him.

"You chatted him up, didn't you? You batted those pretty green eyes at him?"

"Are you jealous, Sergeant?"

He returned his attention to the road, but his neck muscles were tight.

Damn. When had he gotten so anal?

They drove in silence for a while, just the occasional static and chatter on his police radio as they followed the horse trailer.

Dylan stole another quick glance at her as they turned into Fairchild Acres and followed the rig in a dust cloud up the long driveway before branching off onto a narrow farm road and heading for some old stables down near the river.

He had a bad feeling being here on Louisa's farm, his daughter's horse in that trailer up ahead, Megan in his squad car. He was getting in way too deep. Yet it was helping his investigation—the information she'd just given him was invaluable.

He might be able to convince a magistrate to authorize a warrant to access Reynard's accounts.

If he could trace the numbered company back to Louisa, he could then get a court order to look into her finances and payroll records. Damn, he really needed a full task force on this.

He also needed to interrogate Marie Lafayette. But he wasn't going to be able to get at her without a warrant.

"I could talk to Marie if you like."

His eyes flashed to hers. She'd been watching him, reading his thoughts. He cleared his throat. "It's better if you stay out of this now, Megan."

"Why?"

He exhaled sharply. "It is a homicide investigation. I shouldn't be sharing this with you. I shouldn't have let you in this far."

Frustration glittered in her eyes. "I *am* in this far, Dylan. This was my information. I didn't have to tell you."

His jaw tightened as the car bounced over a rough section of road, dust billowing behind them.

She sighed and slumped back into the seat. "You're a stubborn ass, you know that?" she muttered.

He ignored her. "Why are you stabling Anthem all the way down here by the river, anyway?" he asked a little too curtly, changing the subject as they pulled to a stop beside the rig, parked near the water.

"It's quiet," she snapped she climbed out of his squad car, slamming the door.

He watched her stomp over to the trailer, her bush boots dusty, not a stitch of makeup, ponytail sashaying provocatively across her back, her faded jeans hugging her butt. She looked capable, earthy, and more than anything he wanted to make love to her. Right now, down by the willows in the warm sun.

He slammed his own door shut and followed her.

"I didn't want to put Anthem anywhere near Breaking Free or the Thoroughbreds," she called over her shoulder, still angry. "They're way too highly strung."

He caught up with her as the groom led Anthem down the small ramp. "Thank you," she said, taking the rope from the groom.

She turned to Dylan, speaking softly now that she was close to the horse. "She needs a completely stress-free environment, and the sound of the river and the trees down here will be good for her."

He walked beside her as she led Anthem to her new paddock. "No one has used this place for a while so it's pretty peaceful," she said. "I've had the fences repaired, and I had an old pony brought down here for company, a real mothering sort. She'll have a calming effect on Anthem."

Dylan hung over the fence and watched as Megan hand-walked Anthem round the paddock. The groom and driver had left with the trailer, and it was just the two of them and the horses, the wind rustling softly in the willow and pepper-tree branches, the autumn sun warm on his back.

Anthem was literally relaxing in front of his eyes, tension seeping out of her neck muscles and haunches. Even the way the mare held her head showed a growing confidence. He could see Megan was relaxing, too, and Dylan was once again struck by what this woman was doing for his daughter. He was indebted to her, growing more so by the minute. Something close to panic began to whisper through him—he had to step back, draw the line with Megan, but part of him knew it was too late, that he'd gone too far.

"I think it's working," Megan said, dusting her hands against her thighs as she came out of the stall where she'd settled Anthem. "I'll walk her like that a couple of times a day." She swung her long legs over the fence and dropped down beside him.

"Looks labor intensive," he said.

"The vet says it's one of the best things we can do for Anthem's anxiety and depression. Hand-walking provides the physical exercise and release all horses need, but without any accompanying psychological demand. Louisa's vet will monitor the physical side of things, but Heidi and I can work on ameliorating her mental stress. Just being away from the fire scene and the memories will help. I think we can make her well."

He looked down into her eyes. "You sure you want to do this?"

"I'm on vacation, Dylan. My gallery stuff is on hold for a few weeks so I have the time, and yes, I do want to do this." She hesitated, taking in the trees, the river, the farm. "I forgot this part of myself—how much I get from being out on the land, with animals."

"What about the city? That's your thing."

She gave him a wry smile. "What would you know about what my thing is?"

"Well, you *are* going back."

She looked puzzled by his comment. "Well, yes, my life is there," she said. "My job, my friends, my home, everything."

And he had to remember that, he thought as they walked along the river toward his car. He stopped suddenly under a willow, and she did too, that sexual awareness strumming between them again as the dry leaves rustled. But it was different this time. Edgier.

She was watching his mouth, and he became acutely aware of the sound of the water bubbling over small rocks, the breeze lifting fine tendrils of her hair about her face. Time seemed to grow elastic, stretching, long, warm, and he felt himself stir between the thighs. He lifted his hand, burning to touch her, but he rubbed his jaw instead. "I should get going."

But she reached up suddenly, placed her palm against the fine stubble along his jaw, and he felt himself melt inside "Megan—" His voice came out hoarse.

She moved closer, and panic resurfaced. His mind screamed to take her, rip off her clothes and make love to her under the willows. But he grabbed her wrist suddenly, a little too harshly, and moved her hand away from his face, his heart thudding hard. "Megan," he said again, voice low, thick. "I…I'm sorry. I can't do this."

Shock and hurt flared in her gorgeous clear eyes. "It's okay," she said, glancing away, embarrassed.

"Look at me, Megan."

She swallowed, turned slowly back to meet his eyes. His heart twisted at the raw emotion he saw there.

"You need to know something about me, Megan. I don't

do half measures. I don't mess around. I…I can't." He blew out a hard breath of air. "I'm a lifer."

"I know," she whispered. "I can tell."

It was what made him special, thought Megan. Different from all the others she'd met and dated.

And he was warning her, right now, right here, that if she wanted to play this game, she was going to have to be prepared to go all the way. To commit.

And it just turned her on even more.

But was she ready for this?

He was right. She did have another life. A job. One she had to go back to, and fairly soon.

Was she just messing with his emotions? With Heidi's feelings? With her own? Had she made a terrible mistake already getting in too deep?

It wasn't as if she'd really had a choice. It had just happened. And now she was on the cusp—a point that required a decision one way or the other. And she didn't know which way to go.

The radio on his belt crackled.

His eyes held hers a moment, daring her to cross that line. Then he keyed his radio, turning away from her as he answered his call.

It was dispatch. There'd been an incident on the highway. He told them he was on his way.

"I've got to go," he said, turning back to her.

She wanted to tell him to be careful, but she just nodded.

He hung back a moment, willing her to change her mind, to say something.

But she couldn't find the words.

"Thank you," he said curtly. "For doing this for Heidi. And for cooperating in the investigation."

He'd just drawn his line in the sand, she thought, making it clear that her efforts were for his child, for the case, and not for him personally. Not unless she was prepared to play *his* game. To cross that line.

He waited another beat. Then his eyes shuttered, and he was once again all cool cop. He turned, walked up to his squad car, and opened the door.

A soft panic threatened to overwhelm her.

"Dylan, wait!" she called out, running after him. "What… what happened with Louisa in the past? Will you just tell me why you hate her so much? Why this is all so personal."

He studied her for a long moment. A flock of lorikeets darted through the willow branches, unsettling her with sharp screeches. "It was an old court case, Megan, one that involved…some people I knew." He was guarded. His eyes had the same flat inscrutability she'd seen when they'd first squared off over that table in the interrogation room.

"Your aunt footed the bill for an unethical legal defense," he said. "For someone who didn't deserve it, someone who was guilty of a terrible crime."

"Who?" She was deeply curious now. "What defense?"

He glanced up at the smoky Koongorra hills. "It's in the past."

"I don't think so, Dylan."

He said nothing. Then got into his squad car and drove off in a cloud of farm dust.

He'd just cut her out, and it hurt like all hell.

But she hadn't been able to cross that line in the sand, either.

She hadn't been able to make the move, and now he was gone.

Phone held to his ear with his shoulder, Dylan flipped a burger on the barbecue, still steamed about the way he'd handled things with Megan down at the river.

Damn, he wanted that woman.

And he'd gone and cut her out.

It was for the best. There was too much at stake even to think down that road. She was plain wrong for him, and now he needed to focus on his job and on his family. The future.

"Hey, Slugger," he said into the phone, using the tag his buddy Mitch had earned in a dust-up outside the Crook Scale Pub some years back. "Can you ask that gorgeous nurse Jenny of yours what a dance frock costs?"

"What the hell you want with a dance frock?"

"Just ask her, okay?"

"No *wuckers*, mate, but first you've got to tell me why the cop wants a fancy dress."

"Heidi's got a school dance coming up in two weeks." He tossed another burger, flames searing up in a burst of fragrant smoke. "I need to put some cash into her account so she can get something special." Dylan had no idea where in Pepper Flats village one bought dance dresses, let alone how much they cost. He was totally out of his depth here.

"Jenny's on the late shift. I'll ask her when she gets back from the clinic. Say, we haven't seen you down at the Crook, mate. You coming round any day soon?"

"Soon as this APEC crap dies down and I can take a day off." Dylan needed time with his mates again. He needed to get back into his old groove.

And as far away from Megan Stafford as he could.

Heidi came bounding out of the house as he hung up and hooked the phone back into his jeans.

"Dad! Oh, my God, I *love* you guys!" she said, rushing out onto the patio, the old Heidi sparkle back in her brilliant green eyes, her young body lithe with the vibrant energy of a happy child, yet the look of a woman.

It made Dylan smile in spite of everything else.

"I had the best day ever! Anthem is sooo happy." She threw her arms around his neck, squeezing with all her might. "Thank you, Daddy. Thank you so much."

His eyes misted instantly. She hadn't called him Daddy for almost a year now. And be damned if he didn't have Megan to thank for this, too.

"Hey, kiddo," he said with a grin, hooking his knuckle

under her chin, his chest expanding with a surge of paternal emotion. "I'm putting some funds into your account for a new outfit, okay?"

"What?"

"For the dance."

Her jaw dropped open. "I can go?"

He nodded. "I checked Zach out. I think he'll pass."

"You *what!*"

"Just to find out a bit more about who's going to be going out with my daughter."

"I don't believe this. You have got to be kidding me. You had Zach *investigated?*"

"Hey, chook, I'm just being a dad. Gimme a break, okay?"

Her mouth tightened. She crossed her arms over her waist and glowered at him. "Geez, Dad, you could have just asked *me* about him."

He shrugged. "You haven't been talking to me much, kiddo."

She was silent for a moment, thinking about that. And almost as quickly, her outrage was gone. "I still love you, Dad." She hugged him quickly, then rushed back inside.

"Heidi, wait! Where are you going? Supper's almost ready."

"I have to phone Megan," she called over her shoulder.

"Why!"

She stilled in the doorway, looking at him as though he was an idiot. "Because, Dad, she has the best fashion sense ever. Have you seen her clothes? I need to ask her what to wear." And she disappeared through the door.

Dylan swore. This *had* to stop. But it was already way too late. And the irony was, Heidi was happy. Megan had come like a ray of sunshine into his daughter's life. She was the mother—the female role model—Heidi seemed to be searching for right now.

The trouble was, *he* didn't want Heidi filled with artsy

ideas of living in the city. He didn't want her aspiring to things she couldn't have. A life he couldn't afford.

Dylan snagged his bottle of beer and took a deep, hard swig. He slumped down into his deck chair, put his head back and watched the stars, stealing a brief moment of relaxation as his mother fixed the burger buns inside.

But Heidi was already back out the door. "Dad! Guess what?"

"What, chook?" He felt tired.

"Megan has invited me to go shopping tomorrow! The whole day in Newcastle, to help me find a dress. She's on the phone. She wants to check with you."

Dylan swore softly. "Tell her it's fine."

"You…don't want to speak to her?"

"No."

Concern showed in her eyes.

He forced a smile. "Hey, it's all right. You're old enough to arrange your own shopping trip with a friend. I'll put a bit of extra cash into your account so you can take her out to lunch."

He owed Megan enough already.

Chapter Ten

Heidi was pooped, cheeks flushed, eyes bright, her arms loaded with shopping bags as they were seated at the small table of a busy bistro overlooking the wide Hunter River in Newcastle.

The city was a waterfront metropolis on a peninsula bounded by the rolling waves of the Pacific Ocean to the south-east, and the mouth of the Hunter in the north. Rich in culture with museums, galleries and boutiques, Newcastle also served as the bustling port gateway for Hunter Valley goods and was a surfer's paradise with ribbons of gold beaches.

And on this Saturday morning the city bustled with activity and Heidi was on a high. She and Megan had found the perfect dress. Heidi had chosen bloodred, bold and avant-garde, and she loved it to bits. She'd never have picked it without Megan. She trusted her style. She loved everything about her.

She wanted to be just like her.

Megan had taken her to galleries, pointing out the work of

some of the artists she'd represented, and they'd talked more about Brookfield.

Walking past a boutique with magnificent hats, Megan had regaled Heidi with tales of how they dressed up for the big horse races in Sydney wearing the biggest, craziest hats possible.

And on impulse, Megan had laughed, her pretty green eyes twinkling, and they'd gone inside and bought the most gorgeously outrageous hat for Heidi, and it came with a promise. Megan would take Heidi to the next big race at Warrego Downs in four weeks, where one of Louisa's stallions would be racing.

"What about my dad?" Heidi asked as she set her hatbox on the vacant chair beside her.

"What about him?"

"When we go to the races, what will he do?"

"He can come," Megan said, before turning to the waitress and ordering a cappuccino and a mocha plus a slice of cheesecake to share. "If he wants to, that is."

Heidi contemplated Megan again. She adored her large and eccentric designer sunglasses, the way the sunlight gleamed on her hair, the way it was so expensively cut. She wondered if her mother looked anything like that now. She'd be older, but maybe just as pretty and stylish.

She took a sip of her mocha, not something she ordinarily drank, and it made her feel ridiculously important to be sitting at a riverside table with a woman like Megan and a pile of boutique packages at her side. She wished some of the girls from Pepper Flats High could see her now. And the first little seeds of an idea began to grow—what if her dad and Megan started dating?

Then she thought of the divorce papers and got scared, her feelings confused.

"I e-mailed my mother," she blurted out suddenly.

Megan set her coffee down slowly, obviously interested but trying not to show it. "Is that not something you ordinarily do?"

"No." Heidi stared at her cup. "I've never ever spoken to

her, or had an e-mail from her. Not since I was four." She brightened. "But things could have changed, you know? If she got to know me now it would be different. I was thinking, if Dad doesn't let me go to Brookfield, maybe my mother will let me go and stay with her in London. She's artistic, like you. I thinks she looks a bit like you."

Megan lifted her shades, listening, her green eyes serious. "She really hasn't contacted you once in ten years?"

Heidi felt her cheeks go hot, and her body defensive, as if the lack of contact was an indictment on her. As if she wasn't good enough for a mother. "I got birthday cards…for a while." She cast her eyes down. "But when she gets my e-mail, she'll probably write back. I sent her some photos of myself and Anthem, and some of my art. She works for a fancy interior design company, so she may be able to help fund art school in London." She looked up. "That would be cool, don't you think?" She sounded unsure.

Megan leaned forward. "Heidi, when did you send her this e-mail?"

"A few days ago."

"And you haven't heard back yet?"

"She's busy. She might be away."

Megan nodded, sat back. "And you really think you'd like to go to London? Why? It's gorgeous here, and you're close to your dad, and there's Anthem and the riding."

Heidi felt the telltale burn of tears, and her lip begin to wobble. "Dad doesn't care about what I need."

"Oh, hon." Megan reached for her hand. "I've never come across a man who cares so much for his daughter. He's built his whole life around you, sweetheart."

"He's built a jail, that's what. He won't allow me to do a thing. And my gran is wearing me down."

"What's wrong with her, Heidi?"

She pulled a face. "She's got some kind of dementia from something that happened long ago."

"What happened?"

"I don't know. No one wants to talk about it. It's like not talking about it makes it go away. But Gran is losing touch with reality. She gets confused, and lost, and she leaves the oven on, and the water running. She'll soon need to go someplace where someone can care for her full-time, Megan, and my dad can't see it. He doesn't want to."

"He's trying to hold on, Heidi. He'll come round to what needs to be done."

"He's never going to change, Megan! I need to get out of Pepper Flats. I..." She swiped at a renegade tear. "I don't even know if Anthem is going to make it anyway. And I want to see my mother."

Megan leaned forward and took both Heidi's hands in hers. "Heidi, if I can promise you one thing, I promise you we can heal Anthem. You saw her yesterday, how much more relaxed she was? Well, the vet has her physically under control, and trust me, we can do the rest. You and I." She reached out and wiped away Heidi's tear, a soft touch, and Heidi caught her fragrance, realizing just how deeply she ached for the tactile comfort of a mother. How envious she'd been of the other girls who'd gone shopping with their mums, just like she was doing with Megan today. It was making her both happy and sad, and all twisted up inside.

"Hey, this is supposed to be our fun day, Heidi."

She sniffed. "I know." She fiddled with her spoon. "It's not like I'd go to London for long," she said, unsure what she really wanted, because she did want her horse, and to ride. And she did love her stubborn old dad, and all the camping trips, and fishing and bushwalking and bike-riding they'd done together over the years. She loved Muttley, and even though Granny June was a nuisance, she cared bunches about her. She just wanted a chance to grow into a woman now, as dumb as that seemed.

She lifted her eyes cautiously. "Do you like him?"

"Who? Your dad?"

Heidi nodded.

Megan looked away for a while, over the river. Then she put on her glasses as if the sun dancing on the surface was suddenly too bright. She turned to face her. "I like him very much, Heidi." She paused. "You're a very lucky girl, because he's a rare man. You need to cut him some slack."

"He needs to cut *me* some slack."

Megan smiled. "Yeah, you both need to give each other a bit of a break. How about we go get an ice cream upriver before we drive home?"

"Top down?"

"Of course."

They walked toward the Aston Martin, arm in arm, and again Heidi felt rich and beautiful in Megan's company. And more confused than anything.

It was dark by the time Megan pulled into the driveway of the Hastings home. She helped Heidi carry her parcels to the door, a nervous anticipation shimmering in her stomach as it opened, spilling a pool of warm light into the night. But it wasn't Dylan who greeted them.

It was June Hastings.

Megan's heart sank. She hadn't seen Dylan since they'd relocated Anthem, and a strange hollow was gnawing into her stomach.

"Gran!" Heidi gave her grandmother a big hug, and Megan felt herself smile. A change of perspective had worked wonders for the kid.

June frowned at Megan. "Sally?"

"Granny June, this is *Megan*."

Megan reached out her hand, and smiled. "Hi, I'm Megan Stafford. Nice to meet you Mrs. Hastings."

June shook Megan's hand, her frown deepening. "I... thought...you reminded me of—"

"Is Dad home, Gran? Are you coming inside, Megan?"

Megan hesitated.

"Yes, please come in," June said. "It's nice to meet you. Timmy isn't here though. He's at the Crook Scale with his mates. He works hard, needs his night off every now and then."

Megan glanced at Heidi in confusion, then at June. "Is…is that Dylan's nickname?"

Panic flitted through June's eyes. "I…"

"Oh, Gran just likes to call him that sometimes," Heidi interjected, quickly covering her gran's fluster. "It's Dad's brother's name, but Dad doesn't mind."

"I…think I should go, Heidi. We've had a long day, but a great one, right?"

"Yeah, a bonza day. Thanks, Megs. Thanks so much." Her eyes said it all. Megan cupped the side of her young face.

"Anytime, hon. Give me a call whenever you want, and I'll see you for riding tomorrow?"

She nodded.

Megan parked the Aston Martin in the Crook Scale Pub parking lot and sat surrounded by four-wheel drives, a shire utility vehicle and several motorbikes.

Small white lights winked in the branches of a giant gum that hung over a terrace out behind the pub, and live country music drifted through the open doors.

There was no squad car out front, but she recognized Dylan's truck. He was here, off duty.

His world.

His terms. His friends.

This was clearly the local working-class watering hole, a predominantly male, English-style pub where farm laborers, shire workers, paramedics, firefighters and cops kicked back on weekend evenings, or enjoyed lazy pub lunches outside on sunny Sunday afternoons. This was where the battlers—the guys who toiled in the trenches—drank. The folk who did the honest work that kept the world turning, the roads paved, the bush and towns safe. While others slept, or played.

So different from Louisa's and Megan's world.

Or was it?

Where did she really fit? Megan wondered. How would Dylan react if she walked in?

She fiddled with the soft leather on the wheel. She felt honor-bound to go in there, tell Dylan that Heidi had contacted her mother and asked to go live in London. Heidi would see it as a complete betrayal of confidence, yet her father should know, for both their sakes, because Megan could see the child was going to get seriously burned. She was worried Dylan would miss the signs, not understand what was going on. Lose her.

Like she'd lost her own father.

Oh, who was she kidding? She wanted to see Dylan again, touch him. But was she ready?

Megan sat back in the seat and blew out a breath of nervous air.

Down by the river he'd lobbed the ball clearly into her court. She had to decide now if she wanted to cross that line he'd drawn in the sand, and she sure as hell wasn't going to find out by sitting in a parking lot.

She pushed open the door to the Crook Scale.

The pub was packed. There were only two other women in the establishment, both in tight jeans and cropped T-shirts, shooting pool in the corner. The men seated at wooden tables nearest the door stilled, looked up, and fell silent as Megan entered.

She felt conspicuous. She was still wearing the couture dress and high-heeled pumps she'd worn to Newcastle. What she'd give for her old pair of jeans and boots right now.

She caught sight of Reynard Lafayette at a table near the wall, hunched over a mug of beer. He was with Sandy Sanford from Whittleson Stud. Both glanced up. She nodded and smiled, relieved to recognize familiar faces. But Reynard just stared at her for a moment, said something to Sandy. They laughed, and returned to their beer.

"Can I get you something to drink, luv?" an older guy at the table nearest her asked.

"I…no, thank you. I'm looking for someone."

"Anyone special?"

"Dylan Hastings. Do you know him?"

The man's eyebrows rose, and the mood at the table shifted. "Down at the bar," said one of the men with a jerk of his head.

Megan made her way to the long wooden bar that ran the length of the far end of the pub. Television screens mounted above the counter flashed highlights from the recent race at Warrego Downs. One of the men at the bar cheered, punching his fist into the air. "*Yeah, baby!* That's Harrison's filly from Huntington Stud. Bottoms up for Harrison!" The group raised their beers.

Then she saw him.

He was seated on a stool at the far end of the counter in a darkened corner, drinking a draft with a bunch of guys. He was wearing low-slung faded jeans, dusty bush boots. His hair was tousled and a stark white T-shirt molded over his muscles, making her recall the sight of him shirtless. Her pulse quickened. One of the men next to him said something, slapping his shoulder, and Dylan threw back his head and laughed heartily

God, he was gorgeous. Seeing him like this, out of uniform, all loosened up, did unspeakable things to her body.

She inhaled deeply, bolstering herself, and made straight for him.

The guy he was talking to glanced up sharply as Megan entered his peripheral vision, and his mate whistled low and soft. Dylan's eyes immediately shifted to see what had snared their attention.

"Megan?" He stiffened, got up off his stool.

"Hey." Crap, she felt nervous. She managed a smile. "Your mum said I could find you here…she told me when I dropped Heidi off."

His buddies looked at Dylan, curious.

He shifted on his feet. "Uh—can I get you something to drink?"

"A glass of white wine would be nice, thank you."

An exchange of looks and raised brows.

"What kind would you like?"

"Surprise me."

He snorted softly, and she felt even more alienated. She smiled at the guys while he ordered. He hadn't introduced her, and the omission stung. "Hi, I'm Megan." She held out her hand.

"Mitch," said one of his mates, taking her hand. "They call me Slugger."

"You're Jenny's man, aren't you? Jenny from the hospital?"

"Yeah. And you're from the Fairchild place."

"Well, I suppose you could say I—"

Dylan handed her the chilled glass, placed his hand firmly on her waist, and snagged his leather jacket from the chair. He lowered his voice near her ear. "Come. We can talk outside."

He nodded to his buds, and she felt a silent exchange of something she couldn't quite read.

Chill night air brushed the skin on her bare arms as he led her out onto the brick terrace where a gibbous moon hung low and yellow behind the branches of the gums. Megan gave an involuntary shiver as she set her wine on a table.

"Cold?"

"I'm fine," she said, taking a seat on the wooden bench.

"Here." He draped his leather jacket over her shoulders, warm, heavy, the faint scent of his aftershave enveloping her.

The garment felt like him—protective, masculine. A woman would forever feel safe knowing this man had her back.

He sat on the bench opposite her, his rugged features cast in shadow.

"You don't want to be seen with me," she said. "Is it because of the case?"

"It's quieter out here," he said simply. "We can talk."

"Look, I'm sorry I came. I—"

He cleared his throat. "Did…uh…Heidi find a dress?"

Megan smiled hesitantly, relieved he'd opened the conversation. "Your daughter is going to be the belle of the ball, Dylan. We had a fabulous time. You have a great child, you know? A really special family."

He snorted, took a sip of his draft. "Dysfunctional family."

"No. You're wrong. You should see what goes down in the city—"

"Megan—" he said, setting his mug down firmly. "I worked homicide in Sydney, the biggest metropolis in the country. Believe me, I know what goes down. It's why I moved out here. Now I have a kid champing at the bit to go back to the city, to go to school there. Live there. Like Sydney is some bloody Shangri La with all the answers to life."

Megan was taken aback by his tone. "You should maybe ease up on Heidi a bit, Dylan. She has her head screwed on right. She told me about her career goals, and for a child her age, she's really got some stuff together. We went to galleries, and she knows her art. Going to a school like Brookfield doesn't have to be a sacrifice of traditional values, you know. If you don't ease up on the reins a little, you're going to push her away."

He grabbed his mug, took a deep swig. "Why did you really come here tonight, Megan?"

Nerves nipped at her. He'd changed, really closed off since that moment down by the river. She took a deep breath. "Heidi told me about Sally."

He looked up sharply, and Megan leaned forward.

"Look, I know it's not my business, and I really struggled with coming here tonight. But I thought you should know that Heidi has e-mailed her mother in London, and she wants to move there, and go to school there, if she can't attend Brookfield."

He sat dead still, staring at her intently. "Go on."

"She told me Sally has not contacted her once since she walked out ten years ago, and I…I'm just worried Heidi will take a real hit if her mother shuns her now, especially since she's reached out personally like this. I thought you should know, Dylan, so you could be there for her if things go downhill. Because they probably will, and Heidi probably won't tell you when they do."

Music drifted out from the open doors, the sound mellow. Dylan said nothing.

Megan stood up, removed his jacket, handed it to him. "That's the only reason I came."

"You could have called me."

"Maybe I wanted to see you out of your cop uniform, off duty," she said. "To see if you were sewn up any less tight."

A hint of a grin tugged at his mouth. "Well, am I?"

She felt her cheeks warm and was glad it was dark. "Yes," she said quietly. "And no."

"You're not going to elaborate."

She remained silent.

He took hold of her wrist suddenly, and drew her slowly down to the wooden bench beside him. A soft breeze rustled in the gum leaves. "Sit," he said quietly. "Finish your wine with me. Please."

He draped his jacket back over her shoulders as she reached for her glass, uneasy. "Tell me about your own father, Megan."

She looked at him in surprise.

"That's why you're on my case with Heidi, isn't it? You mentioned him earlier, at the clinic. You said you lost him, and I didn't get a chance to ask you more."

She twisted her glass on the table, watching the puddle of condensation darken the wood. "He was a good man, Dylan. Very traditional, almost Victorian in his discipline, and he was the boss in our house, no two ways about that. He was super protective of me, and he didn't want me to date." Megan smiled ruefully. "I sort of ran with that for a few years, not wanting to upset things—he had a fierce temper, and even though I loved him, I guess I was also somewhat afraid of him. Then when I turned sixteen, there was one guy I fell really hard for." Her smile deepened. "He was *it,* Dylan, quite a bit older than me, and he asked me out on a proper date. Dad flat out said no, wouldn't even discuss it. I couldn't believe it. I was furious, frustrated… Long story short, I sneaked out that night, didn't come home until the early hours of the morning. He was up waiting for me."

"What did he do?"

"Nothing. He didn't say one word. And his silence just about killed me. I broke my dad's heart that night, Dylan. He'd given me absolutely no freedom so I ended up rebelling totally, and then he wouldn't talk to me for weeks…" She inhaled. "And then, before we could iron things out, before I ever exchanged another word with him, both my mum and dad were taken from us in a car accident."

"Jesus, Megan," Dylan said, sitting back.

"He died angry with me and it left this big, big void in my life. I know it's not a major deal in the scope of life tragedies, but there's something to be said for finding resolution, and being able to move on because of it. Because when you can't—"

"I know." His eyes narrowed on hers. "I know exactly what it does when you can't find resolution. Justice. A way to move on."

Megan waited for him to continue, but he declined to elaborate. She wondered if he was referring to Louisa, to that old court case.

"You really think I'm pushing Heidi away?" he said suddenly.

She looked up at him. "Yeah, I do."

He rubbed his brow. "She saw I'd signed the divorce papers. They were on my desk. That's what must have set her off, where she got Sally's e-mail."

A strange sense of disappointment rippled through Megan. "I…I thought you and Sally were estranged years ago."

"We were. From the day she walked out. I…" He blew out air. "I never wanted her back, Megan. I never expected her to come back. I don't even know if I could have found it in me to forgive her if she had. Not because she walked out on me, but because she walked out on her own kid. Her child, for Chrissakes. I can't respect a woman like that."

"Why did she leave?"

He sighed, looked up at the branches of the tree. "We married very young, and for the wrong reasons. By the time we realized we weren't compatible, Heidi was on the way. I wanted to hold it together, but I was working a graveyard shift, overtime, and our marriage was falling apart. Then Sally went and had a raging affair with an artist. Some sort of self-validation thing."

He swigged the last of his beer, plunked his mug on the table. "It broke me, Megan. Totally. But like I said, I'm a die-hard. I wanted to at least *try* and put our life back together, so I moved us all back here to the Hunter where I'd grown up. Sally didn't even hack it for one year. The city life was what she wanted, so she left, went to Sydney for a while, hooked up with some wealthy Brit interior designer who got her a job in London. And that was it."

So that explained his issues with Sydney, thought Megan. "And you haven't seen Sally since?"

"Nope."

"Yet you never actually finalized the divorce until the other day? Why not?"

"For Heidi's sake. I never wanted to shut the door for her, if that makes any sense. Even though I could never make it work with Sally, I wanted Heidi to have the chance to know her mother."

She placed her hand softly over his. He was a good man. A really amazing man, and in this moment of revelation, she'd glimpsed the vulnerability under the hard, cool, capable cop exterior, the pain of a single dad who wanted everything for his daughter. He was a man who went the distance, and he'd been burned trying. And Megan thought she might just be falling in love with him.

That scared her a bit. No. That scared her a lot. Because she didn't know what to do about it.

She slanted her eyes up to his. "Why now, Dylan?" she asked softly. "Why did you suddenly sign those papers now, after all this time?"

His eyes held hers. "Because, Megan, I met you. And I decided it was finally time to close that old door."

She swallowed, a hot tension simmering between them, the weight of her decision suddenly growing heavier.

"Thanks, Megan, for coming tonight." He cupped the side of her face briefly, held her eyes. "You didn't have to do this."

"I did," she said softly, every nerve in her body zinging.

"Because of what happened with your dad."

She nodded.

"Tell me about yourself, Megan, your job in Sydney. How'd you get into the art business?"

She inhaled. "Well, I started criminal law at university, but it wasn't in me. It was combative, and I'm not. And it has more to do with strategic game-playing than real justice, or retribution. At least that's the way I see it." She laughed. "I'm too sensitive. Too idealistic. Well, that's what Louisa and Patrick keep telling me. I should have been a social worker. Anyway, I moved over into corporate law, and an art minor."

He looked at her so intensely she felt as though he were

trying to read right into her heart. "I got you wrong, you know? When I first saw you."

She shrugged. "We're all guilty of prejudice. It's human. It's the way we learn not to get burned again."

"Doesn't make it right," he said, watching her so fiercely she thought she'd combust under his gaze.

"No, it doesn't."

"And the gallery business?" He touched the back of her hand lightly with his fingertips as he spoke. "How'd you get into that?"

Megan tried to swallow. "It...suits me." She forced herself to concentrate as his fingers feathered her wrist. "And I'm good at it. I have some very high-end private clients and have moved into auction buying, researching provenance, that sort of thing. The art business has paid well. Very well."

"Would you ever consider doing something else?" he said, trailing the backs of his fingers softly up her arm, higher, his lips moving closer to hers. Megan could barely breathe, let alone speak, think. Desire shivered down her spine, and a tingling started low in her belly.

"I...hadn't...thought of it." Her voice came out a dusky whisper.

He hesitated, his mouth so near hers now, his lids lowering, his hand moving under the jacket, up to cup her shoulder. The sound of music and laughter grew louder in the pub, the wind increasing in the rustling gum leaves as her heart began to pound.

Without thinking Megan reached up, placed her palm against his jaw, feeling the delicious sensation of rough dark-blond stubble under her skin, and heat arrowed through her abdomen.

He leaned forward, his lips meeting hers as he grabbed her suddenly around the waist, pulling her harder into himself, gathering her into his strong arms, against his chest, as if suddenly unable to hold off any longer. She could feel the steady thud of his heart against the swell of her breasts as he moved his mouth over hers. Her world swirled, sucking logic and thought away with it.

She opened her mouth under his, and he kissed her deep, hard, hungry, his tongue tangling with hers as his hand moved down and cupped her breast.

Megan moaned against his mouth as his thumb rasped her hard nipple. Her breathing grew light, fast. She splayed her fingers over his chest, feeling the resilience of firm flesh over rippling muscle as she ran her palm down to the waistband of his jeans. His belly was hard, like iron. She moved her hand lower still, over rough denim where she could feel his erection.

He stilled suddenly, her hand between his legs.

Then he drew back, his eyes dark, hungry, a little wild, and they exchanged a hot silent look. "Come back to my place, Megan." His voice was rough.

I don't mess around. I don't do half measures, Megan. I can't...I'm a lifer...

And suddenly Megan was terrified.

This was a serious decision. For him. For her. Her heart began to race so fast she couldn't breathe, and perspiration broke out over her skin. "Dylan...I..." Her voice hitched. "I...think I better go."

Confusion snaked across his features. He frowned slightly. "Megs?"

She tried to swallow the ball forming in her throat. "I'm sorry," she whispered almost inaudibly.

His eyes turned grave. "This your way of saying no?"

She shakily pushed her hair back from her face, emotion burning into her eyes. She didn't know. She honestly did not know how to handle this, him, where to go from here. Her brain was thick, logic unclear. She stood quickly, pulling her dress straight. Even her legs were shaking. "It's better this way, Dylan."

"Megan—"

But she spun round and all but high-tailed it out of there using the terrace exit instead of going back through the pub again.

A nanosecond longer and she'd have been beyond the point of no return, undressed and in his bed. Her physical ache to have him—all of him—inside her was so hotly intense she didn't trust herself to make the right decision.

Dylan swore, lurched to his feet, and went after her. But he stopped at the terrace gate as he saw the red taillights of her Aston Martin brighten at the end of the parking lot exit, and then spin onto the highway and fade into specks in the night.

What in hell just went down here?

He swore again, kicked the gate post, and turned to go back into the pub, realizing with mild shock his hands were trembling. He fisted them, trying to tamp down his adrenaline, his lust.

It was his fault.

He'd told her he didn't mess around. What in hell was wrong with him? Here was the most gorgeous woman ever, wanting to make out with him, and he was spooking her with his seriousness, his talk of commitment.

But deep down he knew what was wrong.

He'd made this mistake with Sally. They'd acted on lust, and look where it had gotten them both. Look where it had put Heidi. Look at how many years of his life he'd sacrificed.

She was right. It did have to stop. Megan had another life, one she needed to go back to soon, and he needed another beer.

Dylan pushed back through the Crook Scale doors and allowed the warmth and laughter and music and camaraderie of his mates and life as he knew it to embrace him, to swallow him back in and cocoon him from Megan Stafford.

But his mates weren't going to let him off that easily. They slapped him on the back, joking about the hot Fairchild babe, one of them slipping something into Dylan's back pocket.

He took the package out, held it up. "What in bloody hell is this for?"

They all guffawed. "Condoms, mate," Mitch said as he ordered another round. "You haven't forgotten how to use those, have you? We figure any you might have in that bathroom cabinet of yours are well past their sell-by date."

Dylan shoved the packet back into his jeans pocket and silently sipped the froth off his beer, thinking it wasn't funny.

Because they were far too close to the truth.

Chapter Eleven

Bags packed and in the rental car, Megan ran up the Elias Memorial stairs to tell Louisa she was leaving. She'd organized a groom to hand-walk Anthem and found someone on the estate to give Heidi dressage lessons. She'd phone Dylan and Heidi from Sydney to let them know she'd left.

She wasn't ready to face Dylan in person after last night's humiliating behavior. And she knew if she saw him again, things would just get more tangled.

As much as she'd found a lost part of herself in the Hunter Valley, the process was also turning her upside down emotionally, making her question fundamental choices in her life, and she just couldn't see her way straight to chucking her job, her apartment, her friends, her life. Not now. Not yet. Not for a man she'd met only eight days ago.

A man who certainly wouldn't relocate for her.

This was something she needed to work through over time. And if she was truly honest with herself, it would be better for everyone—including Louisa's case—if she moved to the sidelines.

Patrick could stay on at Fairchild Acres and be as pragmatic as he damn well liked about his inheritance, but she needed out.

She'd been kidding herself, anyway—Louisa didn't need her. Maybe on the first day of her arrest she had, but now her aunt had Sydney's top legal sharks swimming around her, and Marie Lafayette was taking good personal care of her.

And Megan sure wasn't going to solve this homicide on her own. She was just causing hassles for Dylan by trying.

But her heart was heavy as she breezed through the hospital doors. And almost immediately she saw Dr. Jack Burgess arguing with Robert D'Angelo near the nurses' station.

Her heart kicked.

Megan slowed, walking purposefully towards the two. But as she neared, Dr. Burgess gesticulated angrily and stalked off.

"Robert?" Megan said, approaching. "I didn't realize you'd be here on a Sunday morning."

Robert D'Angelo, elegantly hawkish in his designer suit, turned to look down at her. "Megan." He smiled easily, his hooded obsidian eyes crinkling at the sides behind his rimless glasses. There was absolutely no sign of the simmering anger in his features that had shaped Dr. Burgess's posture a second ago.

"I was just leaving. Come walk with me." Classic D'Angelo, thought Megan—she could talk to him, as long as she went in his direction, on his terms.

She hastened to meet his stride as he made for the exit. "What was that with Dr. Burgess?"

He paused at the doors, pushed his glasses higher up the bridge of his nose. "Burgess says he can't ethically hold the police back any longer. Louisa is well enough to walk out of here, and has been for the last two days. He was about to call the cop, but I've negotiated a forty-eight-hour grace period,

threatening him with legal action should my client have a
relapse because of his hasty judgment. After forty-eight hours,
he can call Hastings. Which means—" he tapped his leather
briefcase "—I need to get back to Sydney to prepare to file
these papers so I can have that injunction in hand before
Hastings rolls in here with a magistrate in tow."

"What injunction?"

"A court order to pull Detective Sergeant Dylan Hastings
off the case. I have a cooperative judge looking into it for me,
and he happens to have the police commissioner's ear. It's an
unusual move, granted, but a tactic I feel is warranted by a
highly unusual set of circumstances." He smiled. "If we swing
this, Megan, it'll be precedent-setting in terms of the law."

Tension shimmered in Megan. He was relishing this game.
"On what grounds will you secure this injunction?"

"Police brutality, breach of arrest procedure, stationing a
probationary guard at my client's door, lack of due care with
a sensitive prisoner, no separation of custody duties, using a
non-designated station. You name it, we nail him for it. That
officer came close to killing an eighty-year-old woman in his
care, Megan. If I get my way with this judge and the commissioner, that cop's career is toast within less than forty-eight
hours. He'll be damn lucky if he escapes facing criminal
charges himself, pending an internal police investigation."

Fury stabbed through her. "Is this really necessary?"

He studied her from up high, impossibly tall, a slow frown
wedging into his brow, intensifying his bird-of-prey quality.
"Absolutely. The arrest will be nullified, no charges. Nothing.
And any officer who wants to come close to my client after
that is going to need absolute proof. Which, Megan, they
won't have, because my client is innocent. Now if you'll
excuse me, I need to get back to the city before five. With luck,
I might even have this application before the courts by
tomorrow—" He paused, the V-shape on his brow sharpen-
ing further. "You *will* keep this in the family."

She tried to swallow against the dry knot in her throat. "Why do you ask?"

"It's not a request, Megan." His eyes bored down into hers. "It's imperative this injunction comes at the NSW police force from left field. The court order must hit them before they have time to redeploy and take Hastings off the case themselves."

"What if he releases Louisa before this happens?"

His eyes flickered and his lips flattened. "Megan, I cannot stress how important it is that you not talk to that cop about this. Patrick…mentioned he's been trying to use you."

Fury seared deeper into her gut.

"He's not using me."

"If you do talk to him, Megan, if you go making yourself an enemy of my client, I shall be forced to put you on the wrong side of the Fairchild fence." His eyes narrowed. "That means I drag you all the way up to the Supreme Court alongside Hastings. Believe me, you're not going to want the media attention that's going to come with that. Allegations that an NSW detective was having an affair with the grand-niece of someone not even legally in his custody, someone he was unconstitutionally accusing of murder—"

"I am not having an—"

He lifted his hand. "*Especially* if that niece was in town seeking to inherit from that same accused." He shook his head, and tutted his tongue. "The perception of collusion could make for a very messy media business indeed."

Megan's hands balled at her sides, and she felt her cheeks redden. "You're threatening me."

"I'm protecting my client."

He turned and left, the glass doors sliding smoothly shut behind him.

Megan stared at his back in shock, pressure building in her by the second.

She *couldn't* walk from this now.

This would devastate Dylan and those he cared for.

It was her family versus his, and she was trapped slap bang in the middle.

Just as Dylan had warned her.

Megan sped up the mile-long Fairchild driveway too fast. She hadn't been able to force herself to go in and see Louisa. She was too furious. She'd started driving to Pepper Flats instead, her impulse to tell Dylan immediately.

But she'd backed out, turned the rental around.

She knew Dylan would just dig his heels in further if she told him what D'Angelo was up to. That cop was as stubborn and immovable as a bloody mountain. And the last thing Dylan needed was to be plastered all over the media as having an affair with *her* while being charged with police brutality.

Her own minor brushes with fame as a glamorous designer-dressed art-gallery lawyer, coupled with Louisa's notoriety and wealth and the tabloid intrigue of the murder and arson at Lochlain Racing, would only fuel a sordid national media frenzy.

She skidded on a curve as her tires hit loose gravel. Her heart slammed into her throat as she managed—just—to control the slide before leaving the road. She swore, slowed the rental, blood thumping through her.

The best thing she could do—the *only* thing she could think of doing—was to get Dylan to release Louisa. Fast. Before that court order came down.

She wasn't even sure it would help him in the long run, but from the quick flicker in D'Angelo's eyes when she'd posed the question, she figured it might at least throw his injunction for a loop, and he'd have to regroup before mounting another avenue of attack. By then a full homicide squad could be back on the job, and Dylan could move to the sidelines, out of the line of fire.

Damn. She slammed the palm of her hand on the steering wheel. She'd known D'Angelo was gunning for Dylan. But not quite like this.

This was so…personal. So serious. The life consequences so great.

What she really needed was to find the true killer. Within less than forty-eight hours.

Megan screeched to a stop in the gravel outside the Fairchild manor house…and saw Heidi.

She was hunched on the stairs that led up to the house, face buried in her hands.

Tension whipped through Megan as she swung open the car door and ran over the gravel.

"Heidi! What's wrong?" she said, setting her purse down and sitting on the steps beside her, Scout and Blue milling about in concern.

Heidi looked up, swiping tears from her face.

"She still hasn't answered my e-mails, Megan."

"Your mother? Maybe she's away on holiday, hon. Maybe—"

"She's not." She swallowed. "I called her office in London. I worked out the time difference and everything, and the receptionist said she was there, and busy with a client. I asked if her e-mail address was still the same, and she said yes, so she must have got my e-mails, Megan. I sent several, just in case the ones with my photo attachments didn't go through." She drew in a shuddering breath. "I don't know what's going on anymore. I feel all messed up right now."

Megan sighed heavily and rubbed her hands over her face. She was a Gordian knot of conflict, too. "You should speak to your father about this, Heidi. You *both* need to talk. Have you seen him today?"

She shook her head. "He got a call at the crack of dawn and had to rush out before I woke up. He's too busy to talk to me, Megs. Too busy looking after other people."

"Heidi, maybe your mother is just very busy, too."

The teen nodded, although her eyes betrayed her.

"Look, maybe London is not such a great idea. I mean,

Brookfield is so much closer. And you'd still come home weekends to ride, and see your dad. And he could visit you there."

"He *hates* the city! He hates everything about it. And he won't pay for private school. He's got a stupid job—"

"No, he doesn't," Megan said firmly.

Heidi looked up in surprise. "You're defending him?"

"I care about *both* of you."

Heidi studied her in silence. "Thanks, Megs," she whispered.

She smiled encouragingly. "Now, would you like to come inside and call the Brookfield alumni association with me? We can see if they have some bursaries available for next year. And if they don't, maybe we could get your name onto a list. At best you can find out how to apply, what marks you might need, and what they want to see in a portfolio."

"Would you!"

"Of course I will." God, Dylan was going to be livid with this on top of everything else. But it might just be the path Heidi and Dylan needed to take.

"Come," Megan said, getting to her feet and holding out her hand, feeling totally drained. "Let's go inside and get Mrs. Lipton or Marie to fix us some tea, and then we can phone the school."

"But it's Sunday."

"That's okay, we'll find someone to talk to. You know what my mum used to do when I felt down? Lamingtons." She forced another smile. "*Frozen* lamingtons, with tea. It was also Granny Betty's favorite, and you know what? I got the kitchen staff to freeze some when the farm union ladies came round on a lamington fundraising drive last week. Mrs. Lipton told me Louisa still has a soft spot for them herself. Maybe she and Betty used to have them together as kids."

Heidi dusted herself off. "Do you miss your mother, Megan?"

"Always, with all my heart. But I remember the special times, and I carry those with me. The times with Granny Betty, too. Come on, we can gear up afterwards and go down to the river and walk Anthem."

"I shouldn't stay long." She wavered. "My dad will be looking for me. I…I came by bike. I didn't tell anyone where I went."

"You better phone him, then. Leave a message for him to pick you up here. Meanwhile, we can make that call and enjoy some tea."

Marie Lafayette, dressed in a crisp navy-and-white uniform, brought their tea and a plate of the chocolate-covered sponge cakes out onto a stone terrace overlooking the corner of the pool and the estate beyond. In the distance they could see dust being kicked up round the Fairchild racetrack, and along the edge of the patio two cockatoos waddled over dry leaves and grass. Scout and Blue lay obediently watching them from under the wicker furniture.

"I cannot believe you got my name onto the Brookfield bursary list, Megs." Heidi looked simultaneously thrilled and concerned. "Dad should be happy, I…I mean, if he doesn't have to pay. He—"

They heard a noise, and they both spun round to see Dylan climbing the stairs on the far side of the stoop.

"Be happy about what?" His laser-blue eyes zeroed in on her. Megan's pulse rushed.

She quickly wiped a lamington crumb from her lips, trying to stay cool, to let Heidi handle this, but God, he looked good, and she wished again she'd left this morning. Her bags were still in the rental.

Nothing was physically stopping her. She could still go.

Then she recalled the dark reason she could *not* in good conscience leave. She had to get him to release Louisa. Soon. She had to finish what she'd started.

He closed the distance between them, eyes locked fast on hers. "Whose suitcases are in that rental out front?"

"Mine."

"You leaving?" His voice was clipped, eyes suddenly flat.

"I was going to. Something…came up."

He opened his mouth to speak, but before he could, Patrick stepped through the French doors. "Megan, I'm going into Pepper Flats to—" He froze as he caught sight of Dylan in uniform on the stoop.

"What the—you better have a warrant, mate, or you get the hell off this porch and property!"

Megan surged up off her chair. "Patrick, wait. I…invited him."

He turned to his sister. "What the bloody hell do you think you're doing. Megan? Having his kid riding here is one thing, but—"

"Patrick," she said through clenched teeth, her voice low. "This is Heidi."

His eyes flickered. He inhaled deeply, nodded to Heidi. The girl looked mortified. She got up, went to stand at her dad's side, glaring at Patrick.

"Patrick's my brother," Megan told Heidi. "And ordinarily he's quite human." She glowered at him.

"We need to talk, Megan. When I get back from town."

"Sure," she snapped.

He stalked off.

Palms damp, she turned to father and daughter. Dylan's eyes were hard, his posture combative, and Megan inhaled a shaky breath. "I really am sorry. Heidi shouldn't have seen that. It's…it's this homicide. It's getting to all of us. Come, I'll walk you to your car."

Heidi took her dad's hand and they walked in uneasy silence to Dylan's vehicle, Megan's stomach twisting.

She burned to tell Dylan about D'Angelo's injunction,

knowing at the same time that Dylan would just hit back harder, at his own expense. And Heidi's.

Moreover, if D'Angelo found out she'd tipped Dylan off, she had zero doubt he would follow through on his threat to allege that Louisa's arresting officer was having an affair with Megan while on the job.

"How's Anthem doing, Heidi?" he said softly as he opened the door of his ute for her, Muttley wiggling inside.

"Really well, Dad. Megan's been walking her three times a day."

He looked over Heidi's head, caught Megan's eyes.

"And we called Brookfield today."

He stilled. "You did *what?*"

"Megan spoke to someone she knows at the alumni association and she got my name on the bursary list. Isn't that so cool? I just have to send them a portfolio, my marks and an essay saying why I want to go. And you wouldn't have to pay a cent if I got in, because—"

"Get in the car, Heidi."

"Dad!"

"Just do it."

Heidi pulled her mouth into a tight, angry pout and climbed in. He slammed the door shut behind her and stepped right up to Megan. "What the hell are you doing now?" he growled close to her ear, his neck muscles tight, everything about him hard and hot and simmering.

She was edgy herself after the confrontation with D'Angelo, her clash with Patrick, and the sexual frisson between the two of them was literally crackling because of it all.

"Heidi was upset, Dylan," Megan said quietly. "She hadn't heard from her mother. You haven't spoken to her yet, and I just tried to help, okay? Brookfield is a damn sight closer than *London*."

"I hope those bags of yours stay packed, Stafford, because

now you've really overstepped your mark. I want you to stay away from my kid. I told you, I don't want her going to a private school, and I don't want her going to Sydney. So quit messing with her head."

"What is your damn phobia with the city?" she said very quietly, her body humming so close to his. "Is it because you couldn't make your marriage work there? Do you think the big city is going to steal everything from you again? Stop thinking about yourself for a moment—"

"Damn you." His mouth was so near.

"Well, am I wrong?"

Silence pulsed. His eyes tunneled into hers. His breathing became light.

She lowered her voice further, the whole world fading around them. "If you think you'll lose your daughter to the city, you're sorely mistaken, detective. You're going to lose her if you keep this up, if you keep trying to lock her away from the world. Like my father did with me."

He raised his finger, almost touching her chin where the bruise was still dark, so close she could feel the warmth of his breath against her lips. "Just...stay away from my kid." His voice was a hoarse whisper.

"I'm the best damn thing that's happened to your daughter in a while, Dylan, and you know it. What are you really so afraid of?"

His eyes lanced hers. "You," he said, very quietly.

Then he spun, stalked back to his car, slammed the door, and drove off in a smoking barrel of dust.

Megan watched them go down the drive, her jaw clenched, her whole body shaking.

She could not believe how she'd fallen hook line and sinker for that little family in the car barreling down the driveway. Ugly mutt and all.

Damn the stubborn hunk of granite.

Stupid fool. Couldn't he see how his love and protective instincts were quashing the very things he cared about?

She stomped off, the wind beginning to snatch at her hair. The afternoon was getting stormy, banks of bruised purple cloud rolling in, the wind beginning to bend brown grasses in the fields.

Perhaps some time in the ring with Breaking Free would center her.

Dressed in bush boots, ragged jeans and borrowed old bush hat, Megan made her way down to the stables where the sound of chainsaws and weed whackers grated against her already frazzled nerves.

"What's with this racket!" She had to yell over the noise to make herself heard as she entered the stables.

The groom waved to the landscaping crew near the door to shut down their machines. "G'day, Ms. Stafford," he said, pushing his hat back on his head, his face sheened with perspiration.

"Where's Breaking Free?" she asked, looking over at his empty stall.

"We set him out for a bit of a run in the lower eastern pasture, ma'am, while we do the fireproofing up here. We're taking out dead trees near the buildings and cutting down dry grass. There's a serious low pressure cell building north of here, and the estate manager is worried this wind will shift. If that storm breaks and heads this way, it could set off more lightning, more bushfires. If the wind switches and the fires join with the Koongorra fires and jump the river—" He shook his head. "We're done for, then."

"Which one is the eastern pasture?"

He pointed. Megan shaded her eyes, squinting into the sun and dry wind. It was miles away.

"Would you like someone to bring him in for you?"

"No. I can do it myself, thanks," she said, striding into the tack area and unhooking Breaking Free's halter, along with a lead rope. She needed to burn off some frustration.

"There's some outbuildings down there with tack and all, and a bathroom and bunk area," the groom offered, sensing her irritation. "Miss Fairchild has the boxes from her study being stored down there while they're doing the renos, so it's been opened up for a while."

She nodded as she made her way out and began the hike over the dry, rutted fields. The mention of Louisa's boxes reminded her that her aunt had been busy redecorating and packing for her U.K. trip before Dylan Hastings arrived to arrest her out of the blue.

It drove home to Megan how swiftly life could change, how fleeting the good times could be.

Carpe diem, she thought. Or as Granny Betty always said, *Don't save the good things for last, Megs. Life's too short for that.*

Granny Betty had been talking about lamingtons at the time. But Megan was thinking about Dylan.

She reached the pasture fence hot and bothered and climbed over, snagging her jeans on a rusted nail. She halted atop the fence, wobbling as she struggled to pull the fabric free. It tore loose suddenly, and she overbalanced, tumbling down hard to the ground, grating the skin from her elbow as she went. Megan cursed, ignoring the sharp bite of pain as she got to her feet, heart thumping, the hot wind further ruffling her sense of unease.

Then she sighted the gleaming black stallion.

Breaking Free stood like a marble statue near a stand of river red gums, his tail and mane blowing gently in the dry wind.

She caught her breath for an instant.

He was stunning, truly free in spirit. Standing there like that, he epitomized what Megan loved about this wild, broad, sun-baked country of hers. And what she'd missed in the city.

Breathing in deeply, halter and rope in hand, she began to walk toward the stand of massive red gums.

The stallion watched her approach with glinting black eyes. Then just as she got within a few yards, he tossed his head, neighed and cantered a distance away. He stopped and waited mischievously for her again, coat glimmering in the sun, tail twitching.

Megan swiped the back of her wrist over her forehead. She called out to Breaking Free, clicking her tongue and talking gently as she closed in on him again, but as soon as she got within a few feet of the stallion, he did the same thing, galloping off playfully and coming to a stop about a hundred yards away, challenging her to come after him yet again.

Megan cursed, swatted at the omnipresent flies.

She moved slower this time, but the damn process repeated itself twice over.

Sweat trickled between her breasts, and she was breathing hard. She took off her hat, folded it in half, tucked it firmly into the back of her jeans. She meant business now.

She turned away from the stallion and stood stock still. This seemed to interest Breaking Free. Megan could sense him coming closer and closer until she heard the soft crunch of dry grass roots under his hooves right behind her. But as she turned to face him, he kicked back and trotted away, tail held high and defiant.

Damn him!

She was perspiring now, the afternoon starting to wear towards evening, the sun angling low and yellow, but be damned if she was giving up.

She moved fast this time, not watching her feet over the uneven dry ground. But in her haste, she stubbed the toe of her boot on a rock, dislodging it.

A snake, glistening wet-black with a deep crimson underbelly, well over a meter long, slithered from between the dislodged stones and raised its head. Its neck region flattened, and the round beady black eyes were trained dead on her.

Megan froze.

Sweat prickled over her brow and down between her breasts. This one was poisonous, deadly so, and it felt threatened. Her throat turned dust-dry, and she cursed the wind that teased movement into her hair.

She stood as motionless as she could, minutes stretching to eternity, her T-shirt going wet with sweat. And then the snake suddenly slithered off into the desiccated stubs of grass.

Megan exhaled shakily, pushing damp tendrils back from her face. She glanced up, saw Breaking Free watching her curiously from a distance.

And she gave up.

She was too shaken to go after him now.

She shouldn't have even tried.

She'd been unfocused, edgy, doing all the wrong things, driven to distraction by Dylan.

She cursed him.

She hadn't realized quite until this very moment how deeply he'd affected her life. How unsettled she was with her own Sydney existence.

And now Breaking Free had won. Louisa, too, in some ways.

Defeat slumped Megan's shoulders, and emotion burned in her eyes as she walked slowly back over the field towards the outbuildings, hoping to find some water there. Evening shadows fingered across the valley, the wind chilling her sweat-dampened back.

She creaked open the large double barn doors, shafts of gold sunlight revealing dancing dust motes.

Her eyes adjusted to the light as she entered.

The scent was of straw, sand, old leather, but it was clean. Several new horse blankets were folded on a rough bench in the corner, and beside it boxes from Louisa's study were stacked against the wall. Placing the halter and lead rope atop several bales of hay, Megan removed the hat tucked into the back of her jeans and made her way slowly over to the boxes. But an eerie sense of being watched suddenly chased ripples over her skin.

She stilled.

There was someone else in this barn.

Not daring to breathe, she slanted her eyes to the old mirror on the far wall and froze as she caught the reflection of a man behind her.

Silhouetted by the dusky evening light, he stood in the doorway, silent, just watching.

Fear shot sharp and fast into her throat. Reaching for the halter, the closest weapon at hand, Megan slowly turned to face him.

"Hey," he said quietly.

"Dylan?" Her heart stalled, then kicked back to a fast patter.

His face was shadowed, unreadable. He wore old jeans, cotton shirt, boots—no sign of the uniform, no gun belt. No sign of the law-enforcement officer. He looked more the rough renegade.

"You…startled me." Her voice came out a hoarse whisper.

He seemed odd, strangely quiet, predatory, as he entered the barn, his trademark stride bringing him within inches of her until she could scent his aftershave, his warmth, the freshly laundered smell of his shirt. Megan tried to swallow against the tightness in her throat, fighting an instinctive urge to back into the hay bales.

"Wh-what are you doing here?" she whispered, her stomach tingling as he came close, cornering her between the hay bales and boxes.

"Your groom told me I could find you down here." His voice was low, thick, hungry. "What you did was wrong,

Megan, but how I handled it was worse. I wanted—*needed*—to say sorry."

She tried to swallow again, her heart thumping against her ribs. "I…was just trying to help, Dylan. Heidi was all beat up about her mother—"

"I don't want that kind of help."

She moistened her lips. "I'm sorry. I don't know how I got so involved. I…just didn't want to see you two end up like me and my dad."

He watched her mouth, his mood shifting, darkening, thickening. A gust of warm air outside stirred up a swirling dervish of dust beyond the barn doors, and Megan could taste the fine dirt in the air. Dylan placed his hand on her shoulder, sliding it slowly, softly down the length of her arm, trailing a wake of quivering nerves, and her breathing became ragged.

"Why did you run from me last night, Megan?" he said, his voice rough.

"You know why," she whispered.

He encircled her wrist, drawing her close. A small muscle began to pulse at the base of his jaw.

"You packed your bags. Where were you going?"

She moistened her lips again, unable to think. "I…back to Sydney," she whispered hoarsely.

"But you didn't leave."

"I couldn't."

He studied her in silence. Then he feathered the side of her face with his fingertips, tracing the line of her jaw as his eyes probed hers, the question in his touch implicit. "You're something special, you know that, Megan Stafford?" he whispered, his lids lowering as his fingers reached her lips and he touched them.

She could taste the salt on his skin.

Her body began to hum, her belly turning hot, molten. She could barely breathe.

She opened her mouth slightly, allowing the tip of her

tongue to connect with roughened fingertips, feeling dizzy and hot as all logic deserted her.

"And I don't know what the devil to do about it, because I want you. All of you."

Her vision clouded, and he brought his mouth down hard on hers.

Tingling heat crashed through her, her legs turning to water as his mouth crushed hers, his hand cupping her buttocks, yanking her body against his. She could feel his erection through his jeans, pressed hard against her pelvis, and heat shafted low in her belly, making her ache to open to him.

Her tongue met his, slick, hungry, as he shimmied her T-shirt up her torso, yanking it over her head, letting it fall to their feet. He groaned as he felt her skin under his palms, found her breasts, her nipples hard. He unclasped her bra at the front as she kissed him back.

Her breasts swelled free of the lace, his hands cupping them, rough thumbs rasping her nipples. The sensation excited her. She fumbled wildly with the buttons of his shirt, yanking it open, grappling with the buckle of his belt as he backed her up hard against the hay bales. Louisa's boxes crashed down around them, contents spilling across the floor.

But they were oblivious to anything but their urgent, desperate need for each other. They moved fast, furiously, the heat, dust, the fear of discovery heightening every nerve ending in Megan.

Breathing hard, mouth against his, she opened his zipper and felt him swell hot and hard into her hand.

Chapter Twelve

Megan encircled his erection with her hand, massaging him with rhythmic movements as her tongue tangled with his, as her breasts pressed against his chest, his hair deliciously rough against tender nipples.

He loosened her jeans, pulling her panties aside, and slid a finger up into her.

Megan felt her eyes roll back into her head as she sank her weight down on to his finger, feeling him deep inside, stimulating her, his barely controlled restraint exhilarating.

"You sure, Megan?" he murmured against her mouth.

She was beyond sure.

She answered by groping for one of the blankets, letting it fall to the ground. Still kissing her, he began to lower her onto it.

They went down hard, knocking back into a stack of Louisa's boxes, sending more toppling, as they bumped up against the hay bales. Straw catching in her hair, Megan laughed against his mouth as they rolled onto the ground. He stilled suddenly, and sat back, staring at her, his blue eyes darkening to near black.

"You're the most beautiful woman," he whispered, removing bits of hay from her hair. He took off her boots slowly, tantalizingly, and he slid her pants down over her hips.

Her hair a wild tangle around naked shoulders, Megan watched from the blanket as he stood above her and removed his clothes. Before dropping his faded jeans to the ground, he removed a condom packet from the back pocket.

Shafts of golden light from the setting sun angled through the open barn door, painting his skin a gilded bronze as he stood above her, even more powerful in his nakedness than he was dressed in his uniform with a gun at his hips. His torso was muscled, broad, tapering to narrow hips. His thighs were potent, his erection bold, his calves beautiful, strong.

There was no pretense about this man. No apology. What you saw was what you got. All or nothing.

Holding his eyes, she reached out for the condom as she slowly parted her legs to him.

His Adam's apple moved in his throat as he swallowed. He knelt slowly between her open thighs, and she rolled the condom down over his erection, stimulating him with soft, rhythmic movements until his eyes were almost swallowed by dark desire. Breathing hard, he clapped a hand on the inside of each of her knees, opening her legs wide, and he softly kissed the sensitive skin of her inner thighs, moving his mouth higher, and higher, until she began to shake and arch her hips to him, desperate for the sensation of his warm mouth between her legs.

Then she felt his tongue slip into her, and her world swirled. He teased her soft folds, grazing her gently with his teeth where she was so swollen and sensitive that it forced a cry to build low inside her chest and her vision to blur.

Nothing about the outside world mattered anymore. Not

the drought, the mounting storm, the whispering threat of fire. There was no thought, just the sensation of being with him, wanting him, needing him. He lowered his weight onto her, leaning her back as he forced her thighs open even wider with his knees. She felt the smooth, hot tip of his erection, and with one sharp thrust he entered her to the hilt.

Megan gasped, arching her back as her body accommodated him, and he began to move with long, fast, rhythmic thrusts. She met him with urgent, undulating movements of her own, the friction, the heat, the pent-up frustration and adrenaline driving them both higher and higher and hotter, sweat dampening their bodies, her skin slicking against his as they moved faster, desperate, panting until Megan's body went totally rigid…and she began to tremble.

With a sharp cry she shattered, her muscles releasing in convulsing waves, taking control of her body and her mind as she arched her back, digging her fingers into his buttocks, pulling him hard into her.

Dylan sank himself completely into her wetness as he felt her climax around him, her nails digging into his skin as she thrust her pelvis against him with a cry. The sensation cracked his control and he released into her with a powerful shudder, holding her tight against his body, inhaling the scent of her hair, her skin, the straw in the barn, the old leather, in the most exquisite, earthy sexual experience of his life.

Still coupled, they lay, pulsing softly in unison, coming down, allowing the soft sounds of the evening to wrap around them, the breeze cool on sweat-dampened skin, cocooned from the reality they both knew they had to face.

Dylan wasn't sure how this had happened. He'd just come to say sorry.

But then he'd seen her in the barn, tousled and dusty in her jeans, her cheeks flushed from sun, a hot spark of frustration glinting in her green eyes, and those damn condoms had begun burning a hole in his pocket.

It had happened so fast, so naturally. And so damn perfectly.

He rolled off her, propping himself up onto his elbow to look down at her, naked on the blanket, hair splayed in a gold tangle about her face. He teased a stray bit of straw from her hair.

"You fit me, Megs," he murmured, trailing his fingers around the contours of her breasts, her stomach, just absorbing her proprietarily.

She smiled up at him, and a cool whisper of warning snaked through him.

He had to be careful. He didn't own her. She wasn't his. She had promised him nothing. And he felt a tinge of male fear.

Because he wanted to keep her. By his side. Always. It was a fault of his, he was beginning to realize, this need to jealously guard—even cloister—the people he loved.

Maybe it was because his family had lost everything after Liam was murdered in the Koongorra bush all those years ago. Dylan had never gotten over not having been able to save his older brother that day, or identify his attacker in the police lineup.

Even though he'd been only eight, it had weighed heavily on him all these years.

His family might have healed if he'd been able to help bring his brother's killer to justice.

But Louisa had made certain they never would.

Protecting the people he did love, holding them close and within his control, was just part of his psyche now.

But Megan was showing him he could end up pushing his daughter away like that. And maybe her, too.

"You got sunburned today," he said, softly.

An emotion he couldn't quite read sifted into her eyes. "That horse did me in today. I couldn't get near him."

"Breaking Free?"

She nodded, sitting up, reaching for her shirt. "I was frustrated, trying to corner him, bend him to my will. That'll never work with Breaking Free," she said, pulling her shirt over her head. "I should have waited for him to come to me. Been patient." She reached for her jeans.

He arrested her hands. "Wait," he said softly. "Just a moment longer."

The light had faded outside, and through the open barn door the sky was pale lavender, darkening to indigo in the east. Tiny bats flitted almost imperceptibly outside. Reality felt a world away.

He got up and lit one of the lanterns hanging in the rafters. "I want to look at you some more."

A wariness filtered into her eyes. "Dylan—"

His mobile phone beeped in his pants. He held up two fingers for a second as he reached for his jeans, finding the phone in his pocket.

"Hastings," he said.

And the cold blade of reality sliced right into the barn, into their private moment. Dylan's heart sank as he learned the warrant he'd finally received to look into Reynard's financial affairs had just been overturned by a higher authority. Something was going on with this case, something much bigger, and he was not in the loop.

He cursed, flipping his phone shut.

"What is it?" Concern darkened her big green eyes.

"It's nothing."

But it was everything. He was being stonewalled at every turn, making no headway on finding Louisa's accomplice. The only thing he had left to go on was a call he'd received earlier today from a police contact in Melbourne.

Dylan had put out feelers on a couple of employees at Whittleson Stud, Sandy Sanford in particular since Megan had flagged his name.

Sanford had given nothing in questioning, but Dylan had learned he was fairly new in the valley, and that he'd done carpentry work at Whittleson Stud, Fairchild and Lochlain, which gave him access and a working knowledge of all three farms. Sanford's record of past employment also hewed closely to the racetrack business around the country, most recently Melbourne, which had prompted Dylan to place a few calls. It turned out Sanford had been questioned by police in connection with betting fraud, but nothing had stuck.

Dylan needed to talk to him again. He should have been doing that instead of making love to Megan. He cursed to himself, running his hand over his hair, conflicted.

She pulled on her jeans and hugged her knees close, giving a little shiver in the cooler evening air. "What's going on, Dylan?"

He skimmed her cheek with the back of his hand. "Don't worry about it."

"I am worrying about it. "

"I need to get back to work. I might have a lead."

"What lead?"

"I'll know more later." Once he questioned Sanford again. He sat next to her for a moment, touched her face, torn. "Megs…when this APEC stuff and everything is over—"

"Go, Dylan," she said, that edgy look in her eyes intensifying. Worry spiked through him.

"Just…go find the person who did this, okay? And *soon*."

"I want to talk to you, Megs. About…this. Us."

She nodded, features tightening. "Later. Just go do your thing, and let me know…if I can help."

He started to pick up the boxes they'd scattered in their ardor.

"No. I'll do that." She smiled encouragingly, but it never quite reached her eyes. "I need to gather myself before I face the manor house, anyway."

His eyes held hers for a beat, intense. Then he brushed his lips quickly over hers, and was gone.

Megan stood at the barn door, watching Dylan's silhouette move toward the manor house in the distance. Her chest tightened. She felt ill at what could still blow up in their faces within the next forty-eight hours, how badly hurt they could all be.

It was as if her whole world was suddenly hanging by a tentative gossamer thread.

Perhaps she should never have crossed that line and made love with Dylan.

But it had happened so fast and furiously, her body acting apart from her mind, responding to pressure that had been cooking between them for days.

She pressed her hand to her stomach, feeling the quivering butterfly nervousness of an incredible emotion she couldn't quite articulate, and along with it came the foreboding sense that this fragile thing growing between them wasn't going to last beyond D'Angelo's court order.

The need to tell Dylan what D'Angelo was doing gnawed deep. But if Dylan learned there was an injunction coming down, D'Angelo would hear about it. And he'd act on his threat.

Of that Megan was certain.

She'd be responsible for Dylan and Heidi and June being dragged through sordid tabloids, splashed on television news. She'd annihilate any hope of reconciliation with Louisa, and, well, Patrick could kiss his inheritance goodbye.

There was just no up side to telling Dylan. He had to find Sam Whittleson's killer, and fast.

Megan turned back into the barn, the glow from the lantern soft and yellow as she crouched down to scoop up the papers that had scattered from Louisa's upended boxes.

She righted an empty container, gathering a stack of envelopes. But while she was dusting off bits of hay, the name on the envelopes suddenly registered.

The letters were addressed to Kent Oxford, her grandfather, Betty's husband, right here at Fairchild Acres.

Her pulse quickened.

She picked up some more, riffling through them quickly. There were twenty-two letters, all of them to Kent. All unsealed.

Megan was unable to stop herself from reading the words on a page protruding from one of the envelopes. "To my dearest Kent."

Her heart beat faster.

She extracted the thin pages written in flowing, youthful longhand. The letter was dated, incredibly, sixty-four years ago. She flipped through to the signature on the last page.

> All my love, Louisa.

Why had Louisa been writing letters to her grandfather?

Megan checked the envelopes again. They had stamps, but no postmarks. They had never been mailed.

They'd never reached their intended recipient.

Why not?

Why had Louisa kept them?

She glanced at the open barn door, suddenly nervous about being discovered going through Louisa's things. A faint beam of light came from a tractor in the distance as it chugged down to the cottages, hauling a trailer with metal drums. She knew the drums were for storing water because of possible bush fire. But otherwise all was quiet.

It was wrong, but she just could not help herself from pulling loose the sheafs from the first envelope. She turned up the lantern and sat on the blanket, leaning against the hay bales. And began to read.

> I hate it here, Kent, really hate it. I had no choice but to come. My parents were embarrassed by my condition. They said if it became apparent it would ruin me for marriage, and they have high expectations for me.

> They don't want you to know about the baby, which is
> why they took me in the night and told everyone I had
> gone to school in Switzerland. But I want you to know
> where I am, and to know I left against my will. I want
> to run away from here. Perhaps we could keep the baby,
> and some day marry...

Megan's body grew hot. Her eyes watered with increasingly fierce emotion as she read, one page after the other,
while the night outside grew dark.

Astounded, Megan realized Louisa had been writing from
a home for unwed mothers, about to give birth to a baby. *Her
grandfather Kent's child.* Louisa had been sixteen, Kent only
two years older, and a laborer on this very farm, training
under his father, who was then Fairchild's operations manager.

But what about Betty?

When had Granny Betty gotten together with Grandpa
Kent? While Louisa was away, waiting for his baby?

God, would Kent have started seeing Betty if he'd actually
received these letters?

Megan read more, skimming as her hunger for information
outweighed her need for detail.

And as she read, her heart broke. Tears filled her eyes and
ran down her cheeks. Louisa had given birth to a baby girl.

> It was a hard birth. It didn't go well at all. But she
> was so beautiful, so small, when she came out. And
> when I heard that little cry, my heart near burst with
> pride. I wanted to hold her in my arms, just to feel those
> tiny little hands in my own, but they took her from me,
> as I knew they would. I cried all through the night and
> my breasts leaked painfully. And then they came and
> woke me in the early hours of the morning. It was still
> very dark, and they told me my baby girl had died.

Megan smeared the tears from her eyes, the words blurring in front of her. But she read on.

> They said I won't be able to have more children. I feel so empty, Kent. I want to come home and pretend this never happened. I want to see you again so badly. But I'm afraid I have changed. And that maybe you, too, have changed. These months away have felt like years, an eternity. I don't feel sixteen anymore. I just feel hollow.

Megan clutched the letter to her chest. If Kent thought Louisa had just left him without a goodbye, it was possible he'd fallen for Betty over the long months of her absence. And if Betty didn't know about the baby, there wouldn't have been any sense of guilt or betrayal on her part.

How it must have killed the young Louisa to return home and see her sister with Kent. The family rift began to make sense. And so did Louisa. She must have grown bitter over the years, watching Kent and Betty falling in love, getting engaged, marrying on the farm. While those letters to Kent sat hidden in a box in her room.

Megan *had* to believe Kent hadn't known about the child. Her grandfather had been a kind, gentle and compassionate man. She couldn't imagine he'd have hurt Louisa that way.

Or even if he had found out years later, choices had been made. Time had passed that could no longer be rolled back. Pain all round. It must have been what led to Betty ultimately being cut off from the estate.

Megan glanced up, saw it was pitch-dark out. People would be worrying about her.

She returned the letters to the box and quickly tidied up, setting the other boxes right. But the one with the letters she tucked under her arm. She'd take it up to the manor house, go through them all again, slowly, in her room with the door closed.

* * *

After excusing herself from dinner and having a hot shower, Megan climbed into bed, and by the light of her bedside lamp she began to read as the wind intensified, rustling the leaves outside, the scent of smoke once again thick in the air, and the faint plaintive howl of dingoes carrying across the river.

Louisa had literally poured her young broken soul into these unread letters. Her writing was poignant, lyrical, her feelings so deep and stoic for a girl that age.

It was the same age Megan had been when she'd lost her own parents, just two years older than Heidi was now.

Megan's eyes filled with emotion again as she read in greater detail, beginning, for the first time, to truly understand what life events had shaped her notorious great-aunt.

And as the hours wore on to morning, and the howls of hunting dingoes reaching over the valley from the Koongorra wildlands grew closer, it was once again driven home to her that one could never really judge another human unless you had walked their road.

Did Louisa's past condone her present irascible behavior? Maybe not, but at least it allowed it to be understood.

More than anything she wanted to talk to Louisa about this, but she couldn't. Not unless Louisa broached it herself. Megan couldn't possibly let her aunt know she'd gone and read all these letters like some underhanded snoop.

She looked into the bottom of the box, and under some old newspaper cuttings she found a silver bracelet. It bore a single engraved charm—a little racing horse.

Love, Kent.

Megan clasped the bracelet in her hand, thinking of love lost. And choices made. And how she had her own thinking to do.

She carefully placed the bracelet back into the box and removed the sheaf of newspaper cuttings.

The top sheet had a story about Louisa's first big win with Fortune's Lady, the first Thoroughbred she'd bought on her own.

Going against the grain, Louisa had picked a seemingly unpromising filly, but according to the article, she'd glimpsed something in the form of the horse that no one else had. And she'd noticed the gleam of defiant spirit in the filly's eye. She'd picked that horse up for a song.

And once again going against the tide of current thinking, she'd hired a brooding, quiet, and controversial loner to train Fortune's Lady—Banner Mac—a man who listened to horses, not people.

Megan smiled to herself.

Her aunt had a thing for the underdog, for giving the downtrodden a chance to prove themselves and make good. It was the way she thought about this country she loved. She'd told Megan and Patrick when they'd first arrived at Fairchild that Australia's history had bred tough people. Proud people. Folk who didn't need the rest of the world to tell them what to do. The rest of the world like that Andrew Preston.

But, whatever Louisa's rationale, possibly forged long ago in that home for unwed mothers, her later gambles in life had paid off big-time. Banner Mac and Fortune's Lady had taken the international circuit by shock and by storm. And after Fortune's Lady, there had been more horses, more wins. The stables had grown, and after moving into the stud business, Fairchild Acres had overseen the breeding of a long line of champions.

Fortune's Lady had been just that—a mare who had brought Louisa real fortune. And fame.

Smiling, Megan took the next newspaper cutting out of the box and her blood suddenly ran cold.

It was a story about Banner Mac's arrest for the sexual

assault and murder of an eleven-year-old boy thirty years ago—Liam Smith.

Megan's heart quickened as she read, flipping over the page, utterly horrified by what came next.

Mac had stood accused of luring three young boys, Henry Luddy and brothers DJ and Liam Smith, into the Koongorra wildlands, where he'd tied them up in a bush shack and sexually assaulted Liam.

The other two boys managed to escape, making it back over the river to alert authorities.

They hadn't returned in time, however, to save Liam's life.

According to the yellowing articles from the Newcastle and Pepper Flats papers, Banner Mac had been arrested in connection with the crime. His night-time drinking habits, penchant for hiking the Koongorra trails alone, and his general isolation from other members of his community had made him a target of law-enforcement interest. He'd been charged when his footprints and blood type matched that found on the scene.

But Henry Luddy and DJ Smith, both eight years old at the time, had failed to satisfactorily identify Banner Mac in a police lineup. Crown prosecutors had nevertheless taken the case to trial.

Megan frowned, wondering why Louisa had kept these stories. Then when she began to read the next article, she saw why.

Louisa Fairchild had personally retained Bob D'Angelo, Senior, Robert D'Angelo's father, of D'Angelo, Fischer and Associates, to defend her trainer.

D'Angelo's team had decimated the Crown Prosecutor's case, and since this was in the days before DNA technology could be used to match semen samples to the accused, Banner Mac had left the court a free man.

Police never arrested anyone else, clearly believing Mac was their man. Banner Mac had left the country mere days after the verdict came down.

Megan felt ill. The distant howl of dingoes reached her again, and she shivered.

This must have been what Dylan was talking about when he said Louisa had bought justice, setting a criminal free. The Hastings family would have been living in the valley around the same time the Smith boys and Henry Luddy were abducted. Dylan probably went to the same school as these boys.

His hatred made sense.

But would her aunt have defended Banner Mac if she'd thought her trainer might actually have been guilty of this heinous crime? Megan would not believe it.

But what did she honestly know?

Disturbed after reading these pages, and by the haunting sound of the dingoes, Megan pulled on her kimono and made her way down to the kitchen in the dark in search of cocoa.

But as she pushed open the kitchen door, she bumped into Marie, a knife glinting in her hand in the eerily dim night-lights. Megan stifled a scream. "Oh, God, Marie, you scared me," she said, pressing her hand to her chest and laughing nervously as she looked at the sharp butcher knife. "I…came down for some cocoa. I didn't expect to see anyone here at this hour."

"I forgot to start the bread maker," Marie said, setting the knife down next to some sausage. "And I thought I'd have a quick snack before going back to the staff cottages." She looked embarrassed. "Would you like me to make you the cocoa?"

"Oh, goodness, no. Thank you." Megan pulled her kimono closer, opening the fridge and reaching for the milk. "Can I make *you* some?"

Marie hesitated, then smiled. "Sure, I'd love that."

They sat for a while at the kitchen table, nursing cups of cocoa as dry wind rattled at the windows.

"Did you speak to that lawyer again today?" Marie asked

as she sipped from her mug. "Do you think he'll have Louisa home soon?"

Megan hesitated, thinking of her altercation with D'Angelo earlier that morning. "You worry about Louisa a lot, don't you, Marie? You're growing fond of her."

Marie shrugged. "Louisa's been alone a long time."

Marie was right. In spite of her fortune, Louisa seemed to lead a very lonely life, and Marie appeared to have taken a special interest in the older woman.

Megan knew that Marie had lost her own mother shortly before coming to work in the Hunter Valley. She wondered if caring for Louisa was a way for Marie to hold on to something she'd lost.

Then she thought of Dylan's concern over Marie's uncle Reynard Lafayette, and possibly Marie herself. Dylan had noted they both had access to the gun cabinet. And to Lochlain.

"You never did tell me what made you decide to come to Fairchild, Marie," Megan said, raising her mug of cocoa to her lips. "It's an awfully long way from Darwin."

Something in Marie's jewel-green eyes flickered and her shoulders tensed. She hooked a strand of blond hair behind her ear. She seemed nervous. And Megan noted once again how similar she and Marie were to each other in coloring, although Marie was smaller in stature, delicate almost.

"I needed a change after my mother, Colette, died," Marie said cautiously. "Her brother, my uncle Reynard, was here in the valley, and he'd heard about the job at Fairchild. He put in a word in with Mrs. Lipton, who interviewed me over the phone."

Megan knew this from Mrs. Lipton.

"You have the same surname as your uncle," Megan prompted, feeling guilty. But she was asking for Dylan. He needed any help he could get right now, and he wasn't able to talk to Marie himself without a warrant.

"My mother never married," said Marie. "She and her brother were both adopted by the Lafayettes and went by the same name."

Megan filed that information away. "You don't have any other family?"

Marie looked long and hard at Megan. "No. Just us."

Megan didn't press further, couldn't. She felt bad enough as it was. "I also lost my mum...when I was sixteen."

"It's never easy," Marie said softly, "when you love someone. Even if they made mistakes, you know?"

Megan nodded, thinking of Louisa's letters and past mistakes.

Marie looked up suddenly. "My uncle's a good guy, Megan. I know the cops have been questioning him, and he's fickle, a drifter, a bit of a renegade, but he's a good man. To me. He's my family."

Megan studied her, thinking how important that was, the need for a sense of home. Of family.

Belonging.

And what lengths people went to find it.

Chapter Thirteen

It was Monday morning, almost lunch, and the clock was ticking. Megan was getting tense. After visiting Louisa, she'd tried to call Dylan from the Aston Martin's car phone. She wanted to tell him she'd learned that Marie's mother was Colette Lafayette, that Colette had never married, and that both she and her brother Reynard had been adopted. It might give him something to go on.

But the station admin assistant said Dylan wasn't at the station. He wasn't answering his mobile, either.

Megan turned up the radio as she drove towards his house instead. The ABC rural news was reporting the Koongoora fires had flared again in deep inaccessible gullies, and that the low-pressure cell in the north was continuing to build.

She glanced to the eastern ridge, saw the haze of smoke was indeed thicker. Tension whispered through her.

She switched to another station where announcers were talking about rural fire service volunteers attempting a risky backburn ahead of possible lightning strikes if the cell moved south.

Megan turned off onto a side road, and into the Hastings driveway.

But when June Hastings opened the door, Megan found the woman in utter distress, and Heidi on the lounge carpet in her school uniform, knees hugged tight into her chest, weeping inconsolably. There was no sign of Dylan.

Through convulsive sobs Heidi managed to tell Megan she'd finally received a reply from her mother. Sally had outright rejected her, saying she was too busy to have her daughter visit, and that it was not a good idea altogether.

A fierce protective anger welled in Megan's chest as she held tightly the daughter Sally should have been here to comfort and nurture through the last ten years. Heidi clung to her like a small child, body racked with grief, desperate for the love of a mother.

And all the while, June stood wringing her hands and rocking on her feet, features drawn while Muttley yipped and scratched at the screen door to come in as if he was missing out on the high drama.

"Oh, goodness," June whispered. "Is Timmy going to be okay? Is Timmy ever going to come home?"

Megan couldn't bear it anymore, and she took control of the household.

She ushered June into the kitchen and set her to making lemon squash, just to keep her busy. June was easily distracted, and seemed pleased to have a clearly defined role.

Megan then opened the door to let Muttley in, and he bounded over to Heidi, pouncing on her with his front feet, knocking her flat onto the carpet, his whole body wagging and slobbery tongue lolling as he rolled onto her.

"Oh, geez, Muttley, you smelly drover! *Get off me!* He's been rolling in kangaroo poop again, Megs, get him out of here."

Megan stood there bemused for a moment, and she began to laugh. And laugh. And laugh.

Heidi looked absolutely horrified, before a hesitant smile began to creep over her lips, and she began to laugh, too, through her tears. Megan's knees buckled under her, and she sank to the floor beside Heidi, where they rolled around cackling and chortling and being bombarded by a smelly hound who was overjoyed by their sudden camaraderie on the carpet.

Megan sat up, wiping tears from her eyes and pushing her hair back from her face. "Oh, Lord, do I ever stink. We need to clean up here, Heidi. Does Muttley have some kind of tub, something we can wash him in? Do you have any clothes I can borrow?"

Heidi studied Megan a moment, then leaned forward suddenly and gave her a quick kiss on her cheek. Megan's heart crumpled.

"Thank you, Megs, for always being there. I wish you were my mother."

She touched the child's face. "Remember, Heidi, that you are an incredibly special person," she said softly. "And never, ever feel inferior because someone unworthy has rejected you. For whatever reason."

Heidi tightened her mouth, eyes glinting with fierce determination, and she nodded fast.

"Come," said Megan. "We can talk about it some more while we scrub Muttley outside. And boy, are we going to give that dog the bath of his life. He needed one before the poo, ugly old Mutt."

Heidi chuckled, and wiped the tears from her face.

And that's how Dylan found them that afternoon—full of soapsuds in his garden, near the pool, trying to wrestle a wet, soapy and hairy mutt back into the tub, the pooch in question shaking a spray of droplets into the late-afternoon sun that caught the light like sparkling jewels. His mother was happily busy in the kitchen baking. The scent of warm scones was something Dylan hadn't smelled in years.

The sound of laughter, the scents, the peace—they caught him by the throat.

He stood, transfixed, unable to move lest the magic pop like one of those glistening oily rainbows on the floating soap bubbles.

Smiling, his mother came up to his side and handed him a glass of fresh lemon squash. "Did you have a good day, Timmy?

He grinned at her, his heart suddenly warm, expansive. "Yeah, I did." Truth be told, his day had sucked, but this made up for it all.

Nothing could match the sounds of happiness filling his home and garden. Nothing could match his woman—because there was no doubt in his mind he wanted Megan now, completely. She was wearing his shorts, rolled up on tanned, lean soap-slicked legs, his oversized T-shirt plastered over her wet breasts, her hair tangled and damp, her eyes gleaming.

She fit: right into his life, his clothes, his family—everything.

She looked up, saw him and stilled.

His pulse quickened.

Heidi glanced up, too, caught the exchange between him and Megan, and swallowed nervously. She hadn't gone to school today, and she didn't want him to be mad. Slowly, she got to her feet, walked up to her dad, and wrapped her arms tight around his waist.

"Hey, Daddy. Megs is helping wash Muttley."

"I can see that." *Helping in so many ways.*

"My mother e-mailed me," she blurted out, eyes blinking fast, waiting for him to yell, to ground her for a week, tell her the dance was off, ask how and why she'd contacted Sally.

Dylan's chest tightened, but he held it all in. "And?"

Heidi's eyes darted up to his. "You're...not mad?"

He smoothed down her tangle of soaped hair. "What did Sally say, Heidi?"

"She doesn't want me, Dad." She glanced down at her bare feet on the grass, her blue nail polish. "She never did."

"Oh, chook." He crouched down to eye level, grasped her shoulders, looked into her eyes. "You okay with this, Heidi?"

"No." She bit her lip. "Not really." She rubbed her toes on the grass. "I always thought Mum would be there if I ever did pick up the phone. That she was, like, some angel in the distance, always watching me from far away, but just too busy, too special to be here right now."

Dylan was almost afraid to speak. This was the most in-depth conversation he'd had with his kid in a long, long time, and he was afraid if he opened his big clumsy mouth, the fragile moment would crumble to dust at his boots.

"Heidi," he said softly. "I know you saw the divorce papers."

Her mouth tightened, and she cast her eyes down. His heart picked up a notch, worried she'd clam up. "I wanted to talk to you about them."

She looked up again, surprise showing that he wasn't going to berate her for going into his study, opening an envelope clearly marked for someone else.

"I wanted to keep the door to your mother open for you, to keep that dream you held." His eyes moistened. "I *wanted* her to be your angel, kiddo. But sometimes...you just can't force people to be who we want them to be. And we have to set them free."

"Why'd you send the papers after all this time, Dad?"

He inhaled deeply, glanced at Megan, who was studiously busying herself with Muttley in order to give Dylan some time with his daughter.

"Is it because you met Megan?" Heidi asked quietly, fragile hope brightening her features, and Dylan realized that his kid was almost as afraid to crush this moment as he was. That she, too, was seeing Megan in their life.

"No," he said softly. "It's not because of Megs, it's because it was time. It was something I should have done a long time ago, chook. For all of us."

"Dad?"

"Yes?"

"I love you."

He exhaled a sharp shudder of breath, and quickly hugged his daughter tight to his chest, wet soap and all, lest she see the tears burning in his own eyes.

Megan glanced up, and Dylan mouthed the words *thank you* over Heidi's head.

He had a hell of a lot to thank that woman for.

And right this moment, he loved her.

"Dylan, you have got to let Louisa go." It was Monday night, and Megan was wondering how far D'Angelo was getting with his injunction. Once he slapped Dylan with it, everything would explode.

"You know I can't, Megan. Not without any new evidence," he said as he turned some sausages on the barbecue.

"But D'Angelo is—"

He faced her. "Look, Megs, I *know* that guy is after my blood. I'm aware of the firm's reputation as 'cop killers,' but I can't let some legal ass tell me how to do my job. *Nothing* that man does is going to change the way I'm doing things, okay?"

"Dylan, please, just listen to—"

He placed his fingers on her lips, his eyes light and happy. "Not now, Megs, please. Let's give it just a few hours break, okay?"

She nodded, loath to kill that rare and gorgeous twinkle in his eyes, that smile on his lips.

But she had a really bad feeling.

She pulled Dylan's sweater closer around her shoulders, her bare feet warm on tiles that had absorbed the day's sun. She watched him cook over the fire and her lonely flat in Sydney felt a million miles away. He'd tossed her and Heidi into the pool, clothes and all, once they'd finished washing Muttley, and they'd all splashed and laughed while the dog yipped around the perimeter. Dylan was so comfortable to be around, on so many levels. He made her happy in a way she hadn't been in a very long time.

Megan could love a man like this.

He was definitely a keeper.

"I saw some old news cuttings today," she said, leaning against him gently.

"Yeah?" He glanced down at her, smoke hissing behind him as flames flared against the fat of the sausages.

"They were stories about—"

"You ready for the rolls and salad, Dylan?" June called from the house.

He held up his hand to halt Megan for a second. "Yeah, Mum. You can bring 'em out."

He turned to Megan and grinned. "You're good for us, you know that? My mother hasn't been this together in days."

"Heidi said she has a form of dementia."

"Pretty much. Her memory is going as well now. We'll have to deal with it, but it's really good to see her like this." He put the sausages on a plate. "What was that you were saying about newspaper cuttings?" he asked as June approached them with a tray of warm rolls and fresh salad from the garden.

Megan smiled. "It's nothing." She didn't want to break this moment for Dylan and his family by bringing up some horrific old crime. "Come on, Sergeant," she said instead, pinching his butt. "Get the rest of those snags off the barbie and onto the table."

He shot her a look, raising the tongs in his hand and

wiggling them at her. "Careful, Megs, you just might get more than you bargained for."

She leaned up on tiptoes, bussed his cheek. "I hope that's a promise, Sarge," she whispered in his ear, and his stomach swooped dizzyingly, his heart swelling with affection.

Once his mother and Heidi had gone up to bed, Dylan sat with Megan on the porch. The night was deep, the glow from the fire in the mountains brighter than the previous nights.

"You think if that storm comes south it might put the fires out?"

"It's more likely to bring lightning strikes and new fires," he said.

"I hear the APEC protestors are using the Koongorra fires to bolster their climate-change anti-globalization protests."

He snorted softly, reached for her hand. "Megs?"

She lifted her eyes to his.

"Would you consider…living here, in the Hunter?"

Her breath stuck somewhere in her throat. Panic whispered, circled. "Dylan, I—"

"You fit, Megan." He took her hand and placed it on his warm chest where she could feel the solid, steady beat of his heart, and she felt ribbons of conflict twist inside her stomach.

"We could be a family, Megs," he said, very softly. "A good family."

She closed her eyes, trying to marshal thoughts spinning wildly, dizzyingly in all directions—her career, her flat, her friends, everything she had built so carefully. She was immensely proud of what she'd achieved, financially, professionally, and all on her own.

Yet, she'd still been lured out here to the Hunter Valley with the faint hope of finding something more. A sense of family, a place to belong. There'd still been a hole in her life.

She just hadn't expected to find it filled by this man she'd squared off with at opposite ends of the Pepper Flats police interrogation room. Or so soon.

Her heart began to race, and her palms felt damp. She withdrew her hand from his, and she felt his muscles constrict, tension suddenly rolling from him in waves.

What did she want of her life, really?

What woman would turn down a guy like Dylan Hastings? He was so rock-damn-solid. A protector, a lifer who would have your back in sickness and in health.

A man respected in his community. A man with honor, integrity.

Thunder rumbled soft and distant in the hills, the sound of crickets growing louder in the electric air.

"Megan?" The rawness in his voice cut her.

She turned in her chair. "Dylan, I…want to keep seeing you. I…might consider relocating, down the road, but—"

He surged to his feet, went to the edge of the patio, stared in silence at the dark valley.

Her stomach bottomed out. She got up, went to him, placed her hand on his shoulder. He stiffened.

He didn't look at her. "Do you think you could love me, Megan?"

Tightness balled in her throat.

"I'm just getting to know you, Dylan. I—"

He whipped round to face her. "What more *is* there to know? I don't have anything to hide. No games. No pretenses. I told you exactly what I'm about. I told you I don't mess around, but when I fall for someone, I fall like a bloody rock, hard and forever. Megan, I want you." He paused. "I want you now, in my life."

"I need to take it slower, Dylan," she whispered. "I…I need to be sure. I have a lot to work out, with my job and all."

He was silent.

She could literally feel him shutting down as she spoke.

She reached in desperation for his hand, but he was unresponsive. Frustration began to mount in her. "Would you do it for me if I turned the tables on you?" she said. "Move? Just like that?"

"I can't move my family, Megan. You know that. You know why."

"Then you're not being fair," she whispered almost inaudibly, her voice catching.

"It's not just about me, Megan. It's Heidi, her school—"

"She wants to go to school in Sydney," she reminded him. "And there are good homes there for June when she needs one."

His eyes glimmered in the dark.

"Why don't we wait until this homicide thing is over before making any major decisions? I could come to the Hunter for weekends. And you and Heidi could come visit me in the city. And if she doesn't get that bursary, I could set up a private scholarship fund for her. If she goes to Brookfield, it would give you both reason to come—"

"Christ, Megan, I don't want your charity! I don't want her going to that goddamn school." He stared down at her. "And the last thing on earth I want *anything* to do with is Fairchild money."

"Oh, don't try laying that on me now. This has *nothing* to do with Louisa Fairchild. I'm talking about *my* finances, money earned by my own efforts. I am a success, Dylan, in my own right. I struggled hard to get where I've got, and I'm damn proud of it. And *that* is what you're asking me to chuck!"

"Chuck?"

She inhaled shakily. "Yeah, chuck."

"I'm not asking you to chuck anything, Megan. I thought… I just thought you might want to do this. Look, I made a mistake. I'm sorry. It won't work, and I was wrong to ask. We should just end it."

Her eyes blurred with emotion, and her jaw tensed. "You're something else, you know that? Why must it be so all or goddamn nothing with you? Why can't you take your time?"

He turned away, stared at the ominous red glow in the sky.

"Because I don't need time. I've lost years of my life already trying to hang on to something I couldn't have. And it's because it's who I am."

She felt sick. Tears threatened to leak down her cheeks. She glanced up at the sky, blew out a soft breath. "I'm scared," she said quietly.

His eyes flared to hers. "Why?"

"Because it's such a big move for me, and so soon. It's not so simple for me, Dylan."

For him it was.

Dylan nodded. He could see now he'd made a terrible mistake in thinking this might work, that she'd actually consider moving here, becoming part of his family. He could see what he was asking of her.

He'd been rash. Impulsive.

Just like he'd been with Sally all those years ago. Wanting her before thinking it all through, before taking the time to see that it wouldn't work in the long run.

Maybe he was being so damn impulsive with Megan because he knew that if they took things slowly, she'd soon see their lives really were incompatible. And then he'd lose her. Maybe he wanted to tie her down quickly, right now, and hold on to her because deep down he knew he couldn't have her.

He should not have let it get this far.

And he had to let her go, before she imploded his life. Before he ruined hers.

"It's okay," he said.

"What do you mean?"

"I'm sorry. I shouldn't have asked that of you."

"We could take it slow, Dylan."

"It won't work."

"Damn it, what is it with you!" Tears broke their banks and spilled down her cheeks. She spun round. "I'm leaving," she said, making for the door.

"I can drive you."

"Don't bother," she yelled back at him. "I can drive myself! Been doing it for years!"

And he let her go.

He just let her go.

He heard her car door slam in the dark night, and he heard the engine start. Then he heard it fade down the ribbon of road.

Every molecule in his body screamed for him to go after her. But he forced himself to stand his ground.

Once again he'd fallen for what he couldn't have. And it hurt him like all hell. He wanted to smash something.

Fool.

He heard a rustling noise behind him and spun round, thinking, absurdly, she might have come back.

But it was Heidi who stood ghostly in a white nightdress at the door, her eyes dark and angry under the dim porch light.

"You sent her away."

He rubbed his neck, tired. "She wanted to go."

Her eyes began to shimmer. "Why do you have to ruin *everything!*"

She spun and charged inside, up the stairs. He heard her bedroom door slam.

Dylan scooped up the vase of flowers his mother had cut and set on the patio table for dinner, and he hurled it into the tiles. It exploded into a million shards that glimmered in the moonlight, the delicate cosmos blooms lying bruised, battered. Broken.

Beautiful for one fleeting moment, ruined by him the next.

Like his damn life.

Why was he such a goddamn idiot?

Megan swore to herself as she entered the Fairchild hallway and saw Patrick. She'd been hoping to sneak in and bury herself in bed.

"Megan!" he said, reaching for her hands as he came towards her, his eyes gleaming. "We got news—we can bring her home. Tonight! The injunction came through early."

Shock slammed into her chest. She felt dizzy. She shot a look at the hall phone.

Patrick placed his hand gently on her shoulder. "*Don't* call him, Megan. The court order prohibits Sergeant Hastings from talking to anyone from Fairchild, and I'm afraid it names you specifically."

Her mouth turned dry, and she wanted to cry, but she was empty. "D'Angelo named me specifically?" she whispered.

"It's just a blanket thing, Megs." Patrick hesitated. "Hastings can't come within a hundred yards of this property, either."

Her eyes flared.

"Look, I…know you like him, Megan. But—"

She shrugged free of his touch. "Don't worry, there's nothing between us, Patrick." *Not anymore.* "What'll this do to him…I mean professionally?" she asked.

"The way I understand it, it basically means he's off this homicide case and can no longer harass Louisa or anyone associated with her, but D'Angelo plans to take it further. He's pressing for a full internal inquiry into Hastings' conduct."

Megan suddenly felt utterly exhausted.

"You okay?"

"Just…tired. I need sleep."

At least she'd managed to avoid D'Angelo's threat of dragging Dylan and her through the tabloids, she thought as she went up the stairs. That would have been even worse.

But it was a bitter victory.

And a short-lived one.

Chapter Fourteen

Dylan pulled up outside Elias Memorial early Tuesday morning, intending to go straight for Dr. Jack Burgess, who'd called to say today was the day Louisa should be well enough to see him.

He was surprised to find the press massing outside once again, but this time there were more vans, the rural media being joined by the bigger Newcastle and Sydney outfits.

The hot autumn storm was still brewing as he got out of the car, the NSW flag outside the hospital snapping in a wind pungent with smoke—a bad wind, given the sudden directional switch. Dylan's radio had been crackling all morning as the big pressure cell inched farther south. The storm hadn't broken properly yet, but lightning strikes had already started spot fires in drought-ridden bush farther north.

He shut the door of his squad car and put on his mirrored shades, adjusting his gun belt as he assessed the scene.

Taken aback, he realized it was Andrew Preston—Tyler

Preston's cousin from Kentucky—who was holding court on the stairs, Tyler at his side. It looked like the Australian and American branches of the Preston clan had been united by the terrible tragedy at Lochlain Racing.

Also part of the entourage on the stairs was Darci Parnell, daughter of Weston Parnell, the Australian Ambassador to Britain and former owner of Warrego Downs, Sydney's premier racetrack. At her side stood Sam's son, Daniel Whittleson, with his PR consultant wife, Marnie. Dylan frowned at the sight of her.

Marnie had been a thorn in the side of the Pepper Flats police. She'd been instrumental in helping Louisa brush her original shooting of Sam under the carpet some months ago.

Then he caught sight of Megan as Andrew drew her close to him, into the line of the cameras, as he spoke.

Dylan's chest turned tight and cold.

The Thoroughbred set was closing ranks. Us versus them. And Megan was one of them.

He pushed off the squad car and moved nearer the crowd, staying under the leafless boughs of the jacaranda trees that lined the road. He propped his shoulder against the trunk of a tree, watching from behind his mirrored shades, arms crossed over his chest.

"Louisa Fairchild is a vital member of this country's proud legacy of Thoroughbred racing and breeding," Andrew Preston was saying into the mikes. "And here on the steps of Elias Memorial, at the very heart of Australia's stud farm capital, I want to say publicly—" he nodded to Daniel and Megan "—that we *all* stand by and believe implicitly in Louisa Fairchild's innocence."

What in hell? Dylan swore under his breath.

Andrew was buying Louisa's support. And he was using these hospital steps as a bloody photo op, just as Dylan himself had earlier. But this was for personal gain—his run for presidency of the International Thoroughbred Racing Federation.

The election was in two months, and the suave American had been racing neck-and-neck with rough-around-the-edges Aussie media mogul 'Jacko' Bullock, whom Louisa had vocally supported. Louisa had been widely quoted in the press as saying she wasn't interested in seeing some American "seppo" at the helm of the international federation.

But this was a bizarre twist, thought Dylan, watching Andrew put his arm around Megan as he continued to speak. Dylan's head began to pound.

"I hereby pledge my full support for Louisa Fairchild and her family. They have been victims of police ineptitude and deprived of justice because of this current state of emergency."

Dylan pushed off from the tree, wire-tense.

"I will personally be working with the Fairchild legal team to ensure that whoever has caused her this distress and suffering is held responsible for their actions."

So *this* was Andrew Preston's way of bolstering his ITRF campaign? By attacking the NSW police force to get Louisa and her clan on his side? Dylan clenched his jaw. He'd bet his bottom dollar this was Marnie's brainchild. She must have twisted Daniel's arm to get him to stand there.

And it hit Dylan suddenly. This homicide wasn't just about Sam. It was about *them*.

All of them.

The Lochlain blaze and murder *had* to be somehow tied into the bigger Thoroughbred racing picture, perhaps even to this election battle itself.

With all of them standing on the stairs he could suddenly see the links.

Years ago Jacko, a close friend of Weston Parnell, had been instrumental in having Tyler Preston's television program pulled from the air because of Tyler's intimate relationship with a then very young Darci Parnell. There had to be a lot of animosity still lingering there.

Jacko himself was rumored to have done business with associates linked to an organized crime syndicate that ran betting and doping scams in the racing industry country-wide. Andrew Preston, on the other hand, had vowed to "clean up" the industry of such scams. The syndicate would see Preston's win as a personal threat.

Jacko would be the man the powerful crime syndicate needed at the helm—not Preston.

Dylan's pulse quickened as he turned these thoughts over.

Andrew had also recently held his big campaign party at Lochlain Racing, which could have made Lochlain and the Aussie Prestons a direct syndicate target themselves.

Dylan knew, too, that Sam Whittleson had had gambling problems. It was why he'd become so desperate in his fight with Louisa to save what little he had left of Whittleson Stud.

And it wasn't uncommon for people with massive horse-racing debts to become beholden to the crime syndicate.

Could this have happened to Sam?

Could the syndicate have wanted Sam out of the way for some reason? Might they have killed him at Lochlain and then torched the place, striking two birds with one stone and sending a clear message to the heart of Preston's campaign?

Louisa, because she'd shot Sam before, would have been positioned as the perfect scapegoat, throwing police off any syndicate scent.

Dylan had also learned from his Melbourne contact that Sandy Sanford had been investigated for betting fraud, but nothing had stuck. When he'd gone to question Sanford yesterday evening, Whittleson Stud employees had said Sandy had left the valley suddenly. That was when Dylan had learned Sanford had initially arrived in the Hunter with a dark-blue Holden. According to one of the laborers, that truck hadn't been seen for a while.

It was possible, thought Dylan, given the light from the flames and the general chaos on the night of the Lochlain blaze, that witnesses confused a slate-gray truck with a dark-blue one.

Sanford could well have been planted by the syndicate at Whittleson Stud to keep an eye on Sam and do the dirty deed of taking him out if necessary.

Or Reynard and Marie Lafayette could have fulfilled the same function.

All had access to Louisa's gun cabinet and Lochlain Racing. And Dylan had seen Reynard and Sanford together at the Crook Scale.

Jesus! Why had he not seen the possibility of a syndicate link before? *That's* why the NSW police must have received that anonymous call when it looked like they might not have enough to put Louisa away.

That call had come from the damn syndicate itself!

It had to be.

Dylan swore to himself. Never mind a full NSW homicide squad, they should have had the feds in on this.

Now the real killer and the masterminds were still lurking out there somewhere, possibly even standing among the gathering crowd of onlookers on these very steps. He really needed to talk to Louisa, and fast—

Megan's eyes suddenly found his, and she tensed visibly on the stairs, wind blowing her flaxen hair over her face.

Dylan's heart raced soft and fast and angry.

He didn't want to hear another word of Andrew Preston's crap.

He didn't want to see *her*. Not with that crowd. It couldn't be more stark that she and he were from different sides of the racetrack.

And the last thing Dylan needed was to present a photo op of himself having a personal showdown with the entire Preston clan, and then seeing his mug splashed over the papers tomorrow alongside a story of Andrew Preston alleging police ineptitude.

Blood running cold, Dylan stalked angrily round the side of the hospital, aiming for the service entrance at the back.

But as he was about to enter, his mobile buzzed.

It was the Pepper Flats High principal—Heidi was not at school. She'd done this sort of thing before, and Dylan had asked the school to call him direct if she didn't show.

He quickly dialled home.

His mother said Heidi had left for school as usual that morning.

His kid was missing.

Tension whipped tight.

He stormed into the hospital, ran up the service stairs, and into the ward corridor.

The chair where his police guard had been stationed was empty.

Dylan pushed through the door to Louisa's room and stalled.

It was empty. Flowers removed. Bed made. As if no one had ever lain there. *His prisoner was gone.*

"She was taken home last night. I'm sorry, Sergeant. They got a court injunction."

Dylan spun round to face a police officer from the Muswellbrook station.

"What?" *Last night?* While Megan was sitting with him in his garden, when he'd pretty much proposed she spend the rest of her life with him? Had she known this was going down while she sat there holding his hand?

His head began to pound. "Where the hell is my constable?"

The officer came forward, looking embarrassed. "I'm sorry, Sergeant, Peebles had to leave. It was basically a cease and desist, and you're to have no contact with any member of the Fairchild family." He held out a piece of paper apologetically as he spoke. "They're listed here by name." He cleared his throat, avoiding Dylan's eyes. "You're also banned by court order from going within one hundred meters of Fairchild Acres."

He glared at the cop. *His own force knew about this?* And no one had told him? That was when his stomach really turned cold.

His phone started buzzing, and he snapped it open.

"Hastings," he barked, tension strangling his throat.

"You're off the case, Sergeant—"

"What the blazes is going on here, Matt? On what bloody grounds can he get a court order like this?"

The Hunter LAC commander cleared his throat. "They're alleging police brutality, illegal procedure, lack of due care of a sensitive prisoner causing—"

"Why in hell am *I* the last one to find out about this?" Dylan demanded. "Why is my super only calling me *now!*"

"I'm sorry, Hastings. It came out of left field and we're still trying to work out where the force stands with this. It's a precedent-setting injunction. D'Angelo and Associates wound a pretty convincing deal around this one—"

"It's not freaking true."

"He has valid points. We *are* short-staffed."

"And you're going to hang me out to dry on this, Matt?" Dylan's voice turned deadly calm, cool, because he was beyond furious now. With his superior, with the law firm, with Megan, but mostly with himself, because he'd seen this coming down the pipe the minute Matt Caruthers had told him to arrest Louisa Fairchild solo, without sufficient evidence to bolster him.

"We'll deal with it—"

"You mean internal will deal with it."

"We don't have a choice right now. We obey the injunction, and that comes straight from the Commissioner." He hesitated, cleared his throat. "And I want you to come in, Dylan."

The use of his first name hit hard. Not once in his career had Matt Caruthers called him that. And Dylan got a very bad feeling about what was coming next. "You suspending me?"

"Pending the outcome of an internal investigation. I'll need your weapon and your badge. And you'll need to bring the vehicle and your phone and radio in."

Cold nausea washed through him. "Look, Matt, there are angles that haven't been played yet. If Louisa really was set up, as she claims, there could still be a homicide suspect out there. And if she is innocent—"

"Which is the last thing we need *you* saying, Hastings. It'll play right into D'Angelo's hands if you show an ounce of belief she could be innocent of the crime you are allegedly harassing her for. And came close to killing her for."

He fisted his hand around the phone. "That's bull."

"Go home, Hastings."

"There could be a killer—"

"Sergeant, you're off the case." The commander's words brooked no argument. "The state of emergency is lifting tonight, and we'll have a full homicide team back in Pepper Flats first thing tomorrow morning. Make sure your desk is clear, and that the Lochlain files are available."

Dylan hung up, limbs literally vibrating, mouth dust-dry. He swore viciously.

Screw them all.

They could have his gun, his badge, his phone, whatever the hell they liked. He'd done his best. Solo. And he'd done it honestly, in the name of justice. Yeah, there'd been a niggle of doubt in him about his personal animosity to Louisa, and that was all probably going to come out in a Supreme Court circus down the road now, dragging him, his family history, his mother, right back into media spotlight after thirty god-damn years.

But right now, he had to find his kid.

That was the most important thing in his life. They could take the rest.

Without his family, he had nothing.

* * *

By early Tuesday afternoon the storm broke violently in the north, stirring hard downdraft winds into the valley, and filling the Hunter skies with wadded purple clouds. The pressure cell was heading this way now, lighting spot fires along the route, heavy rain vying with flames in a race for supremacy through the Koongorra wildlands. Worst-case scenario, fire would crest over the ridge and jump the Hunter River, already low from drought, sweeping into the farms.

And Dylan couldn't find Heidi anywhere.

He told himself to relax, that she'd probably show when school was out, pretending she'd been there all the time.

After dropping his weapon, badge, squad car and other accoutrements of his job off at the station, he'd been humiliated to have to call Mitch for a ride home.

It fed his rage, and it torqued his worry over his daughter. But he could do little until school was out. In an effort to eliminate the cortisol building in his body from the constant rush of adrenaline, Dylan went for a hard, long run along the ridge across the fields from his house.

Trees were beginning to bow and creak as the hot wind increased, redolent with imminent rain and smoke. A branch from a massive river red gum cracked like a gunshot, splintering down to the ground at Dylan's feet. He dodged as another came crashing down, moving quickly out from under the massive trees known ominously as widow makers because of the way they shed limbs up to half the diameter of their trunk size without warning. He ran until sweat drenched his torso, and his lungs burned raw.

He bent over, hands on his knees, sweat dripping as he tried to catch his breath. The sky lowered sullenly over him, darkening his world.

He'd been locked out.

He'd lost his woman through his own idiocy, and was now on the verge of losing his daughter. Even if he found her.

And a cold unspecified fear fingered him. The same kind of fear that had taunted him when he and Liam and Henry Luddy had been lured into the Koongorra wildlands all those years ago.

Dylan cursed viciously.

It was irrational, he knew, because Heidi had not been abducted. She had not been lured into Koongorra bush by a psychopath.

She'd simply fought with him and run off to spite him for letting Megan out of their lives at a time when she really needed a mother.

Damn. She might even be at Fairchild, with Megan and Anthem. And now he was legally barred from going anywhere near the estate. Or calling the house.

The injunction had specifically named Megan Stafford.

Dylan swore again and kicked at a stump. Injunction be damned.

It was getting late. He needed to find his child before night fell.

He began to run back to his house as the first fat plops of rain bombed to the ground, rolling in the dry dust like small mercurial marbles, water releasing the scent of sand and gum trees.

By the time he neared home, the wind was close to gale force, cracking drought-ridden trees and bringing them down across properties, roads and power lines.

He entered his house to find it dark, his mother hunched over the battery-operated radio, listening to the storm report by the light of a candle.

"The power is out," she said in a thin voice. "Timmy won't find his way home. I'm so worried about Timmy."

Dylan placed his hand on her shoulder. "It'll be okay, Mum. Have you got your emergency bags packed? Like we practiced in the fire drill?"

She nodded, eyes huge.

He picked up the phone, and tensed—no dial tone. He depressed the cradle. Still nothing.

The phone lines were down.

He tried using his personal mobile to call Fairchild. Nothing. Of course there wouldn't be. If the landline to Fairchild was down, he wasn't going to get through via cell phone. And he didn't have a mobile number for Megan.

She'd only ever called him from Louisa's car phone.

He glanced out the windows. It was getting really dark now, the rain coming down in glistening sheets. Be damned—his own force could arrest him if they wanted, but he was going to drive there himself.

He grabbed his oilskin coat and cattleman's hat. "I'm going to get Heidi," he called to his mother.

"Where is she?"

"Safe," he lied, shrugging into his coat. "And I'm going to call Mitch on his mobile, tell him to come and get you if there's an evacuation alert. You be ready with Muttley and your bags like we practiced, okay?"

She nodded. "Be careful. And…bring Timmy home safe."

His throat choked up. "I will, Mum. Don't you worry."

Dylan screeched to a stop outside the Fairchild Manor house and flung open his door. Rain and wind pummeled him as he ran toward the sweeping stairs that led to the entrance.

But before he got to the doors, they flung open and Megan came racing down the stairs into the rain, dressed only in a thin T-shirt and jeans, no shoes.

"Dylan!" She grabbed his arms. "You shouldn't be here!"

Rain drenched her instantly, water sheening her face, plastering her hair and clothes to her body. His heart clutched sharply.

"I didn't come for you, Megan. I came for Heidi."

She looked confused "She's…not here."

"You *sure?*"

Thunder crashed and rolled into the hills. Wind gusted, lashing the rain at them.

"Of course I'm sure."

He spun round, stared into the driving sheen of wind and rain. *Where the hell was she? What game was she playing with him?*

He felt so incredibly alone in this moment.

"Dylan—"

He ignored her, making for his vehicle.

But she ran after him, slamming her hand against the door of his truck as he tried to close it. "Talk to me Dylan! What happened?"

"Heidi's missing. Has been all day." Emotion choked his voice. "Can't find her anywhere."

"Have you checked Huntington Stud?"

"Why would she—"

"Because Zach's there. She's fourteen, Dylan. She thinks she's in love, and she's feeling rejected by her father. It's where I would have gone. Maybe Zach is missing, too. Have you called there?"

He felt like a complete idiot. He was a cop. It should've been one of the first places he looked. But as a father, he'd panicked, developed a blind spot. He looked up into Megan's eyes, the rain coming down thick between them. "Phone lines are down. I'll go there now—"

"I'm coming."

"No. There's a court order. So just stay the hell out of my life—"

"I don't give a damn about that injunction!" she yelled, refusing to let him close the door, rain streaming down her face and hair, plastering her shirt to her body. "This is my problem as much as yours! Heidi is *my* friend. I know her, I can talk to her. I can reason with her where you can't. As much as you care for your daughter, you're a stubborn ass, Dylan Hastings. And I care deeply about you both." She paused. "I love you, dammit."

Dylan's world tilted. He stared at her blankly for a moment, then cursed. "Get some gear!" he yelled, putting the car into Reverse.

Megan raced into the garage, pulling her wet T-shirt up over her head as she made for the cupboards at the back. She had no idea why those words had come out of her mouth at that moment. All she knew was that they came straight from her heart. And it was true. She loved the obdurate hunk of cop, and she was suddenly determined not to let him get away. Ever. She frantically pulled out a mechanic's shirt, yanking it over her head as she reached for an old oilskin and hat. Hopping on one foot she slid oversize bush boots onto her bare feet, and ran out to where Dylan had the car door open and engine running.

He gunned the gas, tires biting into gravel before she even had the door closed.

Dylan drove too fast, fiddling with his personal scanner as he tried to tune into the volunteer-firefighting frequencies. His radio crackled with sporadic reports of fresh lightning strikes as the big storm cell moved south. There was now also a flash flood warning.

"You not on duty?" Megan asked, looking at his clothes.

"Thanks to you."

She stared.

"What? You people had no idea what your injunction would do to me?"

"I know you've been taken off the case, but—"

"Off the goddamn force. Pending internal investigation, I'm suspended. Thanks."

Megan's stomach churned. Oh, God, she hadn't expected him to be suspended off the bat.

"It wasn't my doing, Dylan! I told you to let Louisa go before this happened. I tried to warn you—"

He swore as he swerved round a fallen tree trunk, tires slipping on the muddy road that led to the Huntington Stud farther up the Hunter River banks, farther into the wilder area

of the Koongorra nature preserve that ran along the opposite bank.

Where Liam had been killed.

"You knew last night that Louisa was being moved, didn't
you? You sat there holding my hand, knowing what was going
down while I damn well near proposed to you."

"I did *not* know it was going to come down last night. I only
found out when I got back to Fairchild. Honest, Dylan. I was
praying he wouldn't get it through. I was—"

He slammed on brakes as the bright eyes of a kangaroo reflected the headlights. Rain thrashed at the windscreen, wipers
slashing to keep up, the night black as pitch.

He breathed out.

"Do you realize, Megan, that if your aunt is innocent there
is still a killer out there who could come for her now?"

She gripped the dash as he hit the gas again, tires spinning
wildly in watery mud that ran in rippling sheets over the road.
"Why would—"

"Because whoever might be framing her for murder might
also want his secret to die with her," he said as he wheeled
into the Huntington Stud driveway, bouncing over fresh ruts
running with storm water. "I think this is much bigger than
we all thought. Syndicate maybe."

"What!"

He shot her a look. "Didn't think of that, did you? And
who's protecting your aunt now? In that big manor house in
a blackout storm with no phones? D'Angelo and his briefcase?"

He pulled to a stop outside the Harrison staff house. Mrs.
Harrison came dashing out, the umbrella over her head yanked
by the wind, her face white in the light from the headlights.
"Thank God you're here, Sergeant! Zach and Heidi were seen
crossing the river into the Koongorra this morning, and Zach's
horse just came back. Riderless!"

Dylan got out of the car. "Which way did they go?"

She pointed frantically down towards the rising river. "There's a small bush trail right on the other side of the Hunter that Zach likes to ride. That's where they were last seen on horseback this morning. I tried to call you when it started raining, but the lines went down."

"You send anyone after them?"

"No! I didn't know what to do—" She choked on her next words. "There's no one left here. All the men have gone to fight the fires. Bill and Steve were the only grooms left, and they've taken the horses to higher ground because of possible flash flooding down here. I'm manning the radio dispatch myself with the phone lines down—"

"You got any horses left we can use?"

She nodded fast. "Down there at that shed. Two trail horses and saddles."

Dylan took Mrs. Harrison's hand in both of his. He looked her direct in the eyes, rain drenching him. "Hang in there, Mrs. Harrison. I'll find them."

"Oh, God, please, *please* find my boy." Her eyes were glassy and frantic in her pale face.

"I will, Mrs. Harrison. I will find Zach. Have faith."

And Megan loved him more than ever.

She knew how distraught Dylan was himself, and the news of the riderless horse must have wound him even tighter.

Yet he was able to give a caring touch to someone else in need, zeroing in on *her* child. Megan's eyes burned. She loved this man, and they were going to find these kids, or she would die trying.

And then she was going to find a way to be with him, here in the Hunter.

If she'd learned anything from Louisa's letters, she'd learned that some choices could not be undone. Time could not be rolled back.

She was at a crossroads. A major one in her life.

...

Chapter Fifteen

The river was already swelling, rain driving at them, when Dylan and Megan crossed on horseback in the pitch dark with the aid of a flashlight. They negotiated a wide and rocky area where the water was still fairly shallow, and Megan hoped it would remain fordable on their return. Even if the water did rise several feet over the next few hours, it should spread wide at this point, as opposed to grow deep.

They carefully picked their way up a steep path trickling with water, the gum forest closing around them, hooves sending loose stones skittering down a ravine at the side.

Lightning flashed, splitting the sky apart, starkly silhouetting Dylan on the horse ahead of her. Through the sheets of rain cascading from the brim of her hat, Megan kept her focus on his solid shape. Thunder rumbled a few seconds later—the centre of the storm closing in fast.

Dylan's two-way radio crackled, and she heard him speaking.

"What is it?" she yelled, the wind rushing through the high ops of the gum forest sounding like a freight train now, cracking off branches that crashed through brush to the ground.

"Backburn didn't work! Evacuation orders are being issued for the Upper Hunter," he yelled back to her. "Fire is moving in from the northeast, joining with the Koongorra fires. If the wind switches again, it'll crest over the ridge—we're in for a mega-fire!"

She could smell thicker smoke now, acrid in the wetness. She almost imagined she could hear the distant roar and crackle over the ridge, or was that the wind in the trees?

Panic wedged into her chest. She knew how fast these monster fires could move, devouring every living thing in their path. But she tightened her grip on the reins, impelling her horse forward, fighting her own urge to flee as the trail narrowed upward, and into the path of danger.

Scanning the ground up ahead with the beam of his flashlight, Dylan called out periodically for Heidi and Zach.

Then suddenly he saw it—a piece of shredded yellow plastic fluttering in the branch of a pine that hung low over the trail.

His heart kicked.

He quickly dropped down from his saddle to examine the strip. It was from a supermarket bag—the kind they gave out at the Pepper Flats Mini Mart. The kind he had at home. His pulse quickened.

Holding the reins of his horse with one hand, he carefully panned the dark glistening area under the trees with his torch. His beam lit on another bit of plastic. Same yellow. Same size.

This strip had clearly been tied to the tree, the branches and understory crushed and broken as if a small freight train had gone barreling through.

Frowning, Dylan directed his flashlight farther into the black bush…and saw fine strands of long blond hair snagged in some twigs, blowing in the wind.

Blood thudded into his ears, old memories crashing down on him, hurtling him back to the time he'd led police into an area not far from here in search of his brother. His stomach constricted sharply at the sudden flashback to how they'd found Liam. Sweat broke out under his hat. Hot. Prickling over his skin.

Lightning cracked above them again, and his horse whinnied, jerking back. He tightened his fist around the reins. *Focus, damn it!*

He had to believe.

He'd told Zach's mother to have faith. He had to hold on to that too. He knew from his law-enforcement experience just how powerful hope could be.

Megan dismounted, came to his side, touched his shoulder.

He glanced up at her.

Rain dripped from her hat and she was dwarfed by the huge outback coat, so far removed from the golden art dealer in the champagne convertible. A woman standing right here with him. At his side. In the dark wilderness. When he'd stood so alone for so many years. His radio crackled again, disjointed voices saying the blazes were converging several miles out.

They didn't have much time.

He stood, took her shoulders. "I want you to go back, Megan," he said. "The fire—"

She shook her head. "No. You need me."

He did.

He needed her more than she'd ever know. The macho cop was scared to death about what he'd find, how he'd deal. Just her presence was giving him courage. But he couldn't risk her life.

"Megan," he said firmly. "I'm ordering you to go back."

"You can't order me, so don't waste time trying. Let's find them. *Then* we go back."

She was dead serious. But he could not be responsible for hurting or losing her, too.

"Megan—"

"You're wasting precious time, Dylan." A jagged fork of lightning speared the ground not far from them, thunder exploding mere seconds later, the centre of the storm hovering closer. Wind gusted, scattering a shower of thick raindrops at them. "I'm not leaving, so let's move."

The horses danced nervously, pulling back, whinnying. But Megan held her mount steady and stared Dylan directly in the eyes, and he loved her more than anything.

She was right about one thing.

He'd been strangling the very things he loved most by trying to hold on to them too tightly. He'd been inadvertently pushing his kid to do something like this. And looking into Megan's face in the storm, he made a silent pact—if he found his child unharmed, he vowed to change. He would ease up on the reins. He would give her more freedom. He'd find a way to send her to Brookfield. He would learn to compromise. And he would do whatever it took to win Megan back. Even if that meant taking it slow.

He'd visit her in Sydney on weekends when he visited Heidi. He'd be open-minded about his career. He'd look into new opportunities in the city. He'd do it *all,* if he could find his child safe. Because now he knew what he really stood to lose.

And all he wanted was a second chance.

A chance to make it right.

"Heidi should have left me a note," he said, voice snagging in his throat. "If I'd allowed her more freedom, then she'd have been more open, told me where—"

Megan placed her hand on his cheek. "We'll find her."

He nodded, trying to swallow the burn in his throat.

"There! Look!" She pointed suddenly as another flash of lightning threw the forest into stark relief.

He angled his flashlight under the branches to where she was pointing, saw another piece of shredded plastic. And a few yards farther, where the ground dropped sharply away into a narrow ravine area dense with scrub, was another shred of glistening yellow.

Someone had tied the markers along what appeared to be a barely discernible track down into the ravine. His heart kicked hard.

Was it Heidi? Zach? Were they down there in the ravine, hurt, unable to move? He thought of the riderless horse.

Why on earth would they have tried to negotiate this section down to the gorge?

Not risking the horses on this terrain, Dylan and Megan led their mounts on foot, picking their way carefully down the narrow switchback that grew dense with eucalyptus and olive trees tangled with weeds, morning glory, balloon vines, and toxic scrub as they got closer to the river that snaked down in the gorge.

Then they heard it—a horse.

Dylan's heart began to thump. He discerned the shape of the saddled animal in the trees, the whites of its eyes stark. The animal was terrified. It was tethered to a branch just off the narrow trail.

Another shred of plastic fluttered down to the left of the horse where the ground dipped even more sharply.

Megan moved forward immediately to placate the mare, smoothing the animal's neck with her hand. "Give me your horse, Dylan," she said. "Go ahead while I secure the horses here. I have a flashlight. I'll follow you down."

Dylan hunched low, thorn and scrub scratching at his back and face as he followed more pieces of plastic lower into the ravine.

The incline grew even steeper. "Heidi! Zach!" he yelled, his voice drowned by the wind, the sound of water now reaching him from the gorge.

He half slid, half crawled, cut by thorns. How in hell had she come down here? Why? Where was she? Was the plastic even hers? *"Heidi!"*

Thunder boomed simultaneously with a lightning strike, the storm directly above, the wind a crashing sound. Another heavy branch smashed through the undergrowth, just glancing off his shoulder. Pain thrummed in him. Dylan stilled for a second, swore. A few inches closer and it could have bloody killed him. Then he saw two huddled forms. *"Heidi!"*

She waved. "Over here, Dad! Help!"

Relief punched violently through him as he slid and scrambled down to her.

"Dad. Oh, God, Dad, I *knew* you would come. I just knew it!" She flung her arms around his neck, shivering and wet and white. "Zach's hurt. He broke his leg, badly. His horse spooked at a snake while we were coming down the ravine. He fell, but got caught in the stirrup, and the horse came down on him, crushing his leg." She was shaking violently. "I...I left a trail...with the plastic...I thought I should stay with him...that you would come."

He cupped her face. "You did the right thing."

He crouched down to look at Zach. The boy was deathly white, his leg bent at a horrifying angle. "Hey, buddy. Let's see how you're doing."

"Hey, Sergeant." Zach attempted a smile, but it came out a groan.

Dylan checked his pulse. Thready. His face was cut. He was physically in shock.

"You hurt your back at all?"

"Don't...think so," Zach managed through clenched teeth. "Just...the leg. I can move everything else."

Dylan quickly shone his flashlight through the bushes, looking for something they could use to splint his leg and transport him out. He shouldn't risk moving him, but with the fire coming, and no help to be had from the valley, they had no choice.

"What made you come down here?" he asked Heidi as he picked up a fairly straight stick.

"We saw something glittering down in the river, through the trees. It looked like it could be a car that had gone down from the tracks on the opposite side of the gorge. We were worried someone may be hurt, and we thought we could take the trail real carefully. That's when the snake slithered over the path, and Zach's horse reared, dragging him down here before bolting."

Dylan panned his torch across the dark and glistening vegetation of the gorge, the chortle of the river increasing as the level of the water surged with storm rain.

Then it caught his eye.

A reflection of light. Maybe a mirror bouncing back his beam. The glint of chrome. Heidi was right—it looked like an upended vehicle. He knew there was a remote four-wheel-drive trail up on the opposite end, accessible from another point much farther north along the Hunter. It was possible the vehicle had gone over the cliff on the other side of the gorge.

"Go check it out," Megan said, coming up behind him with her flashlight. "I know first aid, Dylan. I can splint his leg with Heidi."

He caught her eye.

"Go. Quick. Someone could be hurt, and the water is rising."

He scrambled down a very steep section, and then over rock, landing thigh-deep in muddy storm water, the current tugging at his pants. Within minutes this very narrow section of gorge could fill with dangerously swift rapids. He had to move fast. He directed his flashlight along the bank and saw it.

A truck—a battered dark-blue Holden—was partly submerged in the river, the cab sticking out. His beam illuminated the license plate. The first two letters were *N* and *W*—*the same as Louisa's Holden.*

Dylan's heart raced.

Was this the missing vehicle? The one that might have

been mistaken for Louisa's dark-gray one because of bad lighting on the night of the blaze?

Dylan shone his light up the opposite bank. It was almost a vertical cliff, dense with growth. The way the trees grew in this part of the gorge, the truck would not have been visible from above. It could have been driven out here and pushed over the cliff and into the gorge as police roadblocks went up all over the Hunter after the Lochlain fire broke out.

Dylan waded through the swirling water, directing his flashlight into the interior of the cab, which was fast filling as the river rose. There was no one inside, but three empty turpentine cans floated in the cab. The Lochlain arson accelerant had been turpentine. He peered closer, his beam glinting off something silvery white—a CD stuck down behind the seat. He reached in through the open driver's window, and plunged his arm into the water. He managed to snag the CD with the tips of his fingers.

He read the label with his flashlight—Lochlain Security. Adrenaline dumped into his system. It was the missing security footage from the inside of the Prestons' barn, possibly a recording of evidence of the actual murder.

He slid the CD into the breast pocket inside his coat and scrambled quickly back up the bank.

Megan and Heidi were making good work of splinting Zach's leg using strips of fabric torn from a spare shirt Zach had in his backpack.

"Looks like it's the truck from the arson," he said. "Have you got anything in these backpacks I can use to bag some evidence?" he asked, dumping out Heidi's pack.

Three empty beer cans rolled out and clattered down into the gorge. He tensed, glanced at the kids. Megan's hand restrained him gently.

"Let it go," she whispered against his cheek.

He nodded. Megan was right. He had to learn to let quite a few things go. He'd found his kid unharmed, and he was going to turn his life upside down now to keep her that way.

He inhaled deeply, took Heidi's digital camera from the pack along with a second plastic shopping bag that had held the kids' lunch. It was better than nothing.

He scrambled back down, water almost up to his hips now. He tried to wrench open the door, but the current held it firm. He strained in to reach the turpentine cans, got one before the water rose farther, washing the other two downriver. He had to move faster. He managed to open the glove compartment, pulling out insurance papers enclosed in plastic. He photographed the truck as best he could, including the battered plate from the upended front. But now he could also sense smoke thickening, and the sky was beginning to glow an ominous orange. Dylan clambered back up the bank with the turpentine can in the bag tied to his belt loop, convinced that they would find that this truck belonged to Sanford, and that he was working for syndicate connections. The evidence would exonerate Louisa.

"What have you got?" Megan asked.

He placed his hand on her wet face, looking into her eyes. "Proof of your aunt's innocence," he said. "Finally."

No one spoke as Dylan led the way on foot, moving as fast as he could with Zach precariously balanced on his horse and in a great deal of pain. Megan and Heidi followed on their horses.

He prayed they would make it back to the Hunter River in time. But as they found the trail that would lead down to Huntington Stud, fire crested the ridge with a fierce rumbling roar—a ribbon of leaping red-orange flames despite the falling rain. The sense of heat was instant.

"We have to go that way, to the south!" Dylan yelled, running now, stones clattering out from under his feet, the horses close to bolting.

"The river will be too deep!" yelled Megan.

"Then we swim!"

They raced as the fire ate down the ridge towards them, gaining distance. Two kangaroos tore past them, crashing through the undergrowth.

He could feel the warmth of the fire now. *God, would they make it?*

They reached a section of the river much farther south and closer to the back end of Fairchild's nine hundred acres than to Huntington Stud.

The water here was wide and dark, swirling with bobbing upended trees.

The roar and the crackle intensified. He heard a *whoosh* as eucalyptus, dense with flammable vapor, literally exploded behind them.

The others were dead silent, watching him, trusting him not to panic.

"Now! Cross *now!* Follow me!"

Leading Zach and his horse, Dylan entered black water that reflected the orange glow from the fire like swirling molten metal. The current yanked at his jeans and his horse's hooves sunk deep into silt, but the animal was still able to wade. Dylan quickly shucked his coat. He had no choice but to swim alongside his mount. He hoped Megan and Heidi would make it across more easily. They were good riders. Better than him.

"Stay close!" he yelled. "Swim the horses if you have to."

He turned to Zach, deathly pale in the saddle. "I've got you, mate. Relax. And above all, do not panic."

Tension balled in Dylan's throat as the river sucked his feet from under him. He hung onto the mane of the horse, using a powerful side kick to stay abreast. The animal snorted as it paddled, the whites of its eyes wide with terror.

More eucalyptus exploded with a whoosh as fire cracked and leaped down toward the bank. Dylan prayed it didn't grow fierce enough to jump the river to the studs on the other side before they had a chance to escape.

His horse suddenly found footing again on the opposite bank, snorting as it scrambled up through the mud. Dylan found his own feet, water dragging heavily in his clothes as he waded out.

He heard a cry, glanced back. Heidi's mount had lost its footing, and panicked, swimming downstream fast. For a split second Dylan froze, trying to make sense of what was happening in the dark swirls of water.

"Let the horse go!" he screamed.

But Heidi couldn't—her foot appeared to be caught in the tack, and she was being dragged under by the current.

Shock slammed through Dylan. But before he could move, Megan had shed her coat, slid free of her own horse, and was swimming fast with the current towards Heidi, her hat floating out into the river. She reached Heidi, managing to free her leg while avoiding the wildly kicking rear hooves of the terrified horse.

It swam off into the dark, aiming vaguely for the Fairchild bank farther downriver.

Heart in throat, Dylan quickly secured his own horse to a post, and he went in after them, aiding them to shore. The fire was raging along the far bank as they emerged onto Fairchild property, miles away from the manor house.

Megan's horse stumbled out of the water farther downriver, racing wildly over the field silhouetted by the blaze. In the distance, above the roar of the fire, they heard the dull thud of a helicopter.

"Heidi," Dylan said urgently. "Take this flashlight, get on this horse with Zach, and move it!" He knew the pain would be terrible for Zach, but being caught by the fire would be worse. "Alert Fairchild staff. Get help for Zach."

Heidi mounted behind Zach, holding tight to him. The kids' faces were pale and frightened, hair plastered to their heads. Heidi gathered the reins, the horse dancing agitatedly under her, and she hesitated, torn between racing off and staying with her dad and Megan.

"Go!" He slapped the horse's rump and it bolted, the flashlight bobbing into the dark.

He grabbed Megan's hand, caught her eyes. "Ready?"

She nodded, and they ran for their lives. Megan stumbled in boots too big over acres and acres of uneven tinderbox-dry fields. The acrid scent of fire rasped in their throats, lungs burning, the plastic bag containing the empty turpentine can thumping against Dylan's thigh.

As they neared the first set of outbuildings, they paused to catch their breath. Megan bent over, panting, coughing. They could hear the chopper cutting through smoke again, probably taking loads of water from Lake Dingo.

"Thank you," he rasped. "You saved Heidi…you could have drowned yourself back there."

She looked up into his eyes, her face smudged with mud and soot. "I'd rather drown than see you lose your kid, Dylan."

His eyes burned. He grasped her hand, and they ran again, coming over a rise to see generator-powered spotlights blazing out from the Fairchild manor house and bathing everything in white light. A bull-horn alarm sounded repeatedly as black silhouettes scuttled over the lawns.

The thud of the chopper grew deafening, the pilot risking lack of visibility to dump his load just across the bank.

And through the smoke, they saw a wraith-like solitary figure down near the river outbuildings, dressed in ghostly white, a wet towel covering her head, a wet scarf over her nose and mouth. *Louisa!* Guarding her farm with a giant hose that pumped water via a generator from nearby Lake Dingo as fire swept the opposite ridge.

Dylan stared in shock. They raced down to her, and he took her shoulders. "My God, woman, you should be in bed! You should be evacuated!"

"Rubbish!" she spat at him. "I'm fine. I've been bloody fine for days confined to that damned hospital."

They'd been playing him, but Dylan knew it, and he'd

played right along, hoping to find more evidence before charging her and shipping her to prison. His humanity had cost him.

"I sent Heidi and the boy inside," Louisa snapped at them both, her eyes fierce and defiant. "Mrs. Lipton is calling for a medic on the radio. Won't get anyone, though. We'll have to take him in ourselves later. If we can hold this thing back." She glared at the blaze that raged in the hills on the opposite bank as if she could force it to retreat by sheer will alone. "Here, hold this!" She shoved the hose into his hand. "Keep wetting those barns."

"Louisa," Megan said firmly. "You're shaking. This stress could cause you to—"

"I tell you what stress is, girl! Seeing this place go up in flames—" She pointed to her house. "My life. Everything. It's all I've got." Her voice cracked and she coughed behind her scarf, eyes watering.

And Megan understood.

Louisa's love of this farm and her horses had become a substitute for her love for Kent, for her lost baby. She'd built this estate on those foundations of loss. And she'd built it fierce and solid. And she'd done it alone.

"If it goes, I go with it. No bones about that. Patrick has left already—he's helping drive a convoy of horses to the rugby fields in Pepper Flats before smoke gets too thick on the highway. The other horses have been corralled in the emergency pasture near the lake."

Megan glanced at Dylan as it hit her. *"Anthem!"*

"I sent Anthem with Patrick."

For a moment Megan was dumbounded. "You went and got Anthem? Sent her with your best Thoroughbred horses?"

"For Pete's sake, Megan, that horse has been through enough. I wasn't going to let her face another fire."

Megan stared at Louisa.

"I'm no fool," Louisa yelled over the sound of the chopper bearing down on them.

Dylan moved closer to the outbuildings with the hose.

"I knew what you were doing with that cop's kid and that horse!" she shouted. "Mrs. Lipton told me. And who am I to stand in the way of a bleeding heart."

Megan hugged Louisa on impulse.

"What's in the packet that man has tied to himself, anyway?" Louisa said gruffly, hiding her own emotion.

She took her aunt's frail shoulders in her hands and looked into her eyes. "Evidence, Louisa. Evidence that will exonerate you. He's a good cop. He was just doing his job."

Louisa stared in silence, then gave a curt nod.

And side by side they stood there, the three of them, fighting patches of fire that leaped and spotted on their side of the bank. Swatting it with sacks, wetting their clothes and the outbuildings, breathing through cloth that covered their faces, thankful for the fact the grass had been shorn down to the quick in emergency preparations.

Up at the house, farmhands pumped water over the roof and into gutters while grooms kept an eye on the horses racing around wildly in the large cropped pasture near the lake, knowing that if fire struck, the horses would run from it and double back to stand on already burned patches. It was a last resort.

Heidi came running over the lawn to join them. Dylan tried to send her back up to the house. She refused. And this time he let her make her own choice—to stand with the adults and fight. Side by side.

In the dark hours before dawn, the wind suddenly shifted, and with most of the fuel in the wildlands consumed, the fire began to die back up the ridge.

They stood in silence. Everyone on the farm. Soot-blackened, with raw throats, they watched the red monster retreat, leaving a charred, smoking moonscape in its wake.

And as Dylan's hand sought hers, Megan saw a sheen of tears over Louisa's dry cheeks as she pulled the scarf away from her face.

She put her arm around Louisa, and the four of them walked in silence back to the manor house.

Dylan hesitated at the front door, the court order suddenly weighing heavy on his mind, his legal status here in question. Reality intruding. He also needed to make sure his mother was okay, and safely with Mitch as planned.

Heidi looked at him, puzzled. "You coming in, Dad?"

Megan shot her aunt a look.

"Come in, Dylan." It was the first time Louisa had used his name. "I think we could all use a brandy." She held his eyes steadily. "And I have something I need to show you."

Chapter Sixteen

Dylan had managed to radio Mitch to ensure June had been safely evacuated as planned. Now, exhausted and ready for a hot shower, he took the shot of brandy Louisa handed him. They were standing in the Fairchild library where he'd arrested her eleven days ago. It seemed a lifetime had passed since then.

Heidi had opted to go with Zach to Elias Memorial—one of the laborers had also been injured, and the estate manager was acting as ambulance driver. Dylan had let her go, making good on his vow to give Heidi more choice in her life. What he'd really wanted was to have her with him, especially after this night.

"Thanks," he said to Louisa.

They chinked glasses in a speculative truce, and Dylan could not help thinking that this old woman truly was formidable. People half her age would not have come through like this.

"What was it that you wanted to show me?" he said, taking a sip, relishing the numbing spread of warmth through his chest.

Louisa reached for an envelope on her desk. "This," she said, holding it up.

Dylan could see the letter had a red Scottish postmark over the stamp. Megan tensed beside him as she caught sight of it. A cool warning whispered through him.

"They used to call you D.J., didn't they? D.J. Smith. Your brother was Liam Smith."

Megan's glance whipped to Dylan, but his attention remained fixed solely on Louisa.

"This is a letter from a true-crime writer in Edinburgh," she said, meeting his glare with her steel-blue eyes. "She wrote to tell me that a man has been arrested in Scotland, and charged with the abduction and murder of two young boys."

Dylan's pulse quickened.

"This suspect is in his sixties now, and was working the Thoroughbred circuit from Australia to the U.S., Britain and South Africa over the last thirty years before he retired in the Edinburgh area." Louisa raised the envelope. "This crime writer believes that suspect is also responsible for similar crimes in all those countries where he worked." She continued to hold Dylan's eyes.

"Why are you telling me this?"

"She thinks his first murder, the debut killing, may have been one that occurred right here in the Hunter Valley thirty years ago. The victim's name was Liam Smith."

Megan inhaled sharply, touched his arm. "Dylan?"

He jerked away, stepping backwards slightly as memories assailed him. "You let him go," he said, very quietly, rage encircling his heart. "You let Banner Mac go free to kill again. Over and over again. For another thirty years. More innocent young boys. More lives shattered."

She held his eyes coolly.

She was a total bitch, he thought. DNA technology might have convicted Banner Mac had the science been available back then. He wondered if Liam's cold case files still contained any viable samples they could use now.

"It's not Banner Mac they have in custody, Dylan," Louisa said calmly. "It's a groom who used to work on the Morundah Estate farther up the Hunter."

"Who?" he whispered.

"Simon Wake. He left the country at the same time Mac went to trial."

Dylan stared at her, his entire world shifting off its axis, resetting askew.

"You're not much different than I am, Hastings," Louisa said. "We both want justice. Fair and for all. I believed implicitly in my trainer's innocence, and I only wanted Mac to have a fair trial. Prejudice accused him, and prejudice was going to convict him for something I didn't believe he could do. Just as you tried to convict me."

Dylan and Louisa stared at each other, tension humming, two adversaries, just as they'd been the day he'd arrested her right here in the library. Megan stood on the periphery, silent this time.

"I wasn't going to bear witness to that kind of prejudice from the sidelines, Hastings. Just because Mac had a drinking habit—one he kept under control and to himself in his room— just because it toyed with his memory on occasion, just because of his sexual persuasion and the fact that he liked long solo hikes in the bush didn't make him a murderer of young boys."

"You're telling me Simon Wake did this?" His voice was hoarse.

"That's who the Scottish police have in custody."

Dylan swallowed. "Why did that crime writer contact *you?*"

"She's working on a book. She wanted to speak to me as Mac's employer, and because I funded his legal defense."

He took a step back, needing air, needing to get out of here. To think that after all these years, Liam's killer might yet be brought to justice.

Not in spite of Louise, but *because* of her.

"Like I said, Hastings, we're two sides of the same coin. You use the system for your fight. I admire that. But sometimes you need people like me to fight the system. Because the system makes mistakes. Like you did in arresting me."

He rubbed his hand hard across his brow, swearing softly to himself. He glanced at Megan. She'd known about Liam's murder. He could see it in her eyes, hear it in her silence.

"When did you know D.J. was me?" he asked Louisa, but looked at Megan.

"In hospital, when Megan brought me this letter. It made me think of something Megan said. She'd asked me if I knew you from before, and from the look in her eyes I knew someone had said something. Then I got to thinking about your eyes. And I remembered that particular clear sky blue in the young D.J.'s eyes. A brave boy."

Emotion burned behind those eyes now, and Dylan hated himself for it.

"It was the police who let your family down, Hastings, not me. The cops were so bloody pigheaded, and they believed so firmly that Banner Mac was their man, that it stopped them looking further. *They* let a murderer go, not me. I saved an innocent man who could have been incarcerated for life because he couldn't put up the kind of legal fight he needed."

Dylan felt bile rise from his belly.

Louisa had just shown him that he had harbored hatred for the wrong man his entire life, hatred for Louisa herself, and that he was just as capable of prejudice as everyone else.

He'd even judged Megan at face value because of her clothes, hair, the car she was driving, her affiliation with Fairchild, her potential for inheritance. Rocked by this knowledge, and wanting to hide the raw emotion threatening to burst from him, he picked up his yellow package and turned to leave with the evidence that would exonerate Louisa.

"Take this letter, Hastings, read it," Louisa called after him.

But Dylan would not look back.

He was about to lose it, spin out of control, and he wasn't going to let Megan—a woman he loved—see his goddamn tears.

"Do what's right, Louisa," he said as he pushed through the front door and made his way down the steps into a dark morning dense with the acrid scent of smoke, an apocalyptic landscape across the river.

"Dylan! Wait—" Megan raced down the stairs after him.

Still he wouldn't look round.

She grabbed his arm, forced him to turn around. And Megan's heart crumpled at what she saw in his eyes.

"You knew," he said darkly. "You knew and you said nothing."

"Dylan, it's not like that—"

"Oh, and how is it, then?"

Megan swallowed at the bitterness in his voice. "I did try to tell you. I read some old newspaper cuttings Louisa had kept—"

"She kept them?"

"She did."

He looked down at her, his body wire-tense, hot energy rolling off him in waves.

"I...I didn't know it was you and your brother in the articles, Dylan. The cuttings referred to the boys as D.J. and Liam Smith. I know you as Dylan and your brother as Timmy."

"Dylan John," he said quietly. "And Timmy the Tim Tam monster." His eyes began to gleam in the dim morning light. "Liam loved the fact Tim Tam biscuits were named after a horse that won the Kentucky Derby in 1958. He loved everything about racehorses, and he loved the biscuits. He thought it meaningful that Ross Arnott, from right here in the Hunter Valley, was there in Kentucky the day Tim Tam won, and Ross decided it was a perfect name for his new biscuits." He glanced at the charred ridge, the burned and dead forest, like a moonscape in the gray dawn. "I think Liam would have made a great trainer," he said quietly. "It's why he spent so much time with Banner Mac. That's why…"

"Why they thought Mac took him?"

He nodded.

"What happened to the other boy, to Henry?"

"He lost it. He's become a drifter. Drinks too much. Can't settle down. Can't hold a job."

"Was he, were you…abused?"

"Sexually? No. Just Liam. We got away."

Megan could see now why his interest in Louisa had been so personal, so bitter. Why he'd been so determined to arrest her aunt and to make her pay somehow. She saw why Dylan had become a cop. Why he so fiercely tried to protect his own child. The past tragedy explained so much about him. "You had survivor's guilt, didn't you?" she said softly. "You still do."

He said nothing.

She reached up, touched his face. "Dylan, about the other night—"

He shook his head, stepping back, his eyes narrowing. "It's fine." His words were clipped. "I understand. And I need to go, get this evidence in."

He climbed into his ute, started the vehicle. He looked out the window, and held her eyes for a long beat.

Then he turned his head, and he drove off.

Megan watched him go, her heart tearing. She understood this man fully now, and loved him even more, yet somehow she'd just lost him.

* * *

The CD Dylan handed the homicide squad had shown Rick "Sandy" Sanford shooting Sam Whittleson before dragging Sam's body into an empty horse stall and dousing it in turpentine. The abandoned Holden had been stolen near Melbourne and driven to the Hunter Valley by Sanford.

Sanford had finally been apprehended at Tweed Heads, going north into Queensland, and his prints had been a match to those lifted from the turpentine containers found in the abandoned truck.

Once Sanford was shown the security tape, he confessed in an effort to ameliorate charges.

He claimed he'd used Louisa's gun to throw cops off his trail, and he'd dumped the truck in a hurry after he became aware witnesses had seen him fleeing Lochlain. He knew he wouldn't get through any of the roadblocks that had gone up immediately, so he'd driven into remote bush instead. He said he'd returned in an attempt to retrieve the CD from the truck when he noticed it wasn't on his person, but that he hadn't been able to find the disk under the water.

However, Sanford said nothing about who he was working for, or who had fed the false tip to the NSW police.

The feds were now getting involved, investigating Sanford's alleged links to the crime syndicate known to control racing and betting fraud. The feds would also be looking for links to Jacko Bullock and his bid for the ITRF presidency.

Megan got a call from a private client saying the auction she'd been planning to attend in Europe had been rescheduled and moved forward. The piece he wanted was coming up for bid in three days. If she was to bid on it, she'd need to make an emergency trip.

She left for Paris as soon as she could, unable to reach Dylan to speak to him before she went. She'd called his house and his mother had said he and Heidi had left town for a while. June had a nurse staying with her and she seemed confused about where her son and grandchild had actually gone.

To Megan's frustration, the mobile number she had for Dylan was no longer active. He'd handed his phone in with his badge. The new Pepper Flats officer didn't have his private cell number either.

While Patrick stayed on at Fairchild Acres, Megan sat back in her seat on the plane en route to France feeling edgy and unhappy about doing her job. Which was nuts. This was her life.

But her brief time in the Hunter Valley had shown her otherwise.

She'd learned how important family really was to her, and she was ready to make some changes. Big ones. She wanted a garden. She wanted to be in touch with the soil, to ride again. Often. Mostly she wanted Dylan.

But she was afraid he'd shut her out already.

Almost four weeks after the big bush fire, Dylan and Heidi were staying at a Sydney hotel. Heidi had passed the entrance exams to Brookfield, and a space had opened up at the exclusive school thanks to the daughter of a diplomat who'd had to transfer immediately. And because Megan had already gotten Heidi onto the waitlist, she was able to start at once.

Dylan had also managed to secure a place for his mother at a beautiful psychiatric nursing home overlooking the ocean, and he'd been to see some of his old law-enforcement colleagues in Sydney.

The buzz was all about how the internal investigation into Dylan's conduct had been scrapped—Commissioner's orders. Louisa Fairchild and D'Angelo, Fischer and Associates had backpedaled, Louisa instructing her formidable legal team that she'd made a grave error in misreading her arrest situation.

Dylan was blown away by this, not sure whether to be

thrilled or irked by Louisa's and D'Angelo's extensive reach. But it sure as hell helped to have that kind of reach on your side, and not against you.

All he needed now was to see Megan. He had called her and learned from Marie that she'd left the Valley, so he and Heidi had gone to her Bondi Beach apartment. Megan's neighbor told them she'd gone to Europe. Dylan's heart had sunk.

Megan had returned to her life, and he'd come to accept that it really was over between them.

Heidi was dejected, too. But Dylan explained that she and Megan could still be friends, no matter what happened between Dylan and her.

"You're an adult, kiddo. You'll be right here in Sydney and you can see her on weekends. You can go see Gran, too."

"I know. I just thought maybe you and Megan…" She looked away, deciding not to venture there. "It's just that Megan promised to take me to the big race at Warrego Downs. It's coming up this weekend, and I brought my hat and everything."

"Tell you what, chook. You and me, we'll go. I can spend an extra weekend in town with you before I need to get back. How about that?"

The atmosphere at Warrego Downs was exhilarating, the day bright and sunny and cool, the fashions outlandish and the hats spectacular.

Even Dylan got swept up, but mostly by the joy on his daughter's face. Her eyes shone a brilliant jewel-green, and she looked so grown-up and startlingly beautiful in her hat, he was just the proudest dad around to walk with her on his arm. But in his heart, he wished Megan was here for Heidi.

For him.

God, he missed her. She'd become part of the fabric of their lives in such a short time. But he wasn't going to let negative emotion ruin Heidi's day.

They both leaped up from the stands, cheering wildly, making themselves hoarse with hysteria as An Indecent Proposal, Louisa's three-year-old stallion, racing neck and neck, took the win by a nose.

Flushed with sunshine and infectious excitement, they began to mill towards the exit gates with the crowds.

That's when he saw Megan.

In the winner's circle.

She looked like a *Vogue* model in a long, white, backless dress slit all the way up her thigh, a glass of sparkling champagne in her hand. Dylan's heart clean stopped.

She threw back her head, laughing, the brim of her wide hat shading her eyes. She was surrounded by her Thoroughbred "family"—Louisa, Patrick, Andrew, Tyler, Darci, Daniel, Marnie—and their trainers, media clamoring to talk to them all about recent events, photographers clicking.

Dylan had never felt more the outsider.

In a raw flash he could see he didn't fit into her life, never would.

He gripped Heidi's hand, trying to steer her away before she glimpsed Megan. But it was too late.

"Oh. My. God!" she squealed. "Look! Over there, Dad. It's Megan!" Heidi leapt with excitement, suddenly all of fourteen again, and she ran, trying to push her way against the thronging crowds.

Dylan moved quickly after her. "Heidi! Wait!"

The crowds pushed her back, knocking her hat from her head, trampling it underfoot.

Irate, Dylan ordered people back so he could pick up the battered hat. Heart thumping hard, he caught up to Heidi, who stood still and forlorn. She'd been turned back from the winner's circle by security, Megan and her clan having moved on.

"Hey, come here, chook." He hooked his arm over her small shoulders. "Let's get out of this place."

Dylan steered his crushed child away, hating that she'd experienced this rejection.

But Megan glimpsed him—Dylan's sandy head and broad shoulders tall above crowds. He had Heidi at his side.

Her heart pounded, the excitement and color of Warrego Downs fading to a dull blur as her attention zeroed in on Dylan moving swiftly towards the exit gates.

She frantically tried to push out through the crowds, to go after them, but was jostled back. "Wait!" she called out pointlessly.

They were heading out the gates now, weaving fast through the masses.

Blood boomed in her ears, and perspiration broke out over her body. *Damn!*

If that stubborn ass had just called her before he'd left the Hunter. If June Hastings could have told her they were right here in Sydney... What must they think of her?

She needed to speak to him. To Heidi. She needed to get to a phone, fast.

But she hesitated suddenly, realizing she didn't have a number. And she just stood there, staring numbly after them while the crowds closed around her and her heart did a slow freefall through her chest.

No, she didn't need a phone number,

She knew what she had to do.

It was suddenly crystal shimmering clear.

She wasn't going to speak to him.

She would *show* him.

Her actions would speak louder than any words.

She'd already discussed things with Patrick and Louisa. Now she'd just put her plan in motion and show that cop she could be just as ass-stubborn as him.

* * *

Heidi sat in the passenger seat of Dylan's truck and bashed her hat flat as a pancake. "I don't want to go to Brookfield," she muttered as he drove her to the school where she would board from tonight on. "I don't want to leave you all alone in the Pepper Flats house."

He turned into the Brookfield driveway, coming to a stop outside the grand old brick buildings covered in ivy.

He killed the engine and shifted round in his seat. "Heidi, you have a passion. You're damn good at your art, and you heard what the evaluator said about your portfolio." He hooked a knuckle under her chin. "I never knew just how good and determined you were, chook. I needed to do a lot of learning these past few weeks, and the one thing I did learn was that I need to let you follow your heart. I need to let you be your own person. And don't you go worrying about me now."

Her eyes filled.

"It'll take a while to settle," he said, "to make new friends. Change can be scary. It can feel real lonely, too." Boy, did he ever know that right now. "But without taking that leap, you won't become who you really want to be."

Her bottom lip quivered and a lone tear tracked down her cheek.

"Hey, I'll always be there for you, kiddo," he said, wiping the tear away with his thumb. "You know that. And I hope you'll be there for me, too."

She lurched forward and hugged him so tight. "I love you, Daddy. I just wish Megan loved you, too."

His eyes burned. Hell, yeah. But that wasn't going to happen.

He sat back. "We can't have everything we want, chook. Come, let's go get you settled in."

"Will you go home tonight, Dad?" she asked as they walked up the pathway through the manicured school lawns.

"Maybe tomorrow or the next day," he said. "I want to meet with the detectives about Liam's cold case, see whether Interpol is able to use the old DNA evidence. They kept Liam's clothes."

She nodded her head solemnly. He'd told her everything. They'd talked long and often over the last two weeks, catching up and forming a new kind of father-daughter bond. One based on love and a genuine friendship.

He felt richer for it. And he knew he had Megan to thank for it. She had been a ray of nurturing sunshine in their lives. She'd shown him how to break free, and now they had to move on. Alone.

Dylan pulled into his Pepper Flats driveway and sat quietly in his truck for a while.

It was good to have gone to Sydney. It had gotten some of his issues with the city out of his system.

It had been even better to spend time with his daughter, to see her so grown-up, and he'd felt so proud to be with her. They were doing the right thing with Brookfield. He could see it now. And he'd relocate his mother to the nursing home in a few weeks, once she got used to the idea. He was sure she'd be happier, too.

He'd mortgaged his Hunter Valley property to do it all, and he was comfortable with that.

But right now he felt so incredibly hollow.

He stared at his brick house, thinking about the reason he'd moved out here when Heidi was only four. How he'd wanted to build on core values, make a life for her. With a dog and a yard and a pool. Build a family.

He smiled sadly.

He'd done some of it.

And, yeah, sometimes change was hard. Like now.

He opened his door and ruffled Muttley, who came rushing from round the back, his snout and paws caked with fresh dark soil.

"Geez, Muttley." He took the dog's collar. "Let's go see what you've done to the veggie garden this time."

But as he rounded the corner of his house he saw someone bent over in his vegetable patch, digging up carrots, and plunking them into a wicker basket. He stilled in shock.

Megan?

His heart tumbled, and then raced as he walked over the grass toward her, wondering if he was seeing a mirage.

She looked up as he approached. "Hey." She smiled, pushing away tendrils of soft blond hair that blew in the breeze with the back of her wrist.

Dylan was speechless, his mind trying to reconcile this gorgeous woman digging in his earth with the unattainable princess he'd seen at Warrego Downs the other day.

She stood up slowly, dirt on her knees and sneakers, and heat seeped to his belly. His heart thumped faster. "What are you doing here?" he managed to say.

"You mean in the Hunter?" She smiled, angling her head with a mischievous glint in her eyes. "I live here."

"Megan, don't mess with me. Not now."

She came up to him, placed her hand on his chest, soil-caked trowel in the other. "Don't be so serious, Dylan. I've made some changes." She leaned up on tippy-toes and kissed him.

He could barely breathe.

He didn't dare take hold of her, crush her to him as he wished to. God, he loved her, wanted her.

"Changes?" he managed to say.

"Patrick and Louisa helped me put together financing for some acreage farther downriver that I've got my eyes on," she said.

"What acreage?" He looked deep into her eyes, searching for evidence she might be joking with him.

"I've decided to extend my art co-op business out this way. I want to establish a gallery on the tourist track, a place that can also serve as an artist's retreat." Her eyes shone with infectious excitement. "I want somewhere I can host overnight guests in small cottages, and a central dining area where I'll serve fine Hunter Valley wines. I want to have a beautiful, inspiring garden, and maybe a few horses." She hesitated, worry creeping into her eyes as he remained overtly dispassionate, while inside he vibrated, trembled.

She swallowed. "Louisa gave me Breaking Free, Dylan. She saw how I found myself with that horse. And…" She hesitated, voice faltering slightly at his silence. "Maybe…Anthem could be stabled there?"

"Anthem?" What in hell was wrong with his brain? Why did he feel like he was moving through water?

"Heidi could ride him at my place when she comes home on weekends and on holidays. The rest of my private consultancy business I can do just the same from here—the buying, the travel. I'll hire a manager to run the retreat when I'm out of town." She looked into his eyes and touched his hand. "Dylan, I have an appointment with the real estate agent this afternoon. Will you come with me? Just to look at the property?"

"Of course," he managed to croak out, emotion pricking his eyes, his heart beginning to turn goddamn somersaults.

"Will you help me build something here in the valley, Dylan? A family maybe?" She touched his lips with her fingertips. "One little step at a time."

It was an offer beyond his dream.

Dylan had finally found the woman he'd been searching for all his life, and Heidi would have someone she loved, admired, a beautiful role model. A mother.

An old crime had been put to bed. Sam Whittleson's murderer was behind bars, and Megan—in helping Dylan bridge the gap with his daughter—had made peace with her own past.

And ironically, the foes who'd squared off on opposite ends

of a homicide investigation—threatening each other's families and values and livelihoods—were ultimately becoming one family. Because, at the core, they all essentially wanted the same.

"Come," he said softly, taking her hand.

A thrill punched through her stomach as she looked up into his clear blue eyes.

"Come inside, Megs. Come to my bed. Be mine."

And she kissed him, her body melting against his, knowing she'd finally found home.

She'd found family.

Silhouette Desire kicks off 2009 with
MAN OF THE MONTH,
a yearlong program featuring incredible heroes
by stellar authors.

When Navy SEAL Hunter Cabot returns home for some
much-needed R & R, he discovers he's a married man.
There's just one problem: he's never met his "bride."

Enjoy this sneak peek at Maureen Child's
AN OFFICER AND A MILLIONAIRE.
Available January 2009 from Silhouette Desire.

One

Hunter Cabot, Navy SEAL, had a healing bullet wound in his side, thirty days' leave and, apparently, a wife he'd never met.

On the drive into his hometown of Springville, California, he stopped for gas at Charlie Evans's service station. That's where the trouble started.

"Hunter! Man, it's good to see you! Margie didn't tell us you were coming home."

"Margie?" Hunter leaned back against the front fender of his black pickup truck and winced as his side gave a small twinge of pain. Silently then, he watched as the man he'd known since high school filled his tank.

Charlie grinned, shook his head and pumped gas. "Guess your wife was lookin' for a little 'alone' time with you, huh?"

"My—" Hunter couldn't even say the word. *Wife?* He didn't have a wife. "Look, Charlie…"

"Don't blame her, of course," his friend said with a wink

as he finished up and put the gas cap back on. "You being gone all the time with the SEALs must be hard on the ol' love life."

He'd never had any complaints, Hunter thought, frowning at the man still talking a mile a minute. "What're you—"

"Bet Margie's anxious to see you. She told us all about that R and R trip you two took to Bali." Charlie's dark brown eyebrows lifted and wiggled.

"Charlie…"

"Hey, it's okay, you don't have to say a thing, man."

What the hell could he say? Hunter shook his head, paid for his gas and as he left, told himself Charlie was just losing it. Maybe the guy had been smelling gas fumes too long.

But as it turned out, it wasn't just Charlie. Stopped at a red light on Main Street, Hunter glanced out his window to smile at Mrs. Harker, his second-grade teacher who was now at least a hundred years old. In the middle of the crosswalk, the old lady stopped and shouted, "Hunter Cabot, you've got yourself a wonderful wife. I hope you appreciate her."

Scowling now, he only nodded at the old woman—the only teacher who'd ever scared the crap out of him. What the hell was going on here? Was everyone but him nuts?

His temper beginning to boil, he put up with a few more comments about his "wife" on the drive through town before finally pulling into the wide, circular drive leading to the Cabot mansion. Hunter didn't have a clue what was going on, but he planned to get to the bottom of it. Fast.

He grabbed his duffel bag, stalked into the house and paid no attention to the housekeeper, who ran at him, fluttering both hands. "Mr. Hunter!"

"Sorry, Sophie," he called out over his shoulder as he took the stairs two at a time. "Need a shower, then we'll talk."

He marched down the long, carpeted hallway to the rooms that were always kept ready for him. In his suite, Hunter tossed the duffel down and stopped dead. The shower in his bathroom was running. His *wife?*

Anger and curiosity boiled in his gut, creating a churning mass that had him moving forward without even thinking about it. He opened the bathroom door to a wall of steam and the sound of a woman singing—off-key. Margie, no doubt.

Well, if she was his wife… Hunter walked across the room, yanked the shower door open and stared in at a curvy, naked, temptingly wet woman.

She whirled to face him, slapping her arms across her naked body while she gave a short, terrified scream.

Hunter smiled. "Hi, honey. I'm home."

* * * * *

Be sure to look for
AN OFFICER AND A MILLIONAIRE
by USA TODAY *bestselling author Maureen Child.*
Available January 2009 from Silhouette Desire.

Thoroughbred Legacy

The purse is set and the stakes are high…
Romance, scandal and glamour set in the
exhilarating world of horse-racing!

The Legacy continues with book #9

DARCI'S PRIDE
by Jenna Mills

Six years ago, Tyler Preston was on top of the equestrian world…
until one disastrous night nearly ruined him. Now, after years
of hard work, his beloved Lochlain Racing has reemerged. Then
Darci Parnell—the woman who'd cost Tyler everything—walks
into his office and changes his life forever.

*Look for DARCI'S PRIDE
in December 2008 wherever books are sold.*

www.eHarlequin.com

TL19934

REQUEST YOUR FREE BOOKS!

2 FREE NOVELS PLUS 2 FREE GIFTS!

SPECIAL EDITION®

Life, Love and Family!

YES! Please send me 2 FREE Silhouette Special Edition® novels and my 2 FREE gifts (gifts are worth about $10). After receiving them, if I don't wish to receive any more books, I can return the shipping statement marked "cancel." If I don't cancel, I will receive 6 brand-new novels every month and be billed just $4.24 per book in the U.S. or $4.99 per book in Canada, plus 25¢ shipping and handling per book and applicable taxes, if any*. That's a savings of at least 15% off the cover price! I understand that accepting the 2 free books and gifts places me under no obligation to buy anything. I can always return a shipment and cancel at any time. Even if I never buy another book from Silhouette, the two free books and gifts are mine to keep forever.

235 SDN EEYU   335 SDN EEY6

Name _____ (PLEASE PRINT) _____

Address _____ Apt. # _____

City _____ State/Prov. _____ Zip/Postal Code _____

Signature (if under 18, a parent or guardian must sign)

Mail to the Silhouette Reader Service:
IN U.S.A.: P.O. Box 1867, Buffalo, NY 14240-1867
IN CANADA: P.O. Box 609, Fort Erie, Ontario L2A 5X3

Not valid to current subscribers of Silhouette Special Edition books.

Want to try two free books from another line?
Call 1-800-873-8635 or visit www.morefreebooks.com.

* Terms and prices subject to change without notice. N.Y. residents add applicable sales tax. Canadian residents will be charged applicable provincial taxes and GST. Offer not valid in Quebec. This offer is limited to one order per household. All orders subject to approval. Credit or debit balances in a customer's account(s) may be offset by any other outstanding balance owed by or to the customer. Please allow 4 to 6 weeks for delivery. Offer available while quantities last.

Your Privacy: Silhouette is committed to protecting your privacy. Our Privacy Policy is available online at www.eHarlequin.com or upon request from the Reader Service. From time to time we make our lists of customers available to reputable third parties who may have a product or service of interest to you. If you would prefer we not share your name and address, please check here. ☐

SSE08R

Thoroughbred Legacy

The purse is set and the stakes are high…
Romance, scandal and glamour in the
exhilarating world of horse racing!

The Legacy continues with book #11

AN INDECENT PROPOSAL
by *Margot Early*

Bronwyn Davies came to Fairchild Acres looking for work—
and to confront stockbroker Patrick Stafford, her son's real father.
Even after all these years, Patrick still hasn't forgiven Bronwyn
for marrying another man for money. Now Bronwyn can see
what life *could* have been, with him. But the cost will be far
dearer than Bronwyn could ever have imagined….

*Look for AN INDECENT PROPOSAL
in December 2008 wherever books are sold.*